Rhose

Rhose

ANNE BRYANT

Ann Brooks

Bryan Hewartt

ROBERT HALE · LONDON

© Anne Bryant 2003
First published in Great Britain 2003

ISBN 0 7090 7482 4

Robert Hale Limited
Clerkenwell House
Clerkenwell Green
London EC1R 0HT

2 4 6 8 10 9 7 5 3 1

Typeset in 11/14pt New Century Schoolbook
by Derek Doyle & Associates, Liverpool.
Printed in Great Britain by
St Edmundsbury Press Ltd, Bury St Edmunds, Suffolk.
Bound by Woolnough Bookbinding Ltd.

'. . . change in a trice,
The lilies and languors of virtue
For the roses and raptures of vice.'

A. C. Swinburne

In memory of Margaret
who would have enjoyed this story.

A special debt is owed to Jane Anson, editor,
for her unbounded enthusiasm and encouragement,
to Mrs Pat Sherwood
and to the staffs of the Portico and
Chetham Libraries, Manchester.

Contents

Chapter One

Manchester 1760

There were no crowds. There had been large numbers the first week, and a few the second, but on a cold day in February, people had other things to do. With boards, 'A Notorious Bawdy House Keeper,' back and front, Susannah attracted only a few jeering urchins. This was the last day, the last day in gaol, trudging through the mud and slush that was all she could think of: to be out of that stinking 'correction house' – no food, brutal gaolers, contempt even from the other prisoners. Tomorrow she would be out, back to work, but not here, not in Manchester, now that her profession was public. She could shrug off the spittle and the horseshit, but the shame would stick. It would be time to move on.

A pull on the rope jerked her face down into the mud and filth. They had stopped just outside the Wheatsheaf tavern. The constable grinned with malicious satisfaction then pulled her to her feet.

'You can wait there my beauty. See what trade you can pick up today – lift your skirts, deary, let them see what they be missing.'

He tied the end of the rope to the rail outside the tavern, saying, 'You'll not be going anywhere will you, now there's only one day to go.' He sauntered in.

Susannah hoisted the boards, squatted and, with relief, relieved herself, watching the thin trickle mix with the other piss and filth. The rain had eased, a wintry sun was trying to break through. Susannah allowed herself a silent grin as she watched an old client scurry past, respectable in his clerical black. 'If only his flock knew', she thought, but her brief content was shattered by a gang of ragamuffins.

'Poxy whore! Poxy whore! Flash-tail Taylor! Flash-tail Taylor!'

Susannah hunkered down and, resigned, covered her head as the mud and filth spattered her.

'That's enough now, be off with you.' The striking figure of a young woman in grey dress and red cloak strode out of the inn. 'Clear off – you've had fun enough. If I catch any of you again, it's into the pig's midden with you.'

Jeering and still chanting, the lads skittered off, leaving Susannah stained, muddied and wet through again. The other woman bent and helped the prisoner up.

'You've suffered enough, Mistress Taylor. It's those that use you that ought to pay – in more than money.'

'Thank you, Mrs Tinnys. You've done more than enough for me these past months. I'd not have got through without your food and your kindness. You always seem to be near when I need help.'

'Nay, I don't approve of what you've done, but I can't see any of my sex starve. It's a hard enough life for all these days. You're released tomorrow so I hear. Come round to the Ring o' Bells in the morning and I'll see you on your way.'

Susannah was about to thank her again, but the new note of sharpness in Rhose Tinnys' voice cut her off.

'Mind – I don't want you back in this town. I'm not doing this just out of charity. Someone like you brings disrepute to us all. It's too late to mend your ways, but you know what will happen if you're caught again.' With a final nod, 'See you tomorrow', she added, then picked her way through the slush across the street. Susannah sank back down, resigned to waiting for the return of her gaoler.

*

The next day the weather had improved, though an east wind whipped the Irwell into rippling waves, giving the river an evil grey menace. Clutching a bundle of clothes still left to her, Susannah, shivering in her thin check, scurried along the bank, past the Old Church towards the Ring o' Bells. Standing outside the churchyard, above the Tin Bank, the half-timbered building looked across the river to the Salford side, its front commanding Smithy Bank. Susannah cast an apprehensive glance at the dungeon on the Old Bridge and suppressed a shudder. Thank God she had not been put in there. It had such an evil reputation: you could be gnawed by rats, even drowned if the river ran high. But now she was free, keen to be on her way. Liverpool lay downriver and in a busy port there were plenty of opportunities for a woman with her talents. If only Rhose Tinnys kept her promise, she felt sure of a good send-off.

As she approached the inn her heart sank. The door was closed, the shutters still up, at ten in the morning. She had never known this before. She hurried down the side alley, shooing away the scraggy hens escaped from someone's yard. Round the back entry she found the door on the latch and pushed into the kitchen. Something was definitely wrong. There was a fire in the hearth, the stockpot bubbling away, but no bustle of preparation, no aroma of baked bread, just the stale smell of last night's lees. At this time of day Rhose should be in her kitchen, supervising the cook and the pot boy, running between tap room and saloon, hurrying departing travellers on their way, chivvying the ostler. Susannah knew well the routines of an inn like this, but here everything was silent: no spit roast, no dripping tray, deserted.

The door to the taproom swung open, and the maid pushed in backward, carrying a stinking chamber pot, her head twisted hard away from the smell. When she turned and saw the woman in the kitchen, she started, splashing putrid slops onto the floor.

'Now look what you've made me do,' she snapped, glaring at Susannah with her pathetic bundle. 'What are you doing here? Today of all days. You've no right in a respectable place.'

Susannah, unblinking, stared back.

'What's wrong? Why is everything shut up? Where's Rhose – Mrs Tinnys?'

'What's wrong? *What's wrong?*' Her voice was shrill, then suddenly dropped to almost a whisper. 'Tinnys is dying – that's what's wrong. The apothecary's with him now – though he'd be better with a minister than one of them quacks. What's it to you anyway? Be off with you before I empty this over your whoring head.'

'No need to get in an uproar, Mary. It was Mrs Tinnys herself asked me to come. I'm really sorry to hear of your master. I knew he was not well, thought it was just the ague – it's a shame for he was a well set-up man in former days.'

'Aye, you'll know about that I dare say. Well he's not long for this world now.' She pushed her way through to the back door. 'I've told you be on your way – the mistress will not want to be bothered with you now.'

Left alone in the room, Susannah took a quick calculating glance around. Two pewter candlesticks disappeared from the mantelpiece into the bundle. Good candles in the kitchen, she thought, there's money in this business. She eyed the brass pans, the pewter and crockery, licked her lips at the hanging hams and herbs, but before she could help herself to anything further she heard a foot on the stairs outside the taproom door.

Rhose walked slowly in. She was dry-eyed but solemn, her face showing little of the tragedy taking place, but her mouth down drawn. She too started when she saw her visitor. Susannah noticed how quickly Rhose's eyes swept round the kitchen when she found the bawdyhouse keeper alone.

'With William taking this turn for the worse, I'd forgotten I'd told you to come today.'

Susannah murmured some sort of apology, picked up her bundle and prepared to leave.

'No, don't go. A promise is a promise, and I'll be glad to see you on your way. I can spare a guinea and there's a parcel of old linen I had set aside for you.'

She opened up a press in the corner, pulled out a neatly

wrapped parcel. Handing this to the other woman, she added some coins to the pile. 'There might have been more – but I dare say you'll get a tidy bit for what you've already helped yourself to.' She nodded knowingly to the mantelpiece.

Susannah began to protest, but thought better of it, pulling her own bundle closer to her chest.

'I'll not say anything more. I've trouble enough to deal with. Just go – to Liverpool or the colonies for all I care. You've paraded your shame, that's enough.'

'I won't forget this – kindness. I will always be grateful for the way you looked out for me these last months. You've always been generous to your own kind. You're an understanding woman and I hope with all my heart your man has a peaceful ending and, when it's over, you enjoy all you deserve.'

The maid bustled back in, almost colliding with the woman leaving.

'What, you still here? What have you . . . ?' Her voice died down when she saw Rhose by the fireplace. 'Sorry mistress, but—'

'It's alright Mary. Mistress Taylor is on her way. Will you be walking? I may be able to arrange a ride with a carrier.'

'No, thank you. I've a – friend – owns a barge, the *Baccus*. I'll be going by boat.' She waited no longer but hurried out of the door before Mary too spotted the missing candlesticks.

The maid looked at her mistress with puzzled admiration. 'I don't know how you can bear a woman like that – today of all days.'

'She's still a woman, for all her sins – and as much sinned against. As for today, well, we all have our tragedies to bear. As for Mr Tinnys, Mr Agar has done all he could, so it's up to the Lord now.'

'Mrs Tinnys! Mrs Tinnys!' A deep voice called from upstairs – then, more urgently, 'Rhose, Rhose!'

Rhose sighed, then for the first time her shoulders dropped and wearily she turned back towards the stairs.

The funeral took place two days later. The rain this time was unrelenting, a curtain of fine droplets that puckered the water's surface in the bottom of the grave. The simple wooden coffin with its plate, 'William Tinnys born 1724 died 1760', splashed down into its resting place. The minister wrapped his wet vestments around him and scurried away. The small group of mourners, huddled like sheep, began to move off. The young widow and Jonathan Agar, the apothecary, hastened across Smithy Bank to the Ring o' Bells. The two Seddons, Ralph's sexton duties done, waddled with their sailors' gait to their respective taverns, leaving a surly gravedigger to fill in the waterlogged hole. In a gossiping gaggle, trailing behind Rhose and Agar, came widow Rylance, Mrs Royle and Jenny Driver. They were chewing over the brief life and the shorter marriage of the departed.

'He was a well set-up fellow in his plush breeches and fancy shoulder knot when he served the Fletchers. I even fancied him a bit myself.'

Nell Royle scoffed. 'Why, widow, you and a well set-up footman – never! You were happy enough with a common salter. Now I thought Rhose Whittaker would have gone for someone better, she had her chances and she always had grand ideas. My Wilfrid knew her back in Lancaster when he was nothing but a carter and she a jumped up nursery maid, and she wouldn't give him a how d'ye do! Not,' she hastened to add, 'that he was ever attracted that way.'

The other two exchanged knowing looks as they all huddled under the porch of the Ring o' Bells.

'Mind you,' Jenny Driver felt she had to stick up for her employer. 'She was always well spoken, and could read and write. That's how she became housekeeper to the Haworths in Blackburn. Agar was their apprentice then. How else could she have taken up as assistant to him later?'

The other two snorted, 'How else indeed?'

Jenny persisted. 'Now I'll not hear anything bad about Rhose. Wasn't it Mr Agar himself that brought her and William together up at the Fletchers'? Why should he have done that?'

'Why indeed?' the others repeated.

'And when Agar set up in Manchester, she's gone on helping as an assistant when he's had clients among the gentry, being educated as she is. Oh, she's a strong woman is Rhose. She stuck by her man over this last year or two, drunken wastrel as he turned out. And now the apothecary has done all he could for him.'

'Better than a so-called real doctor, I've no doubt,' muttered Annie Rylance. 'Yet look how she's come out of it all. She'll keep the inn going – she's been running it single-handed this past year. It can make money with the right handling, especially with the coach trade building. With her connections to Agar, the gentry know of her. She'll make something of that – you watch, the young bucks will be patronizing the Ring o' Bells before long.'

By now they had rid themselves of the worst of the weather and moved into the inn. The large public room was nearly empty. Mary was doing duty as barmaid; two local hucksters sat close to the sputtering fire, smoking and not talking in friendly companionship. A carrier at the long bar downed the last of his flagon, picked up his whip and, with a guttural farewell, trudged off into the rain. The three women went straight through with a 'how d'ye do' to Mary, shaking the last drops of rain from their mantles. They mounted the back stairs to the private parlour where Jonathan Agar stood with his back to the fire, coat-tails wrapped around his wrists. The room was dim, faint light trickling through the bottle glass windows. The fire alone gave off a reassuring glow. Rhose was standing at the centre table, sorting papers from a battered box, a silver punch bowl standing by. There was an air of strained familiarity between the two.

As Rhose pushed the papers back in the box, snapping the lid closed, her thoughts returned to what they represented. Marriage to William had been a disaster from the start. Their passionate attachment barely survived the first year to be replaced by constant rows over money and liquor. Still it had

15

meant she was soon in control of the inn and she could use the profits as she chose. Investing in Sugar Lane was a risk – if it became known she ran a bawdy house it would be a disaster. Still it was paying handsome dividends. The risk was worth the price to be in charge of her life. Her thoughts were interrupted by the entry of the three mourners.

'My, it's a dark day – in more ways than one,' Nell Royle remarked as she perched on the settle by the window. The younger Jenny sat beside her while Widow Rylance pulled a spindle-back chair closer to the fire, forcing the apothecary politely but reluctantly to one side.

'It's the sort of day makes you wish candles weren't so dear.' She looked meaningfully at the unlit tallow dips on the sideboard. 'Many of us have to make do with rushes.'

Turning to the newcomers, Rhose smiled a tight, wan smile. She had loosened her dark hair so that it fell to frame her high-cheekboned strong face. Her grey eyes showed her tiredness, reflecting the strain of the last few months.

'I'll get some light if you really need it,' she said. 'But for now why don't you help yourself to the punch.'

They needed no second bidding, ladelling themselves generous helpings. Jonathan Agar smiled and said nothing.

'You're quiet, Mr Agar,' said Jenny. 'You're not usually lost for words. I've heard you many a time crying your wares to whoever would listen. You've not much to say for yourself today.'

Suddenly remembering why they were there, embarrassed, she buried her head in her mug and backed onto the settle.

Rhose, eyes now alive, replied for him. 'Mr Agar did more than anyone could for my husband. He may "cry his wares" as you say, Jenny, but he need not for he's a fine apothecary. Remember,' and she emphasized this with a slow turn of the head, which took in all three women, 'I was his assistant when he saved Sir Geoffrey's eyesight. He alone—'

'Now, that's enough Rhose – spare my modesty,' Agar interrupted. 'I am certain that Miss Driver meant no harm. But as it happens, I have been asked to go to the Fletchers again, Sir

Geoffrey no doubt – or possibly Lady Elisabeth – is ill. I'll let you know if I have need of you Rhose. You will excuse me ladies, I must be on my way. If there's anything further I can do for you Rhose . . . oh, and if you do revive the card parties – in due time of course – I would be honoured to be included.'

With a bow to the room, he took up his surtout coat, hat and stick and turned to the door. At that moment there was the unmistakable rattle of harness and squelch of heavy wheels. Nell looked out of the window.

'The London coach is here – near a day late.'

'I'd better go down to see to it. Mary won't be able to manage on her own. Help yourself to the punch bowl while I'm gone. And I have no doubt you would like to stay for a bite to eat.' There was a satiric note to the invitation as Rhose followed the apothecary out of the door. The three tankards were filled before the door had closed as they settled down to a really worthwhile gossip.

Downstairs the street door burst open to a gust of rain. The coachman filled the doorway, shaking his wide-brimmed hat like a dog out of the sea. He flung the sacking from his shoulders and shambled to the fire, the two hucksters hastily backing away from the spattering of the greatcoat. There were only two travellers with him. The older was small and round bundled in an old topcoat, his face seeming ready to burst into smiles, – once it was dry. The other was only slightly taller, yet because of his slim build was more imposing. Removing his slouch hat and unfastening his own topcoat he revealed more fashionable dress, from his mud-smeared light jackboots to his elegant brocade waistcoat.

'Well, I have vouched for the inn and the landlady. I hope they live up to my puffs.'

'Indeed, young man, the blaze of the fire is enough after that journey.'

'Ay, the weather in Manchester has lived up to its reputation, but you'll like it here. There's plenty of opportunity for trade. I think we can do each other a good turn.'

17

'No doubt! I've names, contacts to visit, then we must meet again.'

'You can leave a message for me here and—'

Rhose emerged from the kitchen. 'Ned!' she cried with obvious delight. 'You've come after all.'

'I am sorry I could not be here for the burying. I owed it to William. But, well, I had business on the road.'

'I don't doubt it.' Rhose laughed for the first time that day. 'Come upstairs, there's punch waiting – and Mistresses Royle, Rylance and Driver.'

'Ah, the three graces! What better welcome could a man wish for,' Ned laughed.

'The round man shook himself, beamed round the room, which took no notice of his good humour, shrugged and walked over to the bar.

'Laurence, Josiah Laurence's the name, my dear. Do you have porter in this part of the country?' he asked Mary.

Rhose answered from the taproom door: 'Of course, do you think us backward savages in this part of the world? French brandy, the best port and good wine if you will.'

'I'm sorry if I offended you,' the portly man swept a bow towards the landlady, 'but I've not always found such good provision outside the metropolis. Well then, a pint of porter if you please, mistress.' He turned back to the maid.

Embarrassed, Mary had to confess. 'No porter, sir, I am so sorry. We have to wait for the next carrier to come in. He should be here today.'

' 'Fraid you might have a fair wait,' this from Ned as he followed Rhose out. 'Some trouble I believe coming up from Nantwich.'

'Ah, well, make if half and half then,' and, as Mary tapped the two barrels, the stranger asked, 'and tell me, I've heard that man called "Long Ned". Is that so?'

'Aye.'

Surprised, he protested, 'Why! I'm no giant, and he's little taller than me.'

18

'Ah, that's not why he got the name,' she winked, 'but it's why he's such a favourite with the ladies.'

Chapter Two

Smith's Coffee House

Spring had come at last. Rhose strolled through the blossoming orchards by the river. This was her place to reflect and contemplate the future. The gardens behind Parsonage Bank evoked distant memories of her home in the north. It was softer here, the trees budded and greened earlier, the air clear with a tempting feel of the country. Here was an oasis of natural beauty and calm away from the frantic bustle of the Market and the Exchange. It had been an escape from William's boorishness when in drink, a haven of clean freshness from the stink of beer and food and unwashed bodies. She had been on her own for nearly two months now and although she felt the loss of her husband, she was looking to the future. She missed Jonathan Agar's support and advice. He spent little time at the Ring o' Bells now he was aiming to build a grander clientele. She did not begrudge him that, she too had ambition. This crisp morning air helped to focus her mind, to concentrate on the enterprises she had set afoot and to ponder on the future. While her gown brushed through the long wet grass, her pattens preserved her daintier shoes from the worst of the mud.

She paused on the bank and watched the Irwell swirl away toward the sea. As she glanced downstream she thought momentarily of Susanna Taylor and the barge taking her to –

what? Rhose had never visited Liverpool but she could imagine
the port as a grander version of her own thriving Whitehaven.
Bustling with energy and novelty, the town must provide whatever was needed for sailors spent from the Americas, merchants
bidding for cargoes, all the roistering flotsam of pimps and
bawds, flashmen and smugglers, blades and cutpurses.
Compared to that, Manchester, with all its business, was a
quiet, respectable, unenterprising town. On the surface, Rhose
thought, smiling to herself. Over the last few weeks trade had
revived at the inn, and there was a feeling of optimism in the air
despite the tragedies of the past. Regrets must be put aside. It
was hard for a woman to make her way in this world without a
man apparently by her side. She shrugged and turned her back
on the river. It was time to get on; time to dress more in keeping
with her next call. She hurried along Parsonage into Deansgate.
Passing by the thriving shops and hostelries she nodded to
several acquaintances.

'Good day, Mistress Tinnys, I was sorry to hear of the death of
your husband.' Rhose recognized Dr White. She had met him at
the Infirmary when she was helping Agar.

'Thank you, sir, I'm grateful for your concern.'

Dr White had become somewhat renowned in recent years for
the mummy contained within his celebrated collection. This
curiosity was an elderly patient, Miss Beswick, who was afraid
of being buried whilst still alive. She promised her doctor
£20,000 on her death if he embalmed her body and examined it
once a year. This he duly did, placing the mummy inside a long-
case clock, and had only to open the face on the anniversary of
her death to fulfil the conditions and collect his prize. Rhose did
not begrudge him his wealth, but there was no inheritance for
her, she would have to make her own fortune. At the Ring o'
Bells the sedan chair she had ordered had arrived in the public
room, its men refreshed with a draft of cider. She realized it was
an extravagance as her inn was a short walk from the Coffee
House, but the streets remained too muddy to risk the train of
her new mantua. She had heard that Dean's pigs were out

again, and an encounter with one of those brutes could lead to more than a muddying. When she presented her proposition to Peter Smith she needed to make an impression.

Of the three Coffee Houses in town, Smith's was certainly not fashionable. Perhaps for this reason it was the most popular and attracted a varied patronage. The coffee was drinkable, the liquor cheap and the latest London newspapers available to all. Smith's own publications came hot from the press – and he could provide services not available at Compton's or the Exchange. Even Rhose felt somewhat intimidated as she climbed the stairs to the coffee room. Ladies did not normally frequent such places. There was no outright ban but the gentlemen did not make them welcome – not respectable ladies.

She, however, was here on business and as a respectable businesswoman. She raised her chin, smoothed her underskirt and pushed open the doors. The pall of tobacco smoke, the reek of rum and brandy, the cacophony of sound, which greeted her, froze her in the doorway. Here in a room no larger than her best sitting room was crowded a host of men, drinking, smoking, spitting, talking at the same time, in shirt sleeves and waistcoats, hats hanging on wall pegs. All stopped as though on command as each took in the strikingly handsome woman. Those sitting half-rose, those standing half-bowed. Only one did not move, an elegant but rumpled young man in military uniform spread-eagled over the one settle. The owner, Peter Smith, crossed the room to greet her. Rhose glanced around the assembly and relaxed, she knew them all. At the round table in the centre with its jumble of newspapers, cups, tankards and journals, were the habitués. One of the Seddon brothers, she was not sure which, both were slightly bandy, shortish with bronzed, pock-marked faces and short bob wigs, well-worn and out of fashion. This must be John, the tailor, his waistcoat a little elegant, a little fussy. Brother Ralph still sported the fearnought he had worn in his sailing days in keeping with his manual work as sexton. He was here too, talking quietly in the corner with a still active sailor, Sam Harper. Something being hatched there, Rhose guessed. At the main table John Seddon had been making some forceful point to the apothecaries, Wagstaff and Bue. John Leigh, the druggist hanging on to every word, was anxious to impress his more prosperous colleagues. Joseph Bue was the most distinguished of them because he had connections with the best in town and country. He insolently paraded his political sympathies with a blue and white favour in his coat. A proud man, he was immaculate in a ruffled shirt and dark blue waistcoat. Rhose noted the silver buckles on his shoes. No shortage of funds in his trade, she thought. Rising from the table, John Travis, the Chairman, formally bowed; to him she was a valued customer. It was well to favour inn and tavern keepers who provided most of the trade for his fleet of sedan chairs.

'Mistress Tinnys,' the Coffee House keeper bowed formally in his turn. 'What may I do for you? It is – unusual – for one like yourself to be here, but, naturally, a great honour.'

The room was immediately reanimated. Two men in the corner were noticeably separate from the others, for Molineux and Tobin were excise officers. They had few friends in the room. Yet Smith needed to keep on sound terms with them: any suspicion of smuggled coffee, tea or chocolate, let alone contraband brandy, could mean jail or transportation. Conversation resumed but was more subdued. Around the walls the tables were occupied by other men known to Rhose: John Royle, baker, the Gilbadys, boat builders. In the darkest corner William Makin and Peter Marsden were grumbling at the injustice of life in general and the Court Leet especially. Smith had been reluctant to accommodate them after they had been fined for holding disorderly houses. Everyone knew what went on there in Mill Gate – beggars, vagabonds and worse – a 'common nuisance' it was called. Smith could give it another name, but then, their money was as good as anyone's and they were no worse than many more 'respectable' customers.

'You have fine mixed company here, Mr Smith.' Rhose covered the room with one sweep of her head. 'I hear the fashion deigns

to enter. The young Sir James, old Sir John, even – is it true –
an Earl? You must prosper.'

'I do well enough, Mistress Tinnys.' Smith was cagey. 'You are
not envious I hope – from what I hear the Ring o' Bells is also
prospering. More of the coach trade – a renewal of the card
parties perhaps? And, who knows, possibly the Court Leet might
be looking for a new meeting place. The Old Coffee House is
rather difficult of access at times and becoming rather squalid.'

'Who knows, Mr Smith? However, I cannot count on such
fortune, I must needs try what I may. And that is why I have
ventured into this masculine domain, to seek your assistance.'
She bowed courteously and gave him the full beam of her grey
eyes.

'Whatever I may, of course. Would you come to my private
office away from the hubbub?'

He led her through the smoke and chatter to a door at the
rear leading to a small room packed on one side with cases of tea
and coffee, leaving scarcely room for a desk and two chairs. In
the corner was a pile of magazines tied into bundles, on top loose
sheets of playbills, broadsides and flyers.

'I'm sorry there is so little space, but it is clean – your beautiful clothes will not be spoiled. Had you been wearing your full
hoop I could not have accommodated you at all.' There was a
certain archness in his manner. 'You can see I am not accustomed to entertaining ladies here.'

'Not in this room certainly, Mr Smith.' Echoing his tone. 'Do
not trouble, I doubt this will be a long stay. I have had an idea
for a business, which I am sure will be of interest to you and
should profit us both.'

'Business and profit are words I always like to hear.'

'At the Ring o' Bells we ever had people seeking places.
William, you know had wide acquaintance and we could often
accommodate servant and master to their, and our, advantage.
Now, without him they still come, so I have been thinking of a
practical means of assisting.'

'Ah!' Smith interrupted. 'I was naturally deeply grieved to

hear of Mr Tinnys' death and I can see you may be in need of extra support. You wish me to help through my clientele to find suitable places for your – er – protégés?'

'I had more than that in mind: a more regulated system with your aid. You have your – should we call them "private rooms" above the coffee house.'

He held up a hand in protest. 'Oh, come now, let there be no pretend modesty between us: you have your interests just as I have mine. Indeed, although few know of your connection with those in Sugar Lane, while my name is often bruited abroad. But then I see we may well have interests in common. What do you propose?'

'You are a printer as well as a coffee house proprietor, one with newsmen throughout the county. With my connections through the inn and your press we might produce a list – a gazetteer of persons seeking suitable positions and of those seeking suitable employees.'

'A gazetteer! Yes, I see the appeal. A compendious list of suit-able young maids perhaps.'

Rhose nodded. 'More than that. There are many fine strong country lads who would fill a livery admirably. A well-turned leg on a footman can turn more than an old dowager's head, don't you think?'

'Ah! Capital! Whoever may appeal to a duchess would attract my more discerning clients. For sure my "private rooms" are always in need of well-turned legs. I could tell you such tales of the ingratitude . . . but enough. I doubt not that Alice Rylance would welcome a supply of fresh young fillies. This publication could be an excellent means of recruiting.'

'Make no mistake Mr Smith, my proposal is for an *honest* enterprise whatever the benefits which may accrue to our other enterprises. Servants will be placed, employers satisfied, as for the rest – let the market provide.'

Smith smoothed hand over hand and nodded appreciatively.

'I can see profit in this for both of us and I welcome the oppor-tunity to work more closely with you, Mistress Tinnys. As we are to be business partners, may I not call you Rhose?' He stepped towards her but, with a swish of her skirts, she moved away.

'I would prefer to keep this on a strictly business footing, Mr Smith. Let there be no mistake about that.'

'Oh, I fully understand. I meant no impropriety, my dear.' He retreated behind the desk, riffling through the papers lying upon it. 'How soon would you contemplate the venture?' His voice now had a harder edge.

'As for that, I already have a sample of the information to be published.' She cleared her throat and read in a matter-of-fact tone:

'Mary, fifteen years old, from a good family in Derbyshire. Flaxen hair, 4' 6" high, experienced in kitchen work, very willing to learn. Fresh from the country but desirous of pleasing in any fashion so she may advance herself.'

'Excellent – I'll take her for myself.'

'I think the next more in your way,' Rhose smiled. 'Richard, seventeen years old, 5' 5" high, well made, strong in the arm. Can manage horses, with a good seat. Former employer summoned overseas, reluctant to part with him as he has proved faithful and obedient.'

'Excellent again. I know two or three would favour him.' He had recovered his even temper and prepared to escort her from the room. 'I am convinced we shall be able to come to a mutually satisfactory arrangement. Before long we could publish the Peter Smith List of Manchester Pleasures to rival the London guides. To seal our understanding may I offer you some refreshment? I have been remiss in my hospitality. We could retire to one of my other rooms.' He caught the look of distrust clouding her face. 'Total propriety and privacy, I assure you,' he hastened to add.

'I thank you, I think not. I must go back to the inn; there is much to do there. Do you think you could have Mr Travis summon a chair?'

As Rhose was leaving she passed Josiah Laurence at the door and, with surprise, saw Ned had followed him in. Laurence offered a deep, polite bow.

'Mistress Tinnys, may I call on you soon?' Rhose concurred with respectful incline of the head. She remembered Laurence was now a lodger at John Seddon's inn, and wondered what was afoot. Watching as they made their way to the centre table to join the throng she saw them greeted enthusiastically and there immediately appeared before them brimmers of brandy. Once Rhose had left the room, the conversation grew more animated; tankards were rapidly refilled.

John Travis turned to the newcomer with a knowing smile. 'I see from the London paper one of your name has been bold in his trading enterprise – and caught out in it too!' He pushed the newspaper towards Laurence. There was silence at the table while he scanned the reports of the Assizes.

'A distant cousin, perhaps,' was his casual reply. 'I know nothing of him or his ship the *Pluto*.'

'What is this?' The elegant figure raised himself from the settle, stretched and yawned. 'As an officer at the King's pay, I would know of what you speak. The *Pluto* you say. I seem to remember something of that from gossip at Chatham. A privateer wasn't she?' He stood and strolled over to join the centre gathering, buttoning his vermilion gold-trimmed waistcoat.

'Really, Major Gee, do you, a military man, take an interest in such things? I thought it more a matter for those – gentlemen.' Travis nodded to the two revenue officers, unashamedly eavesdropping on the conversation.

'I assure you that I take a great interest in all that affects His Majesty's government and His Majesty's service.' A rustle of disquiet ran round the table. Apothecary Wagstaff put a restraining hand on Bue's arm and shook his head in warning. Gee appeared to notice nothing, picked up the paper and went on:

'I see from this report that – this – pirate, Laurence, stole cambric and lace from a neutral ship.'

'He must have a maid like mine. Always after such fripperies,' Ned interrupted, glancing round to try to lighten the mood. No one laughed.

'There's no cause to scoff. These were no fripperies – the cargo

27

was worth near a thousand pounds. The man could be hanged for such and deservedly so,' the Major rejoined.

This raised an unsympathetic mutter from the others. Laurence put in: 'That's harsh, Major. He may be none of my kin, but he was no pirate, and I reckon in these times of war there's not much to choose between privateers like him and the King's navy.'

'Aye,' John Seddon butted in, 'with all these taxes and duties and these bolly dogs of excisemen, a man can call nothing his own.'

Molineux started to rise from his corner table, but was held back by his fellow officer.

'Why it's almost treason I'm hearing here,' the Major protested. He was now standing back from the table facing the others, as the atmosphere became threatening. 'Good men have lost their limbs and their lives defending this country from those frog-eaters across the Channel. And don't think you're safe in this God-forsaken North Country. There's not much between here and Ireland. The French have landed there once and could again. Do you fancy being at the mercy of that Popish rabble? You'd lose a lot more then besides a few taxes. We need all the money and men we can raise to keep us strong and preserve our true religion. It was threatened before, remember. I'm not here for my health you know, but to summon brave men to the colours of the Royal Welch Volunteers. We are all proud to rally to the defence of the Protestant cause and our good King George.'

Wagstaff could restrain Joseph Bue no longer. He pushed forward, face flushed with drink and anger. Glaring directly up into Gee's face, he chanted singsong fashion:

'God bless the King! God bless Pretender! But who Pretender is and who is King? God bless us all! That's quite another thing.'

The two faced each other, their eyes with the same fanatical gleam. Others reached out to try to pull the apothecary away. 'Come, Joseph, enough,' someone said.

'S'blood sir, this *is* treason. I see from your favour you flaunt your contempt for the true King.' He leaned forward and snatched the blue and white ribbon from Bue's coat and tossed it to the ground. 'Your Popish popinjay was sent packing with his tail between his legs in 1745. He was taught a lesson and I believe you need the same.' Gee's hand was on the hilt of his sword.

Smith moved swiftly between them. 'Now gentlemen, gentlemen. No bloodshed in here if you please.'

'No, for sure!' Bue's face swelled with rage, his body twisting out of the clutches of his friends. He spluttered trying to get his words out. 'No, but there shall be. This – this – tricked out – fancy molly can take a lesson from my sword. I'll not have the only true king slandered and insulted by a uniformed quean.'

He was cut short by a resounding slap from the Major. Bue staggered back, almost collapsing into Laurence's arms.

'Dawson's Field, sunrise! My friend will call on you to make the arrangements,' Gee snapped. He gave a smart military bow to the silenced company, turned and marched out.

'You went too far,' Wagstaff said. There was a grunt of agreement. 'He may have taken your Jacobite politics but never a personal insult – even if true.'

Bue was still shaking his head, but straightened up, calling for more ale for the whole table. 'I'm not afraid of him. I can handle a sword as well as the next man and someone has to stand up for the cause. It is not lost while Charles Stuart lives.'

It was Josiah Laurence who bent to pick up the trodden favour. He was amazed that these Jacobite gewgaws could still arouse such hot tempers. He dusted it off and, with a mocking reverence, handed it back to the apothecary.

Chapter Three

A Duel

A small group of men gathered at the edge of Dawson's Field across the Irwell on the Salford bank. From the orchard they could make out the clearing below through the dawn mist. The field dropped down through a gentle slope to a level of open meadow with a thin trickle of a stream running through. Here at one side stood an ash, leafless still, and saplings. Across the way was a copse of young bushes and thickets of shrubs and weeds. Major Gee stood motionless under the tree in sleeveless waistcoat and ruffled shirt despite the chill dampness. Several yards away, by the copse, the squat figure of Joseph Bue paraded restlessly, a voluminous blue cape protecting him against the cold. In the centre of the glade, Charles Wagstaff and Captain Johnson, Gee's second, were exchanging words. In the distance a hound barked the morning in. Here all was silence except for the voices drifting upwards through the stillness.

The watchers were the Coffee House regulars together with Ned and Laurence, here to see the outcome of the quarrel between the major and the apothecary. Laurence, yet the outsider, doubted that Bue would go through with it. 'Surely an apology would be enough,' he said. 'I'll bet on it.'

'You'd lose!' Ned replied.

The others scoffed.

'Aye, he's been disappointed since '45,' someone said. 'This is his chance for revenge and dignity. Don't be deceived by his size or his manner, he's a good swordsman.'

'In any case,' Travis added, 'I doubt the major will forgive the insult to his manhood. Buggery is still a capital offence and in the army . . . .' His voice trailed away as they all concentrated on the scene below.

The two go-betweens had returned to their principals. The Major drew his sword calmly and waited. Bue's cloak was flung onto the bushes, revealing the blue and white cockade of yesterday attached to a white sash vivid against his dark suit. Through the curling wisps of mist the two figures appeared to the watchers to be almost something in a dream, but the clash of swords and panting breath were real enough. Major Gee lunged contemptuously at Bue, to be met by a fierce parry and slash at the head. Gee sprang aside, startled, recovered and thrust. The smaller man flicked the blade away, stepped back – and waited. Gee gave him a mocking salute, cut upwards to Bue's left, parried the return, struck across, then stamped forward with a flurry of lunges and feints. Bue, backing, held them all, cut and slashed in his turn. Both now were beaded with sweat, their breath trailing each movement in the cold air.

'Ten guineas on the apothecary!' Laurence cried.

'Done!' Travis replied.

The spectators found themselves further down the slope, out of the shelter of the blossoming fruit trees. No one else spoke.

Below both men had paused. Feet had churned the damp ground, each step now a concentrated effort. The two seconds began to move forward from the shelter of the ash, but Bue struck again. A quick feint to the right then a slash left caught Gee off guard. A rip in the shirt, a brief trickle of blood; his left arm had been pinked. His response was swift: a lunge to the body, cut to the head, thrust to the groin. The apothecary twisted away, down the slope. There was a rally of sword on sword, but weaker, no aggression. Bue regained ground, a flurry of hacks and parries forced his opponent lower, into the dip.

31

Laurence: 'Double it.'

Travis: 'Done.'

Again the two by the tree seemed to the watchers to start to intervene as both fighters backed off, gasping for breath. Wagstaff was halfway down the slope when he heard Bue taunting: 'You even fight like a poxy woman.'

'And you – a jerky Jesuit,' was the reply.

The fog swirled and briefly lifted as the two clashed again, swords locked, eyes glaring. The Major's lean height dominated the apothecary, but it was the smaller man who pushed the taller back with the force of his sword arm. Gee slipped, foot into water. Bue saw his advantage, cut and thrust. The Major's counter lunge clipped past the defence. Bue slithered, stopped, looked down.

Gee's sword had sliced into his stomach. For an instant there was total quiet. All that could be heard was the dripping of moisture from the trees; no birds; no movement; clouds of silent breath motionless above the duellists.

The apothecary sank to his knees, splashing into the water. Major Gee drew out his sword, let it drop to the ground and bent to the collapsed figure. 'I didn't mean . . .' he began. Wagstaff and Johnson stumbled down the slope, apothecary to apothecary, soldier to soldier. Two figures detached themselves from the cowed onlookers. The rest murmured and shuffled uneasily. There was a chink of money changing hands. Bue had collapsed into the mud, his friend held him up from the icy trickle of the stream. Captain Johnson plucked at Gee's sleeve but was shaken off. The Major leant over the bleeding body. 'I had no intention . . . .' He had difficulty speaking. 'Had he apologized . . . .'

The fog had begun to lift, a watery sun sent shafts of feeble light onto the scene. The two Seddons pushed forward, helping Wagstaff to lift Bue's inert body. Johnston retrieved his friend's weapon and took Gee's arm. The Major started to speak to Wagstaff, 'You must get him to a surgeon. I will—'

He was cut short by the Captain. 'Major, we cannot stay. This is a bad business – best return to barracks. Remember we're to Southampton tomorrow.'

Gee shrugged, cast a last desperate look at his opponent, reluctantly donned his cloak and picked his way up the hill.

The other bystanders hurried to join those carrying the moaning body of the apothecary. Voices echoed the Major's words – 'a surgeon', 'he needs a surgeon'. 'If it's not too late,' added Laurence.

'We can take him to the Ring o' Bells, its close over the river!'

'No, Ned,' Wagstaff cut in. 'Get him to his shop, it's not much further and we'll have all the surgeon may need.'

Wagstaff wrapped Bue's abandoned cloak around his friend. The slow procession moved through the orchard, across the old bridge, passed the lock-up and on to Mill Gate. Ned and Laurence slipped away to the inn. News of the duel would soon spread through the town.

In the deserted grove, the sun broke through. In the bushes a blackbird burst into morning song.

The coach, with its attendant rider, stopped on Deansgate outside the Star Inn, adjacent to the dancing master's house. Francis dismounted and helped his mother and sisters alight. Charlotte and Anne, after saying a hasty goodbye, rushed into the house for their lesson with Signori Lucii Fabiano. Elisabeth hoped today would be enjoyable for the girls; the last two months had been a distressing time. Sir Geoffrey had not improved. The message from Bue had an air of urgency and Geoffrey had suggested that a renewal of the girls' dancing lessons, at his insistence, would allow her to go to town without suspicion.

Lady Elisabeth with her son at her side hurried through the streets. They strolled into Half Street and then crossed over to Mill Gate. They stopped outside one of the many hat shops that lined the street.

'I was glad you were going this way, Ma. I was thinking of paying a visit to the Ring o' Bells to catch the latest news.'

'Surely the Bull's Head is the place for that. Your father never came to town without dropping in.'

'Yes maybe if you want politics. I am more interested in the racing. I want to know whom Vulcan will be running against at the Manchester Races in October. Though I don't know of any horse than can beat him on a good day.'

'Off you go then, Francis. We'll meet at three o'clock on Deansgate.'

She watched her son disappear around the corner into Bridge Street then she quickly crossed over and entered an apothecary's shop. Inside was total confusion. Several men were standing around in deep and earnest conversation. They turned towards the door and the conversations petered out on the lady's entrance.

Wagstaff, who was nearest to the door, recognized Lady Elisabeth and bowed politely.

'Lady Fletcher, oh dear, you find us in disarray, nay in despair. Mr Bue has had an accident. Dr Hall was sent for and is upstairs with him now.'

'I hope it is nothing too serious.' Lady Elisabeth hesitated then added, 'I had a letter from him asking me to call today.'

'I'm sorry you have made a special journey, but I fear he is not well enough to see visitors even though expected.'

'I must insist you inform him I am here, Mr Wagstaff, if you would be so kind.'

'Very well,' he acceded, 'but I must warn you it will be unlikely you will be admitted.'

Left alone, several of the men bowed, and one escorted her to a chair hastily placed by the counter. An embarrassed silence descended.

Upstairs Wagstaff moved anxiously to the bed, where Bue, pale and exhausted, was lying. Dr Hall was attending the wound.

'Lady Fletcher is below and insisted I tell you she has arrived. I have told her you are ill, can I give her your apologies?'

Bue rallied to insist: 'No, Charles, I must see her.'

'Please Joseph, you are in no fit state to see her,' interposed

Dr Hall. 'I have patched you up but the wound is beyond my repair.'

'All the more reason to see her now. I have news I must pass to her. You've done your best Edward. I am in the hands of God now. And please ask Lady Fletcher to come up, I will see her alone.'

Wagstaff and the doctor descended to the shop.

Dr Hall bowed graciously. 'I am sorry we meet under such circumstances, Lady Fletcher. He wishes you to attend him. Please try not to tire him. My skill as a surgeon was to no avail. I fear the shock of the wound will kill him.' As Lady Elisabeth climbed the stairs she heard the doctor address the others. 'We'd best all go home. The less said about this affair the better. The constables will hear soon enough.'

Lady Elisabeth saw at once that the injury to Joseph Bue was indeed mortal. He lay exhausted against the pillows. His pallor was wax-like, as if the spirit was gone and only the body continued to function. The eyes were sunken, looking into the distance.

Gently she began to speak. 'What has happened, Joseph? Geoffrey so ill and now you like this.' The tone of her voice revealed the distress she was suffering.

The apothecary dragged his gaze to her face. 'To the first, I'm afraid my passion for the cause, and too much ale, led me into a foolhardy duel with a Major in the Welch Fusiliers. I thank God I was spared long enough to see you. I asked you to call because this letter is for you, from the same hand as the others. Good news I think. You will not be alone long in this matter. I have guarded it well. 'Tis a pity I guarded myself so carelessly.' Painfully he drew the letter from under the pillow.

'Take care, Thomas Miller will come here as he knows naught of you, but I will arrange for him to be sent to Greenwood Lea. Will you ask Edward to come up? He knows nothing of our matter, but you can trust him if all else fails. He has been a staunch supporter – as a young man it was he who took down the heads from the Exchange and buried them. I pray you will be guided by God in all things.'

Lady Fletcher did as she was bid. The shop was now empty save for Wagstaff and the surgeon.

'He is asking for you, Dr Hall.'

'I will attend. Wagstaff, return to your own shop if you please. I can send anyone calling on Joseph to you there. I fear it will not be long.' With a low bow to the lady, the doctor returned to his patient. Wagstaff took his farewell and departed.

Lady Elisabeth, now alone, sat down once again on the chair. A single candle lit the counter casting a pool of light over the letter in her hand. With trepidation she opened it. All seemed overwhelming, how could this letter be of any comfort? As she glanced at the contents, she wished she was with Geoffrey. Quickly she thrust the letter deep into the pocket on the inside of her cloak and left the shop. Drawing her cloak around her as if a shield, she set off for Deansgate.

As the evening gloom descended on Manchester a small round man silently made his way to the rear door of the Ring o' Bells. No one watching would have seen the door open as not a glimmer of light showed as he went inside. Rhose called to Martha that she was not to be disturbed. She led Laurence to the cellar trap behind the bar; below were a labyrinth of interconnecting passages and oak-beamed ceilings. Slate-pierced openings let in a fitful light in the day. To penetrate the evening gloom Rhose lit a lantern and holding it high wove the way through the stacks of barrels and racks of bottles. At the back of the main cellar lay a scattered heap of crates, boxes and the detritus of years. The scuttling of rats, the drip of water and the stink of stale beer caused Laurence to baulk.

'I've not had the opportunity to see to this. The front cellar's good enough but here . . . well, William was a good enough man but in his last days he did neglect his duties. Yet the vaults are sound enough.'

The little man stepped fastidiously through the debris, tapped the walls, felt the beams and had the lantern shine in the corners. His inspection was thorough, pushing aside boxes and lifting a heap of rotting sacking. It fell into woven powder, releasing a flurry of silverfish and cockroaches. He drew back with a cry of distaste, which at once turned to a chuckle.

'Ideal, Mistress Tinnys, no one would wish to explore further. And behind this dung-heap?'

Rhose laughed. 'You're a fly one, for sure. You've smoked me straight away. Come.' She stepped past the rubbish, lifting her skirts as daintily as if attending a ball. Behind the disgusting pile was another opening half covered by a filthy curtain, behind the curtain another cellar. It too looked abandoned. A fallen beam lay across yet more dirty sacking which Rhose drew aside to reveal tubs, flagons and parcels of cambric.

'So, I was not aware you were already a customer. Had I but known we might have come to an earlier arrangement,' Laurence said.

'I had some suspicion of your interest in the trade because of your understanding with Mr Seddon. But I must tell you I have my own, independent, sources.'

'That's Ned, I trust. Indeed, I see that some of these goods could only have come from the Low Countries. But overland routes can bring problems, can you be certain yours is secure?'

'Oh come, you would not expect me to reveal Ned's methods. If you could guarantee safety and, naturally, match the prices, we might also come to an understanding.'

Laurence bent to examine the contraband, then continued his inspection of the cellars, passing out again to study the maze of walls and turnings. 'Yes, this is a very good place and I am seeking other accommodation. The Isle of Man enterprise is prospering with the Liverpool interest. I can guarantee a regular and protected run.'

Rhose stood by him, raised her lantern to highlight his face. His bland boyish countenance sharpened in the shadowy glow. 'We need a firm agreement. The revenue can be persuaded to turn a blind eye to a little brandy or tobacco, even coffee and tea, but a regular run!'

'Now that is why I need more premises. Yours are ideal; close to the river and on the safer bank. There's been too much activity over in Back Salford recently. The Seddons are "obliging" but not so secure, while you, if I may be bold, have respectability, charm and the necessary connections. A financial settlement could be mutually beneficial.'

Rhose smiled in the gloom at the words, which echoed her own on a similar occasion. She walked on through the front cellars to the stairs, talking over her shoulder to the smuggling agent.

'Don't worry. I am sure I can arrange things. The cellars have proved impregnable to such revenue visits we have had, but perhaps an improvement of access through the backside of the inn. Shall we retire to my room upstairs to discuss the matter further?'

'With the greatest of pleasure, Mistress Tinnys.'

'Please, call me Rhose . . . Josiah.'

Chapter Four

The Letter

Spring days were welcome to those who travelled the road. Five o'clock on an April evening and Knutsford Heath was still bathed in sunlight. The slender elder were breaking into leaf and pussy willow seemed to glow. The post rider, Robert Todd, enjoyed the downy scent of the yellow flowers as he trotted quietly along nearing the end of his journey. 'One call, then on to Manchester and we can both rest,' he murmured patting the neck of the grey. He was accustomed to chatting to his horse to keep at bay the loneliness and trepidation of riding through these deserted places. The copses could well hide rapacious enemies. 'Highwaymen and footpads will think twice about an attack on a bright night like this', he reassured himself. Nevertheless he once more checked the horse pistol that lay athwart the saddle.

Then he saw it. A riderless horse stood grazing by the track. As he approached, its ears pricked and, whinnying,it bucked away. There were saddlebags like his own flapping empty at the horse's side. Robert, taking a firm grip on the pistol, spurred forward, scanning both sides of the path. He found the body lying in a hollow a few yards on. The man lay face-down, a heavy russet cloak spread around him. His head lay against a rock, blood seeped from a wound. His left arm stretched along the

39

ground, a riding whip inches from his hand.

'Another post boy – strange', Robert thought for he knew of no others riding this way. 'Was it a fall or was he waylaid?' he wondered as he slid from the saddle. He checked the scrub and brush but there was no one in sight. He bent to turn the body over gently.

The 'body' rolled, sat up and Robert was staring into two unblinking dark eyes. And the unblinking muzzle of a pistol! The face was half-covered with a kerchief, the eyes wrinkled with good humour.

'Now, my lad, quietly does it'. As he stood back the highwayman stooped to pick up the whip while the pistol never wavered.

'You'll hang for this, robbing his Majesty's mail,' Robert blurted out, more astonished than afraid.

'I've had many supposed appointments with hangman Jack Ketch before this,' the other laughed. 'Let's to it. First the brass ticket; I'll be carrying his Majesty's mail so I'd as lief look like a mail carrier.'

He took the distinctive royal badge and pinned it prominently to his own Norfolk cloak. 'Now the boots!'

'What? My boots? Why?'

Robert was pushed roughly to the ground, the pistol waved towards his sprawling feet.

'The boots! It's either them or a crack over the head with Betsy here. Which do you want?' The butt end of the pistol stopped inches from his skull. The post boy hurriedly tugged at the heavy riding boots.

'I reckon it will take some time for you to hobble across the heath barefoot and I need that time. Of course I could . . . .' This time the pistol, cocked, pressed close to his temple. Robert cringed onto the ground, desperately hoping to sink into it.

'That's it, lie down, but face-down. You are welcome to my artistic rock – just pig's blood and water if you were concerned for my welfare. Stay there.' The last was peremptory with fierce menace. Robert closed his eyes and prayed. He prayed hard until he heard horses, including his grey, being spurred away.

Slowly he staggered to his feet and began to limp painfully towards the village. He cursed his assailant with loud and unrelenting oaths. Then he thanked God it had been no worse.

'. . . . And so I left the poor lad to hobble his way onwards.' Ned laughed as he tipped the saddlebags over Rhose's bed in the safety of the Ring o' Bells. Letters, parcels, bills and bundles cascaded over the quilt spilling onto the floor. Rhose joined in the laughter as she bent to rescue the overflow.

'But why the russet cloak, the King's badge? Was that not a greater risk? What if someone had recognized you impersonating a post rider?' she asked.

'Don't you understand? All that people see are the cloak; the badge; the saddlebags. Tell me now how your post boy looks. Eh?' Rhose shook her head. 'Besides who would dream of stopping his Majesty's mail on a bright spring evening? 'Twas the blithest ride I've had for many a day.'

'What of the post horse? Is that safe? A grey you said?'

'Ha, ever practical, pippin. Do not fear, it is with a comrade-in-arms and tomorrow will be on its way to Appleby. The boots will pay for its keep so there's more profit in tonight's adventure than this pile.' So saying he thrust his hands into the heap and pulled out a plump package.

'Deuce take it, look at this.' He held out a fistful of bills of exchange. 'All cut in half and worthless without the other. By my troth, there's no trust anymore. What a sorry pass the world has come to. There was a day when a man's word was his bond and there was true faith in the King's mail, but today these canting London merchants . . . .' Lost for words he tossed the offending papers into the fire.

'Ah, come Ned. There's rich enough pickings withal. Here's a bundle of bank notes worth over twenty pounds. There's faith and trust for you. Who's to know what treasure may lie amongst these innocent-looking letters?'

She brushed her hands over the papers on the bed before resting them on Ned's thighs. She raised her eyes to his and held them with a mocking gaze. There was an instant flash of understanding.

'And what treasure lies atop?' He breathed as they fell together on the rustling pile.

Rhose was up with the sun, her feet scuffling among the papers disgorged from the bed overnight. She stretched and smiled down on the highwayman, still oblivious amid the sheets. From downstairs came the sounds of Mary and Martha about their morning chores. Mary could be heard clattering the pots and glasses of the night before. Martha was rattling the fire-embers into life ready for the day's cooking. Rhose, shivering slightly in the chill, rolled on her stockings and began to pull her petticoat over her head.

The activity aroused Ned who sleepily groped towards Rhose's buttocks. 'Ah, what sweet little cunny', he murmured.

Rhose slapped his hand away. 'Enough of your coarseness, Ned Edwards, it's day and I've a day's work to do. You clear up all this,' she kicked at the mail on the floor, 'and see what is worth something and what is not. Clear it all away before Mary comes up – and you can keep that long cunny-catcher in your breeches.' She flicked at the offending member with a discarded stocking. Hurriedly she pulled on a deep blue grisette skirt and short-sleeved bodice. As she laced up the front of the bodice to reveal the swell of her breasts, Ned sighed deeply. Snatching a large fine white neckerchief she threw it round her shoulders, crossing it to fasten at the front, giving a hint of modesty to her attire. Ned chuckled, heaved himself from the bed and picked up her shoes from where they had landed the night before. With a mock bow he handed them to Rhose as she left the room. Reaching for his drawers, he surveyed the task allotted to him.

Downstairs Rhose busied herself with the routine of the inn. In the kitchen Martha was already well into the day's baking. A goose lay split open ready for the forcemeat stuffing. There was a ham steeping in water by the stew pot. A leg of mutton hung alongside the hobs from the ceiling rack.

'I'll give this a wipe over,' Rhose said as she hooked it down. 'Another day and it will be ready for roasting.' She patted it dry, sniffing for signs of damp or must. 'With a good sauce that could well pass for venison, Martha,' she said with approval.

The cook grunted some kind of answer; at this time of morning she said very little. Indeed she could be grumpy and ill-tempered, but she was faultless in the kitchen.

'There are fresh pigeons in the larder, brought in last night,' Rhose continued. 'I thought a thatched house pie would be a pretty dish for the table tonight.'

'Aye, well. The first batch o' today's baking is in the oven. The next is proving. This here puff pastry I'm doing now, is for rook pie. My Arthur's bringing in a dozen he took yesterday up at Mosley's. But if you want som'at fancy—'

'No, Martha,' Rhose knew when to give in, 'Rook pie it is. We'll fricassee the pigeons for dinner. The "fancy" for tonight can be a real porcupine, 'twill go well with the boiled ham. Elias should be bringing in a catch of rabbits – roast will do for them, I think. I'm not expecting great custom today.'

'Right, mistress. I've tansy pudding and apple dumplings. If our Joan brings them, there'll be forced cherries for tarts.'

'That will serve, Martha. What a godsend it is to have a family like yours.' Rhose knew that the Coopers covered half the country and could be relied on for everything in – and out – of season. The Ring o' Bells owed its reputation for good honest food largely to Martha and her relatives.

Rhose went into the taproom. Last night's debris had been cleared away, fresh straw and sawdust strewn on the floor. Mary was still making her morning racket in the main room. She and the cook were so like their biblical namesakes. Mary liked nothing better than the noise and the bustle of the bar. Nor was she troubled by the 'tousling and mousling' as she called it, of the bolder company. Rhose smiled as she sat to the accounts. Her maid would doubtless be a valuable addition to the 'Servants' Gazetteer' she was producing, but Mary was too valuable to the inn to be parted with. The smile turned to a frown as she contemplated the figures before her. William had ever been prof-ligate with money and, although the inn was beginning to prosper again, it was a hand-to-mouth existence.

Rhose leaned back in her chair and took stock of her assets. Above the bar and taproom there were three 'guest' rooms, her own and the private sitting room, above that the attic with two box-rooms and a cluttered space – hardly enough room to attract profitable trade. Below were the cellars. These promised better with the illicit arrangement with Laurence. Yet she couldn't fully trust the man from the south. She felt secure from the Revenue, but if things went awry, she knew Mr Laurence would take care he did not suffer. Yes, she must take extra precautions on that front.

She heard the first early morning stallholders come clumping in. They would be drinking cider. Later would come the trades-men, then the petty officials, the idlers, the scroungers: ale, porter and, as there was no gin, brandy. Rhose sighed; there was little to be made with these people. Jonathan Agar was right to put the past behind him, to try to move on and up. To get on you needed to cater to Society. Now Sir Francis Fletcher, a coxcomb but well connected and – what was he called? Banton, Oliver Banton, they were the sort that the Ring o' Bells needed regu-larly. Yes, the inn must be brought into fashion.

For a start the main room could be partitioned into 'modesties' like the stylish London taverns – booths gave more privacy away from the hurly-burly of the public bar. Bringing back the card parties could also bring in a better class of trade with tea and chocolate for the ladies. The whole upper floor would benefit from refurbishing for that. But all such improvements required money. A sigh escaped her. True the Laurence enterprise promised well, but she had already doubted that. There remained the 'Servants' Gazetteer' which could be a regular source of income with the collection of fees and whatever arrangement might be made with Smiths' questionable connections. She shuffled the papers together, her problems unresolved.

As though conjured by her thoughts, Mary called from the

bar. 'Mr Smith is here to see you', and the man himself came through the taproom door.

'Good morning, Mistress Tinnys. I thought it best to call before we both became busy with our daytime trade. I have the first issue of the Gazetteer produced to your requirements. I trust you will be pleased.' He proffered a sheaf of broadsheets to Rhose who had risen to receive her visitor. She scanned the sheet while Smith pompously read aloud the preamble:

' "Mistress Rhose Tinnys begs to inform the Public that having many Applications for SERVANTS she takes this Opportunity to publish Information relating to MALE and FEMALE Servants seeking Positions". I think that well introduces the purport of our venture. And note I have taken the liberty of altering slightly your general paragraph thus:

"Also Healthy BOYS of Ages seven years and Upwards and Country-Bred GIRLS of like Ages seeking good Masters to be put to a trade". I perceived the term "country-bred" a more tempting epithet than simply "healthy" again.' Smith's voice was cloying in its deference.

'Yes. Yes. I can read well enough, sir.' Rhose was curt in reply. I see you have also added to my list. I do not recall one Phanny Heap.'

'Ah, no I – acquired – her from John Stewart of Sugar Lane. You may know him?'

'I know of him. Did he not run foul of the law only last year? I am not pleased that you see fit to intrude your business into mine without the courtesy of consulting me.'

'Forgive me. I understood this to be a joint undertaking with a joint purpose. Those who read – know what they read. Is that not so? Otherwise the business is of very little profit and scarcely any at all for me.'

The two now stood facing each other across the table. Rhose's indignation showed in the cold glint in her eyes. Smith's smile curled into a knowing sneer.

'Let us be clear about this, Rho – Mistress Tinnys,' he leant across the table, his thin fingers tapping the Gazetteer; 'you have the connection with those who need positions of whatever description, whether it be maid, cook – or whore; footman, stable-boy – or stallion. The Gazetteer makes them known. My connection is with those who need the maid – or whore. I may even find employment in my own private establishment. Together we may garner profit from both sides, far more than either alone. Now, is that not why you came to me rather than Wheeler and the more respectable printers?' He concluded by pulling out a chair, sitting and contemplating Rhose with calm satisfaction.

She walked over to the window to look out on the river flowing sluggishly below. What he said was true, but his was the world she wished to move from: the world of crude bargaining, of dangerous liaisons – of private rooms and Sugar Lane. Still it was also the world of Ned and his saddlebags. Her mood lightened at the thought of her lover upstairs sorting though all those packages and parcels. She shrugged and turned back to the table.

'You are right, Mr Smith. We profit from our combination. I trust these,' she held up the papers, 'will be distributed widely.'

'My chapmen already have them in hand.' He stood but was interrupted by the door bursting open.

'Oh, lud!' Jenny Driver stopped in the doorway only to be scrambled forward by her companions. The three women crowded in, no way abashed by their intrusion, despite their exclamations of apology.

'We had no mind to interrupt an intimate conversation.'

'We came only to tell you the dreadful news.'

The voices fell over one another. Jenny slid purposefully to Peter Smith's side. Nell Royle straightaway fumbled at the papers on the table. Mrs Rylance plumped into the nearest chair. It was she who took up the tale.

'Did you hear? Last night the post rider was held up at pistol point by a whole gang of masked men and robbed of the mail. Lord, in broad daylight too.'

'And that's not the worst of it,' Martha interrupted. 'They held him down and stripped the boy stark naked and left him to freeze to death on Knutsford Common.'

Alice Rylance was keen to get back to the story. 'He was trussed up to a tree stump and only got free by biting through his bonds, brave lad. Then he limped into the village a-bleeding from his wounds, poor soul.'

'I've never known him anything but limp,' Jenny giggled.

Smith smiled in his turn. 'I trust he kept clear of the gorse and brambles; they'd not do his manhood any good. And I doubt he'll be riding so soon.'

'Whoever did it will swing for sure.' There was a vindictive relish in Alice's voice, and more than a hint when she added, 'and those who hide 'em.'

Rhose faced her down. 'If they are ever caught.'

Martha had picked up one of the Gazetteers. She thrust it at Widow Rylance. 'You've had the learning,' she said, 'Does that word not say "Heap"? Is that Phanny?'

'It does indeed. Listen to this. "Phanny Heap, an Experienced and very agreeable personage",' Alice chuckled, ' "of refined manner" – refined manner indeed – "with all qualities needed to adorn a gentleman's household". Well, what stuff. And here', she pointed the words out with a stubbly finger, ' "a fine singing voice and supple of figure".'

Martha cackled out loud and the three could scarcely contain themselves.

'Why, she's supple enough with the lads. But she likes 'em stiff,' said Alice.

'And the only time I've heard her sing is when the stiff un's in play,' added Jenny.

'Now, Ladies,' Smith had to intervene, 'there's nothing to prevent an unfortunate from wanting to better herself. She has a desire to move out of such a place as Sugar Lane.' He frowned and raised an eyebrow in a pointed stare at Alice and Jenny.

'There's respectable folk live there as well,' Alice was indignant. 'We cannot help the reputation some establishments have around there. We get none but the finest gentlemen, eh Jenny?'

Jenny was paying no attention but laboriously spelling out

another of the Gazetteer's entries.

' "John B-arr-ing-ton. Twenty-one years old". What's it say, Alice? "Can dress gentleman's hair in the newest taste",' she read out, 'and he's willing "to serve any gentleman". D'you think he'd serve me?' Jenny burst into giggles once more.

Rhose decided it was time to end this speculative chatter. 'He's far more likely to settle for someone of Major Gee's persuasion, if you remember him. A likely candidate for one of your particular rooms, Mr Smith?'

The printer bridled at this direct attack. He gathered up the bundle of papers; bowed formally and moved to the door. 'I think we have agreed on our business, Mistress Tinnys. I shall see that these get the widest circulation. I have no doubt the enterprise will be profitable to us both.' He bowed again. 'Ladies.'

When he had gone Martha warned, 'I trust you have a long spoon to be supping with him.'

'I am well aware of his reputation, but I need his assistance in this. There is money to be made from the placing of servants. As for the other, need I remind you that everyone has two ears and only one mouth?' There was menace in her voice and her warning look took in all three. They nodded in understanding.

'We know your meaning,' said Alice Rylance. 'It may be that we too profit from your Gazetteer. I for one am always in need of a green goose, such often tempts the jaded pallet.'

Jenny pouted and protested: 'I've never failed you yet. I'm no draggle tail.'

'No my poppet.' Alice patted the young girl's cheek. 'And I'd trust to you to put the young ones through their paces.'

Rhose was becoming more restless as she grew concerned to know how Ned progressed upstairs. She let out a theatrical sigh and ushered the three harpies to the threshold.

'I fear I must leave you ladies. I have an inn to attend to. See Mary on your way out, there'll be a bottle for you.' With some mock ceremony she chivvied them to the bar before hurrying up the stairs.

*

In her room Ned had whisked away evidence of last nights' robbery save for the saddlebags thrown casually on the bed.

'Rich pickings, pippin! Close to two hundred in notes and bills I can exchange through Rupert the notary – and letters of interest, particularly this.' He tapped a small letter on the side table. 'Read and give me your thoughts.'

The letter was addressed to Joseph Bue. Ned settled on the edge of the four-poster while Rhose read:

Swan with two necks, Lad Lane London

Mr Bue

I arrived in the roads yesterday. It was strange to leave the East Indies after so long a time with the uncertainties ahead. We had fearsome storms after leaving Ceylon and took two months before we anchored at Table Bay at the end of December. The ship had lost men and many were sick but we managed to set sail by end of January for St Helena. And so by the Azores, Madeira and Lisbon to England, which we joyfully saw about five o'clock in the afternoon three days ago. I have some business to attend in London for some Madras merchants. I am booked on the coach leaving here Friday for Manchester. All being well I arrive Monday evening. Perhaps you would do me the honour of taking supper with me. It's fifteen years since I saw Manchester still I expect the Royal Oak still flourishes. I plan to go straight to see my family. Then to find our treasure. I trust her guardians and I will be in agreement as to her future. Such a jewel must be carefully displayed at last. My best service and hearty prayers.

Thomas Miller

When she had finished, she stood lost in thought.

'Well?' Ned rose. 'I must be away, but I needed your opinion before I left.'

He put his arm around her and drew her to him. She

responded with a light kiss and looked up at him, her forehead creased in deep concentration.

'Fifteen years takes us back to '45 or '46. A mysterious child – a girl – but what is the connection with an apothecary like Bue?' She was talking to herself, turning the paper over in her hands, Ned apparently forgotten. 'And Thomas, who is Thomas Miller? I smell intrigue – I scent money!'

Bright-eyed, she threw her arms around the highwayman's neck, forcing him backwards once more onto the bed, then running her hands up the inside of his thighs.

'Thomas's jewel's a treasure, I know it, I know it – and, as we minded before there's more treasure here, and mine for the asking I trust!'

Chapter Five

Greenwood Lea

As Jonathan Agar set off up Smithy Bank, he pressed hard under the walls, the first floor overhang providing some shelter. Quietly cursing to himself at the filthy state of the streets, he gave the odd pig a kick when he stumbled over it. He turned into Smithy Door and realized the town was busy in spite of the awful weather. The drummer from the Royal Welch Volunteers was beating for recruits to go to the Bull's Head. Glancing into the Shambles where the crowd was pushing and shoving he decided there was no time to visit the inn to hear the latest gossip. The Exchange too had best be avoided, though one could learn useful snippets by imbibing in the Long Room. He could brook no delay if he was to reach the Fletchers' and return tonight. He hurried on to his shop.

'The Sign of the Unicorn' in Back Alley was small though well stocked and fitted out. A counter along one side, with a chair next to it, allowed for consultations with his customers. Behind on shelves were majolica jars containing herbs, spices and galenicals together with ointments, syrups and electuries. These latter preparations were made in the rear compounding room. Opposite, more shelves held leech jars, glazed drug rounds and bottled preparations. A flight of stairs between the two rooms led up to his living quarters above.

'Matthew, I want you to deliver the cordial to Mrs Bayley in the Square. Assure her the liquorice will aid the cough, and the melissa and hyssop calm the chest. I will attend her tomorrow when I return from the Fletchers'. Be sure to let her know where I am going as it will be the talk of her tea table.'

With a quiet 'Yes sir' Matthew slipped out of the door.

Jonathan Agar gathered up his cloak from behind the counter. Sir Geoffrey was his most valued client; his entry into Manchester's polite society. It had been a most auspicious day when he was first summoned to Greenwood Lea. Henry Haworth of Blackburn had been the cause; he had long tended the Fletchers. As a young apprentice he had accompanied his master there. The Haworths, apothecaries for nearly a century, had considerable wealth. By coming to Manchester he had hoped to make his own fortune. Still it meant loosing his connections and starting afresh. The Holy Well near Blackburn was well known as a cure for eye diseases and 'Agars Blackburn Collyrium for the Eyes' used this belief. It was indeed fortunate that the Haworths had been selling it – Sir Geoffrey insisted on trying it – and he had been summoned to attend the patient. What better recommendation could a medicine have than a puff from the local gentry. The sales were increasing satisfactorily and his other remedies were starting to be known. It was now a toast to the tea table and the coffee house.

Reaching down his saddlebags, which hung behind the counter, he packed several medicines and herbs his experience led him to think might be necessary. Matthew slipped quietly back into the shop.

'All done?'

'Yes sir.'

'Good, I shall be back before nightfall.'

Agar left the shop and crossed to the Buck and Hawthorn where he stabled his horse and pony. The ostler saw him entering the yard and saddled the chestnut with speed. He knew Jonathan Agar was not one to be kept waiting. Agar admired his horse, Peru, as it was led out. It might be flim-flam but a fine horse impressed the public and convinced them he was a man to be trusted. He would ride through the busiest part of town even if it meant taking longer. It was good for business – a successful apothecary had to be seen round and about. There would be people to speak to. Let them know he was going to see Sir Geoffrey Fletcher.

Rhose met him by the Ring o' Bells. How fine she looked in her riding habit, he thought. It reminded him so strongly of the days when they rode together regularly.

'Much like the old days, Jonathan?' Rhose's thoughts obviously mirrored his own. 'You on your fine horse while I trot behind on the pony!'

Agar chuckled. ' 'Deed so, Rhose. You were naught but a girl then but now – why a handsome young woman, a lady of property even.'

'As you say. Yet, I'm content to be in the saddle again and I'll not deny I welcome the chance to meet the Fletchers once more.'

They turned their steeds past Chethams, then over the Irk out into open country. The sight of the apothecary astride his horse before her brought back memories. Those days had been her first taste of freedom, freedom from the tyranny of someone else's household. It was freedom from 'yes, ma'am', 'no, ma'am'; freedom from the lecherous pawing of the 'master', or worse the fumbling groping of the 'young master'. A shiver went through her at the memory of those days in service.

'Not cold surely?' Agar had noticed the tremor as he dropped back to her side.

'No, merely an unquiet memory.'

'Ah, none of those now. It's a new life before you. Time to shake off the past.'

Rhose nodded in reply as they trotted on in silence. A new life perhaps ... she was her own mistress now, and mistress of others: the inn, Sugar Lane. Yet these were still part of the past; what could she make of the future? Ally herself again with the apothecary's art? What future in that when no one would take a woman healer seriously – unless she was old and wrinkled. A highwayman's doxy? No, she was sure the future held more, however satisfying Ned's pleasuring. She smiled to herself, enjoying the sun's warming rays now breaking through the veil of clouds.

Agar turned the horses off the road and down the steep rutted lane that led to the house. A stand of trees guarded the house from the road, their bare branches offering protection from the worst of the winter gales. Greenwood Lea was an old-fashioned rambling house built of the local stone. The house seemed part of the landscape, the steep cliff to the rear making it all but invisible from the road. The front with its mullioned windows looked out over the valley. As the horse clattered into the cobbled yard, Robert the stable-boy came out to meet him.

'It's good to see you, Mr Agar, the master is taken real poorly.'

'Thank you, Rob, take good care of the horses.'

Hannah the maid opened the door, welcoming them both into the kitchen. They had been watching for him – someone must indeed be ill.

'Hannah will take you through.' This from Mrs Rigby, the housekeeper, who was sharing a herbal ale with the cook in front of the kitchen fire. Leaving his hat and saddlebags on a chair, they followed Hannah through the passage leading to the hall. Waiting there were the ladies of the family, Lady Elisabeth, Anne and Charlotte. All usually so bright and cheerful, had an air of despair.

'He is in great pain, Mr Agar. The doctor has been and can do nothing. Sir Geoffrey insisted you should be called. The doctor protested but as Sir Geoffrey said, "If the King can send for an apothecary so can I". He is upstairs. Follow me if you will. You are welcome too, Mistress Tinnys. Girls you must wait here in the great hall. Francis is with his father.'

Passing his cloak to the maid, the apothecary followed Lady Elisabeth up the broad oak staircase. He motioned Rhose to follow. As Agar passed the large window at the top of the stairs he glanced out over the gravel terrace at the back of the house toward the orchard and valley beyond.

'Fie, Mr Agar, this is no time to admire our view. Sir Geoffrey is in here.'

She had opened the door to the bedroom. With a slight bow to the lady, Agar entered the chamber.

The heat in the oak panelled room struck him a blow. Despite the fine day, a fire was blazing in the immense fireplace and Clegg, the butler, was adding more fuel. The curtains were closed and the room lit by several candles. Francis who was sitting next to the bed, rose and crossed the room. Agar noticed that the usually immaculate son was somewhat dishevelled.

'It is well you have come. We are losing hope. The doctor bled him, as it seemed only to be an inflammatory fever, but to no avail. A second bleeding gave him no manner of relief. He's suffering from flushes of heat, loss of strength and appetite and a heavy sort of respiration. The doctor says he has a weak pulse. He tries to rise but is taken with a very great faintness so he must be returned to bed. Now he is in great pain.'

'I shall examine him and the portions of blood that were drawn if they were kept. Draw back the curtains.'

Francis did so, noticing for the first time Rhose standing at the threshold. With a curt bow he moved towards her. She returned greeting and moved to the bedside.

Agar slowly considered the blood, then his patient. The diagnosis seemed correct. Though exhausted, Sir Geoffrey was free from delirium. His tongue was black and his breath stank so it was horribly offensive even at a great distance. He was weak and trembling. Blistering and volatile cordials would certainly kill him if the illness didn't. Agar turned to Rhose.

'I am going to recommend the Bark in frequent small doses with Elixir Vitrioli and syrup of red poppies. Claret and red Port with about half water, he can drink at pleasure. You will find the Bark, elixir and syrup are in my saddlebags. Prepare them immediately if you please. Clegg, will you assist Mistress Tinnys.' They descended to the kitchen at once.

'Will he survive?' Francis sounded anxious.

'I trust so. I'll send Matthew this evening with an acid decoction of seville orange rind, roses, cinnamon water and Japon earth. I'll attend early tomorrow. If all is well then, a small dose of rhubarb should help to carry off any injurious matter.'

'My mother blames me for this. I came back late the other night from Manchester. Father had gone up to the road convinced I had fallen from my horse in a state of torpor. He was soaked through and a day later developed the fever. Lord, they fuss over me. I shall ride back with you, an evening at Smith's coffee house will improve my spirits and Matthew can attend me on my return.' He turned to the door, shouting for the butler. 'Clegg, send Jeremy to my room, I'm returning with Mr Agar, and warn Rob I shall need Emperor ready in half an hour.'

Rhose busied herself with the prescription, pulverizing the bark and placing it in a card box, the lid bearing Agar's personal monogram. She poured the elixir and the syrup into two small bottles from the larger bottles that had been carried in the saddlebags. The housekeeper and the maid watched in silence. She hurried back to the stairs to find Charlotte anxiously waiting.

'I did not know that you still worked with the apothecary; Mistress Tinnys.'

'Occasionally, I was once his assistant and came as nurse when he attended your papa. I think I have not lost my skills in mixing the potions.'

'A many-talented woman, I have no doubt.' Anne emerged from the sitting room.

'Mayhap Charlotte you could follow a similar profession when you leave our household.'

Charlotte blushed and stepped away.

'A young lady of Miss Fletcher's background would have no need of such menial toil. I had none of her advantages.'

'Advantages, yes, advantages indeed.' Anne paused, looking meaningfully at the younger girl. 'But we hold you from your "menial" duty. My father should not be put at hazard by girlish chit-chat.'

Rhose mounted the stairs to find Lady Elisabeth had entered the room. She was standing by the bed, smiling down at her husband. She moved to allow Rhose to carefully administer the first doses. 'I hope this will begin its work soon, Sir Geoffrey. The red poppies should help ease the pain before too long.'

Agar explained carefully what he had prescribed, and that Matthew would be bringing the decoction later that evening.

Lady Elizabeth took Rhose by the hand. 'It is a relief to find you with us again, Mistress Tinnys. You were always so kindly a nurse.'

'Thank you, Lady Elisabeth. I am pleased to do what I can, but the inn takes all of my time now that I am on my own.'

'Yes, I was sorry to hear of your loss. A widow's life is not an easy one.' A look of sadness filled her eyes and there was a reassuring clasp of hands.

The door to the room was flung open. 'Ready, Agar, let's go. Don't worry Ma, I'll be home soon with Matthew and the medicine.'

His startled parent looked across the room at her only son. He was now the veritable beau attired in a purple coat with a blue and silver brocade waistcoat and cuffs, shining white stockings and black leather shoes with red heels and intricate silver buckles. On his head was a powdered brigadier wig, the queue tied with a large black satin bow. His mother felt something akin to shame that he could be so unfeeling towards his father. Francis was anxious to go. He had spent a fortune obtaining the latest wig from France and was determined not to allow anyone in Manchester to upstage him. Deuce sir, he was determined to be the talk of the coffee houses.

Agar turned to the others. 'But what of Mistress Tinnys? I would not have her return alone.'

Lady Elisabeth assured him that if Rhose would consent to stay the night and help with the nursing, she would make sure she was accompanied to town the next morning. With a deep bow Agar said his farewells to the Fletchers and left the room. Clegg was instructed to see that Rhose was furnished with a room. With a last sympathetic look at the patient, she followed the butler out of the door.

Lady Elisabeth moved closer to her husband and gently took his hand in hers. They listened to the sound of the horses' hoofs in the yard and then they were lost as they ascended the lane.

'I hope the pain is easing, Geoffrey. I must talk to you about Charlotte. What would I do if I were to lose you now? I know we have talked of her future often but we always thought she would be married and away from here. She would no longer be our responsibility.'

Sir Geoffrey gave a deep sigh. 'I know my dear. She has been a great trust. A marriage must be arranged. With Anne spoken for it will seem natural. You must choose a loving man who you can trust with the secret.'

Elisabeth sat by the bed holding Geoffrey's hands as she gazed into his haggard face, relating all that had happened. Slowly she read the letter.

March 1759
Mr Bue
Your letter arrived with its dismal news of my sister Mary's death and I thank you for all your kindness to her and her child and your staunchness to the cause. I am glad my niece is safe hidden with friends and cared for by a willing family who will keep the knowledge safe and secret. I have soldiered with Clive through his victory at Plassey and risen through the ranks but now hope to return home. I am applying for my discharge and pray I may set sail for the Cape of Good Hope and England in October. My best service and hearty prayers to you.

Thomas Miller

'What shall we do Geoffrey?'

'There is nothing to do but wait, my dear.'

'How long will it take to come from India?'

'Two months . . . four months? I have no notion, there are so many things that could happen, storms, light winds. Still he could be here soon, then we will decide what to do. Thomas is Charlotte's kin though lowly born.'

Anxiously Lady Elisabeth thought of what that might mean. 'Thomas's is a terrible tale. Joining the Prince then being taken prisoner at Carlisle. He suffered terrible tortures before he was shipped to India. Thank goodness no one knew about Mary. At least we did not have to see his head on the Exchange in Manchester like Deacon and Sydall.'

'True, but at least we knew he was alive from his letters. I have waited for him to arrive at our door ever since. Let us pray he is in good health. As to those letters, we must burn them, Elisabeth. If I should survive naught is lost. It could be fatal for you if they were found. The country has not forgotten the Jacobite threat and persecution may come again.' Geoffrey collapsed against the pillows.

Elisabeth crossed the room to the desk and took two further letters from a secret drawer. She glanced at them as she moved towards the fire. The first letter had come from Thomas as he was about to board the ship at Spithead, telling them of his dreadful time after his capture at Carlisle. The second was from India. She paused as she read this letter one more time.

March 1753

Dear sister

I have not had a line from you since I have been in the East Indies though I have wrote several times. I should be glad to hear from you that I may know how you and everybody does. I don't know rightly who to write to so I send this letter to our mutual acquaintance Mr Joseph Bue, the apothecary in Long Mill Gate to apprise you of how I have fared since I came into this country. I have learnt a lot of soldiering against the French and against robbers who are detrimental to our trade. The natives are cowardly and very ill disciplined and we have driven them from their walled city and captured their king called the Nabob. The general came and gave liberty to all who had an inclination to stay in the company service. Worried for my safety and yours if I returned so soon I accepted the bounty of forty rupees and enlisted. We joined the few troops left to defend Fort St George, the fleet having sailed. There came word that our main force at Trichinopoly was besieged by the French together with many native troops of Chandra Sahib and they begged assistance. The new governor allowed our Captain Clive to attempt to capture Chandra Sahib's capital to draw him off. Two hundred of us together with three hundred sepoys succeeded and after a desperate siege reinforcements arrived and saved us: we were but eighty left together with 420 sepoys. We are now famous as the veterans of Arcot.

I hope you will be glad enough to let me hear from you at the first opportunity, as I have not had a line for six years. The child must now be grown and I pray that you manage well as always. Hearty prayers, your loving brother

Thomas

Elisabeth thrust the papers into the flames. Within a minute they were consumed. She returned to the bed, sat by her failing husband and so began her vigil through the night. It was not long. By morning Francis was the master of the house.

Chapter Six

At the Ring o' Bells

After his father's death, a pall of gloom had descended on Greenwood Lea. Francis, pleading business in town, escaped to Manchester. Lost in reverie he strolled down Mill Gate to the Ring o' Bells, passed the towering bulk of the Grammar School. A group of the blue-clad boys were splashing in the gutters of the road. He jabbed at them with his cane: 'Out of the way! You'll muddy my breeches – off with you back to your lessons. You're a set of idle scholars, don't you know. Your masters will hear of this.'

Laughing, the boys kicked up the foul water and ran jeering back towards the school. Francis waved his cane impotently, then was forced to jump back as a phaeton clattered past at great speed. Further annoyed, he watched as it turned into the yard of the inn, which was his own destination. The owner deserved a good caning, he thought, so he followed the vehicle into the inn yard.

Much to his surprise he saw the phaeton being pulled into the large barn next to the stable. Curious he drew back under the archway where he could watch unobserved. Long Ned came out of the barn followed by Rhose who carefully shut and barred the door. Ned's chestnut horse in a lather of sweat stood in the middle of the yard. He led it over to a stable by the arch and they went inside. Where was the ostler? This unusual behaviour piqued Frank's curiosity. He had heard rumours of Ned's nefarious activities – did this confirm them? Hidden in the recess of the arch, he strained to hear the conversation.

'Really Ned, it's dangerous to come like this in daylight. Who knows who could have seen you? I know you like to live dangerously, but it will end badly one day,' Rhose remonstrated.

'Don't worry my pippin. I just need to lay the wheels low awhile. I had a nasty fright last night. I took a drive up the Bury Road and hid the carriage in a copse, changed and rode out. A likely mark happened along and a few guineas were my reward – perhaps a present for you my love. When I went back to the wood the phaeton had gone! 'Sdeath, what a fright! The biter bit!' laughed Ned.

'Where had it gone? Who had taken it?'

'I rode on and came across two cowmen dragging it into town. They were taking it to the constables. Fortunately a tall tale of highwaymen robbing me, disrobing me and, oh yes, a guinea for their troubles, persuaded them it was mine. It would have been a different story if the authorities had been involved. It seems I must plan a different tactic for next time.'

'Thank heaven you were not taken. I'll send the ostler out to take care of the horse.'

'Yes, Rhose, then you can take care of me. I promised you a present; the one I had in mind involved one for me too.'

As they came from the stable, Ned pulled her to him in a rough embrace. Watching her laughing as she broke away, Francis realized she was far from the reluctant lover. Damn, he thought, he had planned an assault on the same lines himself. The grieving widow should have been glad of his attention. Perhaps he'd think again; he had no fancy for Long Ned as a rival.

'I shall look forward later to your "great gift".' Rhose walked to the back door. 'Now I have paying clients to look to, though they cannot compete with your attractions, my dear Ned.'

The highwayman kissed Rhose tenderly on the back of her

neck and strolled out of the yard. Francis emerged from the arch, walked to the front of the Ring o' Bells, pushed open the door and made his entrance.

Inside the fuggy air reeked with a miasma of spirits and tobacco, the rank sweat of men's bodies and the more appetising odour of food. At a corner table sat three butchers, aprons and arms stiff with blood, the unmistakable stink of offal keeping others at bay. At the fireplace a carter, whip negligent in his hands, leant against the mantle, backside to the fire. The rest of the room was crowded, sitting and standing, with hucksters, traders, chandlers, market men and idlers, all gossiping in their own small groups. The sawdust floor was pockmarked with tobacco spittle and the dregs of spilled drinks. A lurcher gnawed at a discarded bone by his master's legs while he and his fellows tucked into veal cutlets and neck of mutton. Overall there was the noisy clamour of talk and chat and dispute punctuated by the coughs and splutters of drinking men.

Francis paused, waiting for the deference due to him among such a throng, but there was no bowing and scraping here. He was forced to elbow his way to the bar. There, a round little man was the centre of attention of a gathering of respectable looking tradesmen.

'. . . I knew the apothecary could not last the day. Dr Hall did his best to save him.'

'They certainly keep to their own,' muttered a lean, gangling individual at the edge of the group.

'What mean you, Mr Loftus?' Laurence asked.

Embarrassed when all eyes turned to him, Loftus shrugged. 'Heigh ho, everyone here knows about that Jacobite connection, Hail and Bue and Deacon – and Byrom and—' He stopped as soon as he saw Francis nearby.

'What? What?' Laurence persisted. His listeners, aware of the presence of young Fletcher, shuffled and began to move away.

'No, don't go. I would hear what cully has to say.' Francis leaned an elbow on the bar with an exaggerated languor. 'Were you to link my good family name with that traitorous crew?' His tone was light, but his dark eyes carried menace. Loftus dropped his head, avoiding the younger man's threatening gaze.

'Now, what is all this?' Rhose bustled in from the back. 'Why, Frank – I beg your pardon – *Sir* Francis, it is many a month since we saw you here, and it is an honour to see you. What may I get you?' Rhose's welcoming smile conquered all; calm was restored to the bar.

'Why thank you Mistress Tinnys – your best brandy if you please. And whatever my – friends, here are drinking.' Josiah Laurence bobbed back to take centre stage while Loftus took the chance to slip away into the crowd.

'I was merely recounting the terrible tale of the rencontre between Mr Bue and Major Gee . . . perhaps you have heard?'

'Damn, was it he you were talking of?' Francis was now all attention.

'Aye, a few words in the coffee house, a challenge, and Mister Bue lay at death's door.'

'I had heard of some squabble at Peter Smith's but thought it not serious.'

'Serious enough,' the druggist Leigh put in. He was eager to show his own importance in the affair. 'Gee called Bue a traitor . . .'

'Some may say it's true,' a voice murmured.

'And Bue impugned,' Leigh continued, lingering over the word, liking the sound of it. 'the Major's, er, masculinity.'

Francis barked a laugh: 'Ha, he was well known for visiting Smith's private rooms, it's not the wenches he was bum-tickling. Beg pardon, Mistress Tinnys.'

'Be that as it may,' Leigh was keen to finish his story, 'I saw it all at Dawson's Field, the Major laid Joseph's guts open and Dr Hall couldn't put 'em back.'

'But what's all this got to do with Deacon and Byrom and the rest?' Laurence asked, not noticing Francis's newly glowering face.

'Why they are all of the Jacobite clan! Do you not remember

the executions back in '46? They were down your part of the country. Two heads, Deacon's and Sydall's, came here to be spiked on the Exchange as a warning to us all. 'Twas Dr Hall secretly took 'em down at night. A real scandal it was.' Leigh was carried away with the urgency of his tale. 'Why many high-stomached families were involved, some say even Lord Mosley himself. Then there was the Reverend Clayton, John Byrom, John Dickenson, and even Sir Geoffrey. . . .'

Too late he realized his mistake. Francis's hand closed round his throat as he pushed him back over the bar, face to face. He jerked back at the evil breath from the other's rotten teeth, but held his grip. He growled into the druggist's ear: 'Have a care, you poxy rattle, or you'll have my boot up your arse.'

'Now Sir Francis, I'll have no violence in my inn if you please.' Rhose was quick to intervene. 'As for you John Leigh, that's enough of your babbling, better settle your score and be gone. Well gentlemen, what will you have? There's food aplenty, stew on the fire, coneys and ham.'

Leigh threw coins on the counter, glared at the young elegant and shouldered his way to the door. At that moment it was thrown open to a burst of song:
'See how the starveling Frenchmen strut
And call us English dogs.'

Three very smart fellows stood on the threshold and in full throat finished:
'We shall show those braggart foes
That beef and beer give heavier blows
Than soup and roasted frogs.'

This brought forth a ragged cheer for the singers who presented a remarkable spectacle. Two of the newcomers could not be more contrasted. One was as wide as he was tall, in short plush frock with metal buttons, almost shabby in its plainness. The other was a tall rake of a youth, elegant in cut-away coat and tight-fitting waistcoat, bright buttoned and silver piped. The third wore a riding coat of dingy brown with top boots scuffed and muddy. They all carried beaver hats elegantly; their short bob wigs glistened like fresh snow. Together they resembled a set of library steps.

The smallest of the three waddled towards the bar, arms open wide. The throng instinctively parted before him.

'Why Francis, I was sad to hear of your loss. A good man gone! Yet how fortunate to meet you here even if I find you cavorting with a riff-raff of ragamuffins, rapscallions and chaw-bacons.' This was said with a cheerful countenance and rounded off with: 'No offence meant gentlemen.' His widespread arms took in the whole assembly, his hands waving in almost royal acknowledgement. 'Give them what they want, Mistress Innkeeper, provided it's good British ale.'

There was a thundering of tankards as the potboy and barmaid scurried to get and fill the orders. Cries of 'Thank your honour', 'Death to the French', and the like drowned out the grumbles of those still feeling insulted.

'Jemmy, by God, what brings you to town?' Francis responded to a polite touching of hands and the sketch of a bow.

'Why, to see you of course!' the three chorused. At the bar the others drifted away leaving the four a significant space.

Francis turned to Rhose: 'Let me introduce my friends. Mistress Tinnys, the Right Honourable James Falkner of Guilden Sutton – well known in Cheshire for his liberality, his ostentation and his quick temper, and an infrequent visitor to this town.'

'Charmed, ma'am.' He reached chubby fingers across the counter briefly clasping Rhose's hand.

'Oliver Banton, Esquire, of Grappenhall, sportsman, dilettante and, as you can see, not a fashion plate. And finally, young Robert Johnson of – damme if I haven't forgotten where you do come from Bob, my lad.' Francis quirked an eyebrow, grinning up at the tallest of the three.

Johnson blushed and stammered, 'Th – th – that's not fair, you know I have trouble with m – m – my, oh devil take it! F – f – f—'

'Frodsham,' laughed Banton. 'Don't tease, Francis. We must

pay our respects to our charming hostess.' With this he took Rhose's hand and gave a deferential kiss all the while holding her gaze in his. He would have been handsome but for the ravages of pockmarks over his face.

'I much admired your entrance gentlemen,' she said. 'A fine patriotic song.' She removed her hand from his but the glint in her eye was encouraging.

'Indeed ma'am,' Banton replied. 'We learnt it from that one-legged old soldier that begs by the Dark passage. 'Tis newly minted to celebrate our late victories in North America.'

'Th – thanks to the *late* General Wolfe,' Johnson added.

'Why, a hit! A p – p – palpabie hit.' Falkner clapped the younger man on the back. 'Our ingénue risks a sally.'

'Not the S – S – Sally you tumbled last night,' Johnson came back with a neighing laugh. The others joined in.

'Trawling the bagnios and flogging houses of Liverpool again, Jemmy? One whore's never been enough for you, has she? What's happened to the faithful Emily? You've never sent her packing at last?'

'Why Frank, the slut has been bilking me these past four months! I put her out with what she came in – bare-assed. Egad! You should have heard the weeping and wailing. I told her what my granny said to me: the more you cry, the less you piss.'

There was a renewed round of laughter followed by calls for more drinks. Rhose had left them to their banter and was busied round the room, a friendly smile for all. Josiah Laurence at a table by the fire motioned her over and they were soon in close conversation. Those nearer the bar made no effort to hide their interest in the young bucks' chatter.

'What of you in that petticoat household of yours?' Banton asked. 'I caught a glimpse of a most charming biddy out with your sister the other day. How goes that campaign?'

'Yes, Charlotte, bewitching and ripe for the plucking! I'll have her one day and that soon, contrary little minx though she is.'

'Come, come, we have not come to talk of whoring and dally-ing.' Falkner dropped the bantering tone. 'I'm putting up my fine Cheshire fighting cocks for a Main next month. We're here to meet with Major Stapleton at the Boar's Head to settle the date and the purse. Will you come, Frank, see all's done fairly?'

'Why did you not say so at first? We could have saved time and breath. Pox on it! I will come with you to see you Cheshire coves don't diddle my honest countryman. On the way you must teach me that brave patriotic song – how did it go again?'

'Why, we'll take you to the very fount. The old soldier that got his left leg blown off at Quebec, or was it Williamsburg?' The Honourable James tossed down the last of his brandy.

'Right leg, Arcot,' Banton protested.

'I'm certain sure it is his left. He has his crutch to that side.'

'N – no. Oliver's right – it's right, his right,' Johnson put in.

'Twenty guineas says it is his left,' said Falkner.

'Thirty it's right.'

'I'll go fifty with Oliver's,' said Francis.

'Match you both,' Falkner led the way into the street adding, 'He will be down by Smithy Door now and, zounds, if he's still got that left leg I'll chop it off myself.'

When they left a murmur ran through the room. There was no doubt the habitués felt more comfortable without the gentry, although it was clear to them that Rhose Tinnys welcomed such custom. A few heads turned to see how she reacted to the departure, but she was too intent on business with the little man up from the south.

The four friends strolled round the corner to Smithy Door continuing the dispute over the missing leg. They were disappointed to find the old soldier gone from his usual spot. The narrow street was packed with the jostling crowd making their way to the market.

'Deuce take it,' James protested as he was pushed aside by a bevy of loud laughing women. 'There's an uncommon lot of common people even for market day.'

'Did you not hear there's a thief in the p – p – pillory, damme,'

Robert cursed his stutter bitterly, 'Splendid entertainment for a sunny morning?'

'Indeed, fine entertainment for the mob to come and gloat.' Francis pushed his way roughly through the crush.

Johnson's tall frame and long neck enabled him to see over the bustling throng and he looked down with amused condescension on his plump companion. Then he cried, 'Why, I spy your man, Jemmy, there on the corner of the Shambles.'

Standing by the butcher's stalls stood a large imposing figure in scarlet regimentals. He was in conversation with a lean young man, soberly dressed in a black tight-fitting coat and immaculate white stock.

'Major, Major!' James bellowed the length of the street. 'A word if you please.'

The military man turned, his florid face beaming in a welcoming smile. 'Why James! I was just on my way to our meeting. How fare your Cheshire fowls? Ready for the slaughter, what?' His guffaw turned heads and seemed to embarrass his companion. 'Just having a quiet conversation with young William Jones here. Have you met?'

'Know him well,' Francis interrupted, clapping the young man on the shoulder. 'Banking alfresco, eh, Will?' He laughed when he saw the other's puzzled face. 'A frenchified term, my boy, means out of doors.'

'Indeed not.' William was on his dignity. 'A chance meeting, that is all, you know well we conduct our business on King Street.'

'Enough of this, gentlemen, if you please.' Oliver was becoming restless. 'This is not the place for an exchange of pleasantries.'

James deliberately withdrew a kerchief from his sleeve to dramatically cover his nose, before waving towards the swill swirling towards the central gutter.

'Point taken! James! Lets remove from the stench.'

The Major agreed and they moved into the relative quiet of a side alley. He continued apologetically, 'Can't stay, military matters, don't you know. Delighted to meet but can't stay. Must get this cocking business settled though.'

Oliver suggested they meet in a week's time. 'It will give us the opportunity of the spectacle of your suitably named Beadle, James Birch, administering a flogging to two of your miserable soldiers, Major.'

The other grumbled an explosive protest: 'Not mine, by gad!'

Robert intervened. 'A p-p-p-public f-f-, damme, flogging – splendid entertainment for a summer morning.'

'Well said, Bob, I hear . . . money.'

With this the group separated, William Jones taking Francis to one side. 'I was most distressed to learn of your father's passing. The family must be deeply mourning.'

Francis mumbled something in reply.

'Do you think it would be permissible for me to go to pay my respects to your mamma and the girls?'

'Most uncommon kind. *Mama*,' he stressed the word with irony, 'will be receiving after midday. Anne and Charlotte would, I'm sure, welcome such courtesy. Now, if you will forgive me, I have my own financial affairs to attend to.'

Will watched him go. Despite the sadness of the occasion he looked forward to a visit to the Fletchers'. Whatever the situation, he was always happy to spend time with Charlotte, the only girl he had eyes for.

Chapter Seven

At the Whipping Post

The morning sun glinted through the overhanging roofs of Smithy Bank as Rhose and Ned set out toward the Market Square. Soon they found themselves bustled along by an animated throng of noisy citizens. Everyone seemed to be there, abuzz with chatter and eager anticipation. Hawkers shoved through the mêlée, crying their wares, fruits and pies, fresh fish and rotten tomatoes. Smith's newsmen waved scandal sheets in the air, bawling their latest 'horrid' ballads in the faces of all the passers-by.

'The whole town's out to see the fun,' Ned remarked as he took Rhose's arm, fending off the crush of a rabble of draymen.

'I'd not call it "fun",' Rhose protested. 'Yet there's not many can resist a public flogging – ho there! Take care with that sword, else my man will make you use it.' A gallant, already half-cut, had tangled his dragging scabbard in her full skirt. With an approving smirk and a mumbled apology he reeled away.

'Ah, it's *my* man now, is it? Off with the old and on with the new, my pippin.' Ned gave her waist an affectionate squeeze. She broke away half angry, half smiling.

'No, 'twas merely a way of speaking to fend off bully-boys. I'm a free woman now. I'll have you remember that. There's no one owns Rhose Tinnys.'

'So be it. And Ned's not one to own anyone or anything, you ken that. Free and easy, a roving eye and a roving . . . blade.' He laughed. 'But you know,' the language was mocking, the tone serious, 'we're a lot alike, you and me.'

A rumbling murmur rippled through the square followed by an expectant hush. A passage was roughly driven through the heaving mass and two men were led and pushed to the staging of the whipping post. The Constable's men strapped the two high to the pillory and ripped off their shirts, exposing their skinny backs to the gaping onlookers. A wave of groans and cheers greeted the powerful figure that next strode out holding high the whip. A lone voice sang out, 'Give 'em a taste of the whip, thy bannybegger will show 'em, Birch, me lad.' The Beadle turned and grinned, cracking his whip in the air.

'I'll not stint today,' he bellowed.' He let out a great roar, echoed by the crowd, as he stepped up to the prisoners. The Constable read out the charges against the two felons, soldiers who had stolen a watch and a tankard from the Dog Inn.

'Poor fools,' Ned's voice was subdued, 'to be caught for such paltry things.'

'It's harsh, but I've no sympathy for those two. An inn-keeper's life is hard enough with the likes of them stealing from honest folks like Jed Perkin.'

'Ay, Rhose, they knew the penalty and Jed can spare little. I only relieve those of what they can well afford.'

'Like His Majesty's mail.' Rhose scoffed and her companion grinned. There was a stir among the folk around them and Rhose started in surprise. The two Fletcher sisters were coming through the crowd. Anne was stalking, head high, ignoring the stares and mutterings. Charlotte tripped behind, head averted, clinging to the older girl.

'Why, Miss Anne, Miss Charlotte! This is scarce the place for you.'

'Mistress Tinnys,' Anne inclined her head, 'had we realized

what was to take place we would not be here. Our brother was to have escorted us from our dancing lesson to the Byrom's an hour ago. When he did not arrive we decided to make our own way. I cannot understand what has become of him.'

'Surely you are not here for this degrading spectacle?'

'No, indeed, we are visiting Phoebe Byrom – my – my wedding preparations, you know. It may be good to see justice being meted out to those who deserve it but Mama will be horrified that we were exposed to the crowd.'

The first blows were struck as though to reinforce her words. The whip lashed first to right then left. One of the prisoners screamed, the other moaned, teeth biting deep into his lip. The crowd bayed for more blood. Birch paused, strutted around the post then delivered a mighty thunderclap of the whip above the heads of the crowd. A howl erupted, then he turned on his heel and resumed the flogging with greater vigour. The soldiers shrieked in the agony of bright weals scarring their backs. Their bodies shuddered as the lash bit into the flesh and the blood flowed. Charlotte and Anne clung together transfixed. The younger girl buried her head into the other's shoulder. Anne could not drag her eyes away from the spectacle. The hiss and slash of the blows kept time with the rhythmic chanting around them. The prisoners sagged against their binding thongs, blood coursing down their backs, soaking their breeches. Rhose found she had put both arms around the girls in a vain attempt to shield them from the sight.

'Come away with me, Ned's strong arm will find us a way.'

'And so they shall come away but with me!' A new voice cut through the racket. Standing behind them, one hand resting on his sword hilt, was the missing brother. He was elegant in dark brown brocade, his wig impeccably powdered, a smile belied by the anger in his harsh blue eyes.

'What my dear sisters are you doing in this rabble?' He saw Rhose bridle. 'Oh, not you, Mistress Tinnys! For you I have the greatest respect and admiration. It is this raggedy mob. . . .' His glance flickered meaningfully toward Long Ned.

73

'Frank, please take us away from here. Why did you not come to meet us as Mama instructed you? Making our own way we got caught up in this frenzied crowd. It's all your fault!' Anne moved to grasp her brother's arm.

The flogging had ended, the prisoners were being cut down and dragged away. Birch, beaming and sweating, snapped his whip one more time, drops of blood splashing the gloating spectators.

'Well, 'tis over. Thieves have got their just rewards. And then there are others might meet a more fitting end – the end of a rope.'

Frank's sardonic look travelled the full length of the highwayman. A flush of anger crossed Ned's face to give way at once to a mocking smile. Their eyes met in open challenge. It was Frank who first dropped his gaze. Ned, saying nothing, shrugged and turned away.

'Time to go, I think. Come Anne, Charlotte, let me protect you from this tatterdemalion crew.' He put his arm around the younger girl, plucking her almost fiercely from Rhose's clasp, who could not help but notice how Charlotte flinched at her brother's touch. She gave the girl a comforting pat and was rewarded with an appreciative smile. The performance over, the spectators began to disperse, some laughing and joking, others in a sombre mood. The cries of the hawkers and chapmen once again filled the square. The Fletchers were soon lost to sight hurrying toward the Byrom establishment. The shop, an impressive black and white timbered building, faced the square. It had been long owned by the Byrom family and was renowned for its 'Manchester wares', fabrics and trimmings that graced the fashion of the town. Francis waited a few moments to see the girls safely inside then turned back to the Square, making for John Shaw's punch house to look for his cronies.

Charlotte and Anne climbed the stairs, where Beppy Byrom and Lady Elisabeth examined rolls of fabrics. Phoebe was nowhere to be seen.

'Where have you been? I have been so worried. To think you

might have been in that crowd below. Why did Francis not bring you sooner?'

'Oh, yes, thank goodness you're safe. Your mother was most concerned not to find you here when she arrived.'

'We were quite safe, Mama. Mistress Tinnys took care of us until Frank arrived.'

'Well, now you're here at last, we are to discuss the wedding over tea. Phoebe thought Beppy might be of use too, I hope you don't mind.'

'Not at all, we can catch up on all the latest scandals. Mama needs help to see my ideas on fripperies are kept within bounds.'

Charlotte stood at the open window of Phoebe Byrom's sitting room and looked out at the Shambles; it was a view she had always found exciting. Today was different, now all she could think of was the soldier's screams, the blood and then Frank putting his arm around her. She shuddered as she turned back to the room. Phoebe had now appeared with the maid, bringing in the tea.

'Why, girls, your mother has told me you watched the whipping. Whatever was your brother thinking of? Those two soldiers were lucky not to be sent to the colonies. I suppose their regiment needs them still. There is so much crime. My problem is shoplifting; women usually do the stealing. They often come in pairs or more. They ask my assistants to bring several samples to the counter then they try to divert them. If they do – well – they stuff my best fabrics up their skirts and walk calmly from the shop. I've known fifty yards to disappear, you wouldn't believe what they can hide, aprons, cloaks, petticoats and gowns have all gone missing. I mark all my stuff so I can identify it if we catch them. The latest report is of clothes being taken from lines at night in the gardens behind Market Stead Lane. The owners are so angry they have installed mantraps and warned the offenders so in the *Manchester Mercury*. I think that too generous, we need to catch one or two to teach them a lesson.' Phoebe's tirade ended and they settled to a dish of tea.

'Shall we discuss your dress now, Anne?'

'Yes please, can we look at your fabrics and lace?'

'Are you going to the Infirmary Ball?' interrupted Beppy. 'I hear all of Manchester will be there, not to mention families from the districts.'

'Oh, yes, we are looking forward to it; it will be Charlotte's first. We hope the weather will be kind so we can dance in the gardens as promised.'

'Yes, I am so excited. Anne has given me one of her old gowns; it's lavender silk with a cream embroidered stomacher and petticoat. Lady Elisabeth suggested we buy some lace from you to make new cuffs for the sleeves. You must have been to many balls Beppy. What are they like?'

'My father didn't approve of balls especially after one degenerated into a fight between those for the Prince and those for the King. It was an exciting time in Manchester when I was your age.'

'Do tell Beppy. What did you do?'

'Well, we used to dress in the colours of our persuasion. My dresses were always blue and white, the Prince's colours, a white-hooped dress with a blue sash. My friends and I were all mad for the Prince. It was all quite innocent until he came to Manchester on his way to claim his father's inheritance.'

'Did you meet him?' asked Anne. Both girls knew her story by heart but loved to hear Beppy tell it again.

'Of course, as you well know, but I shall tell you again if Phoebe and Elizabeth can bear to hear it.'

'Don't mind us my dear, we shall go and check on the shop and Elizabeth can choose the fabrics for us to examine. With all the excitement in the square it would be an ideal opportunity for thieves to distract the assistants.'

'I was twenty-three that year, 1745. Lots of families began to pack up and leave town. Lord Warrington was sending his plate away. The bellman went round Manchester forbidding anyone sending provisions out of the town. I was in this very room with father and Aunt Phoebe when about three o'clock the strangest trio rode into the Market Place, two men in highland dress and a woman behind one of them with a drum on her knee. She was a strumpet – you could tell. They beat up for the Prince, calling for volunteers and so they took possession of the town.'

'What of the Prince, did you see him too?'

'Next day at eleven, we came up here again to watch the rest arrive. At about noon he appeared – walking in Highland habit – I nearly swooned to see him. The bells were ringing and fires lit, the whole town was illuminated. Next day I put on my white gown and with Aunt Brearcliffe saw the Prince get a-horseback. Later we went on to the Palace where the Prince was at supper in the great parlour. Everyone was exceeding civil. Secretary Murray came to say the Prince was at leisure and would see us. We were introduced and kissed his hand. I was the envy of my friends. Dolly and the Miss Levers still talk of it, to have stood so close and kissed his hand.'

'Oh the Prince sounds so romantic, so handsome and charming, he would have made a wonderful king,' said Anne.

'Don't be going around saying things like that, my dear. It would be taken amiss by many we know. It was all a long time ago. It became very unpleasant afterwards too. By the New Year the bonfires and the bells were for his defeat at Carlisle. My favourite cos Jemmy Dawson was taken and later hanged. Yes, it was a sad ending for the Manchester Regiment.'

Phoebe entered the room followed by Lady Elisabeth and the maid carrying rolls of cloth. 'Come everyone, we will discuss the trousseau.'

The ladies seated themselves around the table and the conversation began in earnest. The merits of silks, brocade, and damask were all examined. White with silver trimmings was the height of fashion so Anne declined dresses in yellow or blue as passé. Phoebe agreed. She had just received a consignment of French silks and there was a beautiful white watered tabby among them. It would make a sac dress of great style. Silver trimmings to the gown and petticoat, with silver embroidery on the low cut stomacher would be exquisite. A white hat with blond lace and pointed shoes in the same fabric as the dress would complete the ensemble. Anne was delighted when she heard her mother agree to the proposal. The list became endless: bed gowns, negligées, nightdresses, riding clothes . . . did she really need so much? The ladies took a turn around the room before proceeding to discuss dresses for Lady Elisabeth and Charlotte. They would be in blue brocade with silver embroidered facings and robings.

Suddenly Lady Elisabeth stopped the conversation. 'What time is it? I told Francis to be here by three of the clock. Surely he is late?' At that moment the maid entered the room.

'I am sorry to disturb you madam, but a young man is below who wishes to deliver a message to Lady Fletcher.'

'Show him up, Lettie.'

Moments later a good-looking young man was before them, bowing courteously.

'Why, William, I can guess what message you bring. My son will no doubt be late.'

'Worse than that I'm afraid, Lady Fletcher. He sends word that you are to take the coach home without him. He has been detained on business.'

'I can imagine. Horse business no doubt. He is incorrigible. Still we have to thank him for the pleasure of your company William.'

William Jones bowed again. He had been glad to deliver Frank's message if it meant an encounter with Charlotte Fletcher.

Charlotte smiled at Will; she had seen him often at Greenwood Lea. He was always cheerful and didn't mind the teasing he took on account of his red hair, now hidden under his wig. Anne was always reminding her that the Jones's were bankers as well as teamen. He could prove a most suitable match and mama seemed to like him very well. Charlotte blushed at her thoughts. Will only noticed how becoming the colour was to her cheeks.

'Are you going to the Infirmary Ball, ladies? It will be the event of the season I think.'

'We were just discussing the very thing. We are all going, though Phoebe and I will be with the old ladies playing Bezique.'

'That's excellent news. Perhaps I can claim a dance now with the young ladies? I hear you have been taking dancing lessons this winter in town.'

'Frank tells you everything I suppose. Still Charlotte and I would be pleased to accede to your request. He also tells us that you would make us an excellent partner,' Anne answered coyly. This time it was Will's turn to blush. Both young ladies fought back smiles as they sought to spare his embarrassment. Lady Elisabeth came to his rescue. Anne was right, she was very fond of the young man before them. Geoffrey had thought the family a suitable one, and William a good match for Charlotte. Perhaps she could further the affair at the Ball. His mother and sisters were sure to be there. Many a union was proposed over a game of cards!

'We will look forward to the meeting. Please give our best wishes to your family. Your mother and I can reminisce on the balls we went to in our youth as we watch you taking turns around the floor.' Will bowed to the assembled company and announced he must take his leave.

'Please ask Lettie to let us know when our coach arrives. We too must be on our way.'

With a final glance at Charlotte, accompanied by a shy smile, William left. Charlotte's smile in return was noticed by all.

Within several minutes the Fletchers were installed in their coach and on the way home. The conversation on the way was of weddings, though the forthcoming ball was not far from everyone's thoughts. It was dark by the time they pulled up in front of the house. Rob rushed out to help them down. Mrs Rigby had the door open and light flooded out to illuminate the steps.

'I've made a little light supper and laid it by the fire, ma'am. I thought you'd be glad of a bite to eat when you returned.'

'Thank you, Mrs Rigby. We are indeed. Francis has stayed in

town so you may retire now if you wish. The bedrooms are warmed I trust.'

'Everything is as you instructed. There is a letter on the dresser. It came this morning, ma'am.' Lady Elisabeth collected the letter and brought it over to the fireside where the candles burned brightly. With relief she saw it was addressed to her and from the Robinsons.

'Who is it from, Mama? What does it say?'

'Be patient Anne. It is from George's mother. They will all be coming to the ball except Sophie. Her time is due in August and the doctor has advised that she should not travel even though it is such a short distance. Then we are all invited to return with them to Holywell House after their stay. They are planning a soirée to introduce you, Anne, to the neighbouring families. She is hoping that their cousin from York will also attend. You haven't met him since you were all children. Do you remember? Francis, George and John locked you and Charlotte in the attic and you cried so loud we heard you in the garden.'

'I remember,' said Charlotte with a shudder. 'They told us the attic was full of giant spiders, we thought we would be caught in an enormous web and eaten alive.'

'Yes, boys can be horrid. Thank goodness George at least has grown into an attractive man. You can't say the same for Francis, can you? His only attribute as a brother is that he has some rather pleasant friends, don't you know.'

Charlotte laughed. 'Perhaps John has improved like George, then mama may have the pick of several suitors for me.'

Elisabeth smiled to herself. Charlotte was indeed growing up. She really must arrange to talk to the Joneses. Her small dowry was a drawback, but they could afford not to ask for a substantial amount. Connections with the gentry, even those as minor as they were, would be important. She had high hopes on that score. Francis could not object, his financial requirements made a bride with a large portion his priority as he had said often enough. Even though she knew he desired Charlotte, he was not foolish enough to want to marry her. The sooner she was spoken for the better. Her uncle might have different ideas for her, but a good match would be difficult to overturn.

'George sends you his regards, Anne. His mother says he has been over to York to buy you a wedding gift. I wonder what he has chosen? Your father bought me the gold locket I always wear. I'm sure it will be something you'll treasure as much.'

'He asked me what I might like. I said I thought a row of pearls would look lovely with my wedding dress. I told him naught about what it would be like of course. I hope he will oblige me.'

'It would be so romantic if he did, Anne. It's a pity you can't run away to get married; a clandestine ceremony is quite the thing. It's not far to Scotland. Imagine you and George in a barouche with Frank in hot pursuit. Don't you think that would be exciting?'

'Really, Charlotte, that is quite enough! I know it has become fashionable in some circles to have a secret ceremony but we won't entertain the idea. I see I must take more note of the novels you and Anne have been reading. Perhaps they are not as innocent as I supposed.'

'I was only teasing,' Charlotte gasped. 'Please don't think Anne has ever suggested such a thing. It's just my foolish imagination.'

The ladies proceeded with their supper. Their discussions ranged far and wide over who should cater for the wedding feast and what it should consist of. Who should be invited and who should not. Exhausted by their busy day, it was a happy trio who climbed the stairs to bed, Anne thinking of George and her pearls, Charlotte of her possible redheaded beau and Elisabeth of the cost of a second wedding before too long.

Chapter Eight

Fighting Cocks

Thomas Miller stepped down into the yard of the Ring o' Bells, both coach and passengers covered in dust. Relieved to be spared any more shaking, Thomas thanked the fates that fine weather had meant a swift journey. After the rush of London the countryside had appeared green and lush, splashed everywhere with foams of white blossom. The towns he had passed, Derby and Macclesfield, mirrored London – new houses and industry growing apace. If only the roads could be so improved! Now Manchester the same! The talk on the coach was of the war with France and the expansion of trade in spite of it.

Crossing the yard Thomas wondered if Bue would be at The Royal Oak later to meet him. His single-minded dedication to a cause had been the mainspring of his life. Now he was about to embark on a like course again, hopefully with more success. As he pushed open the door, faces turned to see the passengers from the coach, paused to examine them, then turned away again. Thomas approached the bar:

'Good day, I'm looking for a room and victals, a porter to quench my thirst.'

Mary glanced at the newcomer. 'Porter's no problem, sir, but as for the rest you're out of luck. The towns full of visitors for the cockfight and we're full up. You'll need to try elsewhere. Do you still want the porter?'

'Aye, lass, I've a thirst on me after that dusty journey.'

Mary obliged him. After downing the drink Thomas returned to the street, passing Rhose in the doorway.

'Who was that, Mary? I don't recognize his face.'

'A stranger wanting a room! They've been coming in all day. We should have cockfights more often.'

Turning up Mill Gate, Thomas came to The Feathers, entered and put a gold coin on the counter.

'I need a bed for the night.'

The man with a quick glance at the coin, smiled.

'James Hodgkinson, landlord, at your service, sir. A good journey I trust? We've rooms if you need them and supper, too.'

'Aye, landlord, as I said, a room for the night's what I need.'

'Follow me sir, we've a good room on the first floor and you'll not need to share. The boy will bring your bags.'

Hodgkinson led the way, wondering who the stranger could be. He'd chanced that he could pay for a private room even though he'd flashed his coin. He had the air of a soldier about him. Still the town was full of strangers, the more the merrier he thought.

'This your first visit to Manchester, is it? You'll find it a lively town.'

'No, though I've been away some years.'

Thomas was shown into a shabby room overlooking the street. He'd seen much worse in his travels.

'I 'ope this will suit you, sir?'

'Indeed. I'm expecting to meet Joseph Bue, the apothecary, at The Royal Oak, perhaps your boy will be able to show me the way?'

'Well, dear me. You'll not be meeting Mr Bue this side of the grave I'm afraid. Killed in a duel he was, in March, by a Major in the Welch Fusiliers. The talk of the town it was at the time. Insulted the Major after he'd taken offence at Joseph's choice of sovereign, if you take my meaning.'

83

Thomas was stunned. To have come so far and now be thwarted at the last seemed beyond belief.

'I'll take my supper in my room. Damn me this news is a great shock. Perhaps you might know who is dealing with Bue's affairs.'

'Well that's 'ard to say. A singular man was Joseph Bue. No family that I 'eard of. You'd best seek out one of the town's apothecaries. Jonathan Agar dealt with the business after his death I 'eard tell.'

'And where might I find him?'

'I should go to the Bulls' Head in the morning. He's often there and after he's sure to be at the cocking. All the town will be having a wager. As I said Manchester's a lively place. But the Bull's Head's your best bet. I'll send supper up straight away, sir.'

Once arrived, the food was as dreary as the room. Thomas, exhausted from the journey, soon fell into a fitful sleep, hoping that somehow Bue had left the information he so desperately sought.

The bills were all over town. 'A Main of Cocks will be fought at the New Cockpit on Monday, Tuesday and Wednesday, 26, 27, 28 of June for ten Guineas the Main and two Guineas a Battle between the Gentlemen of Cheshire and the Gentlemen of Lancashire.'

Most of these gentlemen seemed to be crowded into the Bull's Head when Thomas arrived. He pushed his way through the crush wondering how to pick out the apothecary. All sorts and conditions of men jostled and smoked and drank. Four young bucks were seated at a centre table. Sir Francis Fletcher had the flushed looks of one who had been drinking deep already. James Falkner, short, squat and dandified was holding court to the others, his easy drawl cutting through the hubbub around him. Thomas caught the end of his cockfighting story.

'. . . just would not fight. Treated each other like little milk-sops a'walking in Ranelagh.'

'So, why not p-p-p-put in a hen. That'd stir 'em up,' the long lean Robert Johnson suggested.

'Well said, Bob, me boy. Just the advice I offered – but what do y'know?' He paused, dramatically.

'Oh come, Jemmy, don't stretch it out. We are urgent to see that cock of yours blooded today.'

'Oliver, Oliver, when will you learn patience! The birds are only now being weighed, there's time enough to finish my story – and for another flagon of ale.'

Francis, the fourth of the group, responded to the heavy hint. 'More of your best, landlord, and be sharp.' His words were slurred, his colour high. Another barrel was tapped and four brimming tankards slopped onto their table.

'Curse you,' Francis snapped, 'You've spilt on my new cuffs. This lace came straight from Holland. I'd give you a sound thrashing if it weren't—'

'Now, Frank,' Oliver held him back, 'let's not spoil Jemmy's story. I for one wish to hear the tale of the cocks that would not fight.'

'Aye,' Bob agreed, muttering half to himself, 'and if that lace came from Holland, it was by way of M-M-Man.'

Francis took a swig of his drink, glared at the landlord's back and turned towards his companions. James Falkner had become restless and rose from his chair, tankard in hand. He paused, with a sweeping gesture spilling ale right and left.

'Such was the hullabaloo in Chester when, as young Bob so wisely advocated, when the hen was placed in the pit for the two reluctant cocks, what do you think? The two game birds, gentlemen to the last, politely took turns to tread her. Not a sign of rivalry.' With an explosive laugh, he left through the back door followed by Robert and a crowd of interested spectators.

Francis, still incensed at the damage to his finery, lingered at the table with Oliver solicitously trying to move him. Thomas had by now attracted the barmaid and began to ask for the apothecary whose name he had forgotten. Instead he mentioned

Joseph Bue. The sound of the name rekindled Francis's anger and he blazed round at the newcomer.

'Bue! Bue! That traitorous, jabbering pissfire was dealt with as he deserved. Damn Jacobite canting crew – damn 'em all to hell.'

Desperately trying to quieten his companion whose outburst was attracting black looks and angry murmurs, Oliver muttered, 'Hush Frank, remember where we are.'

'Aye, I know full well we're in a den of perjurers and traitors. Look there,' he gestured toward a high chair, set prominently against the wall. 'The Throne,' he scoffed, 'where the Scotch prick pretender plonked his "royal" backside.'

Francis and Oliver were now isolated amid a sea of angry faces. Thomas felt his own temper rising and stepped forward to the young men. The murmuring had died. An ominous silence pervaded the bar. Suddenly Frank, mouthing further insults, hurled his tankard at the chair. Thomas, now almost face to face, started to reach out. The crowd began to move in as Francis half drew his sword. Oliver eased Thomas aside and stood between them. His hand closed firmly over Francis's, forcing the sword back into the scabbard. He turned to the menacing group, holding the other as in a vice.

'Gentlemen, 'tis the drink talking, not the man! As you can see, my young friend here is a good Whig but a poor drinker.' He tossed a handful of coins on to the table. 'Landlord, see that all drink a toast to the King – whoever they think he may be.'

With this he marched the still livid and struggling Francis to the street door. 'No cocking for you my bellicose friend, and none for me neither,' he sighed as they left.

Turning to the landlord, Thomas, the unwitting cause of the furore was anxious to learn what had provoked the outburst. He repeated his enquiry for an apothecary associated with Bue who might have news for him.

'So, it was Bue's name that stirred Sir Francis into one of his rages. He likes not to be reminded of the sympathies of many here – not forgetting his own father. Some say he has ambitions beyond the county and needs to please his political masters. But you may see for yourself how the "auld cause" rouses fierce passions even now.'

Indeed the inn was full of clamour. Some were cursing the dandy for his attack on the noble Stuart line. Others praised his loyal stand for the Hanoverians. Where drink flowed freely, squabbles were growing more heated. Thomas was cautious in reply.

'Well, I'll not be drawn into present quarrels. I've served my time in the country's service and all I seek is a quiet life and reunion with my family. So – the apothecary, Ackem, was it?'

'Jonathan Agar's the man you'll be looking for. He's a very different fellow from Joseph Bue. One on the way up yet does not neglect those he knew. He it was who tended Sir Francis's father at the last. He was here earlier in the day. I doubt not that you will find him at the cocking.' He raised his voice to the bar in general: 'And, gentlemen, those who wish to see the first battles had best be on their way. There will be enough blood and feathers there to satisfy your fighting instincts. Better at the pit than here.'

Thomas followed the throng to the new destination. A passage led into the Bull's Head yard and from there a back lane entered Cockpit-hill. More men were coming up Market-stead-lane and the two streams flowed up the hill. The cockpit was a wooden building in the centre of a square of houses, the walls following the lines of its surroundings. Inside Thomas was met by a restless expectancy for the first of the Main. James Falkner was again holding forth as the centre of interest. His bulk alone commanded attention and his voice carried in praise of his contender.

'Look at him! Is Tawny not a true gamecock? His thick long neck, the round black breast, beak and claws one ochre colour, straight from a breeder's manual. Who could bet against such a paragon?'

'Well, the M-M-M-Manchester m – m oh, curse it. The betting's on Major Stapleton's red. He's taken four battles in a row,' Robert protested.

'Ah, nought but half-bred, ill-walked dunghill things, I'll warrant.'

The cocks were being shown off to the animated crowd. The Masters of the Match, Falkner and Stapleton, leant on the rail at opposite sides of the platform ring. They bowed courteously to each other. The Major threw down a bag of coins.

'Fifty guineas, two to one the red.'

Jemmy responded with, 'One hundred and fifty, three to two.'

The Teller of the Law high in his seat took charge of the proceedings. 'We are ready to begin. No more wagers gentlemen. Setters, cocks to the mat.'

The crowd, restless until now, settled into intense silence. Those ranged at the back craned forward, those at the front elbowed for positions.

The setters holding firmly to their charges placed them back-to-back in the centre of the mat. Red and Tawny were equally matched, a solid four and a half pounds of sleek perfection, clipped wings and tail, long slim heads shorn of feathers. The setters withdrew behind the rail and the teller began his count. There was a cry of anticipated thrill as the two cocks turned, beak-to-beak, necks stretched in ferocious rivalry. Like two experienced prizefighters the two circled and tussled, testing each other out. Their wings flapping, beaks darting and silver spurs catching the light, they were high coloured gladiators sparring for an opening.

It was Red who struck first. A jab of its spur drove Tawny to the mat, its wings flat, its head twisted sideways in defence. The crowd's murmur rose to a howl of triumph. Falkner pounded the rail, his voice raised above the rest.

'Damn me, man, he's fast. He's fast in the mat. Free him, blast you, free the poor devil.'

The setters stepped into the ring. With expert speed and caution the Cheshire man freed his bird's claws enmeshed in the mat. At once Tawny was up and in the air. The Lancashire setter released his bird and retreated to his position.

The battle was now met in earnest. The crowd hushed then

cried with glee when spur struck cleanly. No one had eyes for anything but the combatants fighting viciously and tenaciously, tiny in the centre of the twenty foot ring. Red began to tire. Its wing dragged down to the mat, the striking claws lost their force. The end was stark, brutal. Tawny struck. The sharp vicious wing quills raked the other's eyes. The spurs, already flecked with blood, struck again and again. Red, spread-eagled on the mat could not move. The fatal heel slashed. The head was down, blood dribbled from the beak. An exultant baying rose from the ranks of the spectators as they crushed to the barrier to see the victorious cock raised head high in triumph.

'Two guineas to the Cheshire Gentlemen,' the teller announced dispassionately, his voice almost lost in the general uproar.

'And a hundred to me,' laughed Falkner as he patted the setter on the shoulder, slipping a guinea into his hand. 'The Main will be ours, mark my words.'

'Don't crow too soon,' Major Stapleton came round to congratulate the winner and hand over the stake. 'I've a grey stag of three pound ten will match any of yours, weight for weight.'

'So you say. Come then, let us set the stakes over a flagon. Are you with us Bob?'

With that the three pushed their way to the door, the crowd already pressing forward for the next contest.

Thomas had watched with detachment. This sport compared ill with the ferocious matches he had seen in India. In the lull between battles he enquired after Jonathan Agar and a tall, elegantly dressed figure at the back of the room was pointed out. He approached and briefly explained his dilemma to the apothecary.

'Yes, Bue! He was a fellow practitioner who met a sad end. He was ever something of a fanatic and splenetic. It was a duel without point. I doubt not that Major Gee will have it on his conscience wherever he may go. Still, what is it you want with me?'

A pair of cocks was being introduced into the ring and the

noise rose to welcome the new battle. Thomas led the apothecary to a corner, striving for greater privacy. 'Should we go outside, Mr Miller so that we may talk more freely?' Agar offered. 'This sport is not altogether to my taste, but it is well to be seen by the fashion.' He indicated a number of elegant young men standing eagerly by the ringside and others more foppishly lounging at the rear.

'It is the same the world over,' Thomas said. 'Much that is important in business and society is hatched at such sporting occasions. I could tell you much of Indian nawabs and English traders.'

'And there's the Manchester copy,' Agar pointed to a huddle cut-off from the spectators. 'I am not certain whether Mr Laurence is a nawab or a trader, but I know he is deep into something.' Thomas noted a little round man in the centre of the group in urgent conversation with two bandy-legged individuals. On the edge, a figure wrapped in a cloak and wearing a slouch hat, listened intently. He agreed with Agar, they were up to no good.

'Now, what was your business with Mr Bue?' Agar asked as they reached the open air.

'I would rather not speak of such matters as yet. I had hoped that he might have left a letter or some communication for me. I cannot know whether he was aware of my return but trusted he may have prepared for it.'

'Charles Wagstaff was more closely associated with him than I, but he very wisely disappeared after that – unfortunate affair. I found nothing in his shop or home connected with your name. Naturally I did not enquire too closely into his personal effects. He had no family and no apprentice. If Wagstaff returns, perhaps.'

'Thank you, I cannot wait. I am on my way to find what has become of my family. I have had no word for nigh on fifteen years. I know not whether my parents be alive or dead. I was hoping that here I might – but no matter. I will come back and enquire further.'

'Wait. I remember now, there is Dr Hall. He was with Bue at the end and they were of like persuasion. I suggest you seek him at the new infirmary where he attends daily.'

'Dr Hall you say. Thank you, sir. I head northwards tomorrow but, all being well, I should be back soon.'

'God speed, Mr Miller! I trust you find your family well and prospering. If I hear of anything you can find me at the Sign of the Unicorn in Back Square.' As the two men left they passed the group of men with the 'Manchester nawab'. Thomas was surprised to see a man wearing a fearnaught waistcoat and slop hose, had joined them. It was the unmistakable dress of the common seamen he'd spent so long with on his voyage.

'Look here,' Ralph Seddon was saying, 'we've provided you safe haven, good storage, regular custom. We do not like it that you deal now with Mistress Tinnys at the Ring o' Bells. No offence, Ned!'

'None taken, Ralph! You'll excuse me, gentlemen, I needs place my bet for the next main.' Ned moved away to the ringside.

'You had the excise in seventeen days ago,' Laurence barked. 'Had I not been forewarned you and your brother could be on the way to Tyburn or the Americas by now. Without our friend Twigg's barge we could not have unloaded so swiftly.'

The craggy-faced bargee grunted in agreement. He thrust out a gnarled fist, opening and closing thick fingers.

'As long as that's well greased, I care not where the *Baccus* docks. I've contract with the Liverpool merchants and need settle for sure this end of the business.'

'And I assure you, Mr Twigg, at "this end" as you call it, the Ring o' Bells is the safest place you will find and Rhose – Mistress Tinnys – is above suspicion. With Ned's contacts in the country, tinkers, sturdy beggars and the like, the goods are moved fast. Please!' He silenced the protest of the brothers with a wave of his hand. 'I am not inexperienced in these matters. The Kentish Owling business ran well, but times are leaner down there.'

'And the climate hotter,' Ralph intervened. 'We know well why you came north. Your own kin peached on you. 'Tis a poor family that does not look after its own.'

There was a brotherly nod from John. 'Fear not, I will remember you both in the new settings. Like Twigg, I have arrangements with the Liverpool Merchants. Only this month I heard proof of their hold on the Isle of Man trade.'

Twigg let out an appreciative guffaw. 'Our fame's spread then? We saw off the Liverpool customs in smart manner. Cap'n Daw will remember his beating in Douglas and his crew sent packing. I was there with Sam Harper to help unload and saw the whole thing.'

Sam took up the story. 'There was a Dutch ship in Ramsey Bay. The cargo of spirits and lace was destined for the Liverpool Merchants' Company, and on to Whitehaven, Liverpool and Chester. The customs' sloop came over to seize her but we were well prepared. Oh! It was a fine sight to see.' His brown scarred face twisted into a satisfied smile of reminiscence. 'As the customs men prepared to board we rowed a longboat to the seaward side of the ship. Then our men hauled captain and crew off the sloop, gave 'em a good beating and,' he broke into full raucous laughter, 'clapped 'em all in gaol!' The others joined in the mirth.

'Strange customs you have up here,' broke in Laurence. 'An independent fiefdom not fifty miles from the mainland, yet the revenue can't touch it. God bless the Duke of Atholl who owns it. My trade could hardly prosper without him.'

'Or without my command of the river,' Twigg grunted. 'I can bring in whatever you will to wherever you will. It must be near the water, this inn you say backs on the river, that's fine. Now let us talk money.'

'Not here, friend. We need be more private. Your quarters at the Black Swan, John?'

'But what of Rhose Tinnys, and her gallant, the highwayman?' Ralph asked.

'No need to worry on that score. Ned's a born criminal and you can leave her to me.' Laurence's portly figure waddled confidently away.

Chapter Nine

The Hanged Man

A thin misty rain drove people from the streets after the cock fighting. At the Ring o' Bells Ned and Josiah were leaning against the centre counter, Rhose was sorting mugs and tankards, checking barrels and bottles. The only other person was an old man and his dog dozing by a smouldering fire. The two men were in earnest conversation settling details of Laurence's smuggling enterprise. Ned had the air of one waiting to be convinced, a note of protest creeping into his voice. Josiah was calm and persuasive, a hand resting on his companion's shoulder. A partial smile crossed Rhose's face, alert to the ups and downs of the discussion.

'Ned, Ned! I tell you there's no danger as great as you take on the road whenever you ride. Why, a wary coachman, a foolhardy dandy, a pair of dazzling eyes, even a lame horse, they could any of them spell the lock up for you – any day or night.' A protest was cut short by a wave to silence. 'Think of it. You touch nothing. I'd not have you carry any of the – the trade – yourself. All I need is to use your connections. I know you have a web spun throughout the county, a web of like-minded fellows, of lookouts, hideaways, safe taverns. The trade would pass through them as easy as – as easy as a skiff through smooth seas. And the profit, man, think of the profit.'

' 'Tis very well for you to say. I need no gypsy to tell my fate: I'm for the noose or the colonies at best.'

He glanced round at the sound of Rhose's gasp. She shook her head and stepped over to him. He held out his hand and grasped hers. Laurence gazed intently into his tankard.

'Nay lass, don't be afeard. You know as well as I what risks I take. Your Ned's not for the gallows yet awhile.' He turned towards his companion. 'But I know my trade. I can handle a sword and a pistol, I can ride a horse and I can gamble, but take to water? That's not for me.'

Josiah laughed. 'It shan't come to that. What I need from you, Long Ned, are names and places, your name to open doors and shut mouths. Oh, I could do it without you but with you . . . the north would be ours.'

'You talk to fine purpose, Josiah, I can see why you prosper. I promise I'll think on it.'

'That's as much as I can expect for now. We'll talk more. But remember the gravest danger is on the water.'

'And in my cellars,' Rhose stepped away looking squarely at the smaller man.

'As for that, I am sure.'

A stranger banged back the inn door and stomped into the room. The noise roused the sleeping man, his dog scrabbled up yapping. The newcomer swept off his cloak revealing a tall, slender figure in clothes that had seen better days. He flung the cloak over a chair, sending it crashing to the floor. The dog backed under his master's chair snarling. The stranger, ignoring both chair and dog, nodded to Ned and Josiah.

'Filthy weather, goddamn this country! What hellish roads, Three hours for ten miles. Blast the eyes of all cross-eyed carriers! Did you ever know such people?' He cast his glance around the room, not expecting an answer. 'Here, wench, have you a decent brandy here?'

Rhose's indignant frown changed in an instant into a deep curtsey. 'Why, indeed, good sir. The best French brandy if you wish, sir.'

Ned's angry intervention had been stopped by a brief nod of her head and a quick reassuring smile. Rhose tripped to the back of the inn with a provocative sway of her hips. The stranger eyed her with a lecherous grin.

'A fair strumpet in this benighted place. If I have time here I could welcome a tumble with her.'

A warning cough from Laurence once again cut off Ned's response.

'You've come far, sir, in this inclement weather?' Josiah asked.

'I've been five days on the road from Oxford first by coach, and then after my baggage disappeared, by carrier. God or the Devil knows when I'll get to Kendal. Ah, thank 'ee, my dear.'

Rhose had returned with the brandy and an even deeper curtsey. 'Why, sir, 'tis a pleasure to serve a gentleman from the south.'

'And a pleasure to be served by so charming a creature.' He leaned over, crooked a finger under her chin then dropped his hand towards the swell of her breasts. She slapped the offending hand, said, 'La, I'm not one of those,' tossed her head and turned away.

'Our northern lasses don't take kindly to such familiarity,' Ned growled, 'whatever may be your southern manners.'

'Now, no unpleasantness gentlemen.' Laurence sought to calm the two glaring men. 'It took me some time to come to their ways when I arrived here. Now I find I am content. Like you, sir, I hail from the south of the country. Josiah Laurence at your service.'

'Charles Jonstone, at yours. I surely meant no offence. Your health Mr Laurence, and yours too, my man.' He gave a grudging nod to the still-angry Ned. 'I have had such ill luck so far and so little courtesy on my journey it leaves me out of temper. Can you tell me where I may hire a horse, I'd as lief not venture further with any of your carriers? I need press on.'

'You do not propose to go further north this night do you?' Laurence sounded most concerned.

'Why, what's to prevent me?'

The little man winked at Long Ned as he raised his tankard

to his lips before replying, 'Oh, naught to prevent you, but north from here is dangerous country indeed. Is it not so my friend?'

Ned took up the hint. 'Yes yes. The roads are worse even than those you complain of. Between here and Preston are the worst in the county – in the whole of England. Take my word for it, I've ridden most of them. I've known an entire coach disappear down one of the potholes, scarce a body saved.'

'That's true. Many's the tragedies I've heard from travellers through here.'

Rhose had returned to join in the banter. 'And there are the highwaymen and footpads, bloodthirsty creatures, preying on the unwary – as like to slit your throat for threepence or a silk handkerchief.'

Ned grinned an acknowledgement. ' Pah, I've no fear of such lowlife. I'm armed and have seen off worse.'

'Mayhap, but that's not all.' Rhose dropped her voice and plucked at the stranger's sleeve. 'There's spirit lights tempting men from the path to their doom in the marshes. There are boggarts, evil spirits to taunt and haunt and monstrous black dogs roaming the moors. . . .'

Jonstone laughed pulling his arm away. 'Such tales are for children and the faint hearted, superstitions worthy of peasants and clodhoppers. I'm not to be frightened by demons and ghosts.'

Rhose continued: 'So you say, but you ride over evil ground and treacherous water. There's Jenny Greenteeth out there.'

'A fine strapping wench, I've no doubt,' the newcomer scoffed.

Rhose stood back, aghast. 'Don't mock. She lies deep in pools and still waters, hair whispering through the weed, waiting, waiting. Then her arms reach out, grasping and pulling down into the muddy depths to her smothering bosom.' Her own arm writhed silkily across the counter to grip his sleeve again. He jerked back.

'A fine warning!' He laughed once more. 'I'll know not to entertain any wet green ladies. I've no truck with such nonsense.'

'So I thought before I came here,' Josiah said, warming to the theme, 'but you know "there's more in heaven and earth" . . . remember 'tis not long still witches flew over Pendle Hill.'

'Well, I'll not delay my journey for such countrified nonsense. I'm for the north whatever you say.'

'You may laugh,' it was Ned's turn with the stories, 'but I know there are terrible things in this world and out of it. Ride forth if you wish, but keep clear of brackish water – Jenny Greenteeth is a fanciful name but drowning's a nasty death.' He paused then clapped the stranger on the back. 'And stay away from Pendleton Moor, wherever else you may ride.'

'Tha'd noan get me oop thear o'neet, for luv nor brass.' The old man reared from his chair then slumped back after this outburst. The others turned to him, startled by his sudden interruption.

'What?'

Ned translated: 'He means there's nothing would get him to go there at night. So take warning from one who knows. No one's looked on John Grindred's remains and stayed sane. He was hanged nigh on twelve months ago for the brutal murder of a wife and two sweet bairns. He's never rested quiet. There he hangs still, flesh all pecked away, a few rags flapping in the wind. I've seen it by daylight and it's a horrid sight,' then, ' "I'd noan go thear o'neet" myself.'

'Surely you, Mr Laurence, do not believe any of this?'

'Well, Jonstone, I too was a doubter but I've heard tales would make your hair stand up.'

'The skeleton walks, I tell you!' There was conviction in Ned's voice. 'it howls and it dances and grabs anyone near. If they don't die of terror, they're gibbering and crying fools ever after.'

Jonstone looked around the faces, all with solemn expressions of deepest concern. Rhose in a dramatic gesture, clasped her hands to her breast and, white faced, looked ready to faint.

'Oh, Ned, don't! Just the telling of it frightens me so.'

'What primitive superstitions!' Jonstone thumped the counter. 'I'd have expected better of you sir, an educated man. As for the others brought up in this God forsaken place, I am not surprised they put faith in such outlandish things.'

Ned dropped his hand over the other's fist. 'I'll put money on it.'

'What do you mean, man?' Jonstone pulled away, turning to face Ned.

'This. I'll wager you two – no – ten guineas you have not the courage to go to Pendleton Moor this night.'

A scornful laugh was the response. 'I'd go and shake hands with this Mr – Grindred, did you say? – to show there's nothing in this taradiddle.'

'Ten guineas?'

'Ten guineas, you'll be with me? Or will you "noan" come brave the ghost?'

There was a mocking smile.

'I would had I not other more pressing business.'

Rhose stepped forward in an apparent fluster of anxiety. 'Oh, please don't do it, sir. It is not worth ten guineas, nor a hundred. Oh, don't do it, I pray you.'

'Calm yourself my dear. No harm will come to me and I have a mind to teach these bumpkins a lesson. Yet how will I prove my wager without your gallant, eh?'

'I can be a witness,' Josiah put in. 'I would see justice done for your sake. I warn you, I've no mind to match your bravery. I'll take you to the place and watch from a distance. I have no wish to make acquaintance with a skeleton.'

So it was settled. As the inn began to fill with the evening crush Josiah took the stranger to hire a horse leaving Ned and Rhose chuckling – and the old man once again snoring.

It was near midnight, scudding clouds crossed the moon as Laurence and Jonstone trotted through the shadows of the trees. Josiah was recounting the tales he had heard from the Seddons and their cronies; tales of witches and warlocks, death lights, sprits and demons. The night seemed to be filled with mysterious voices, the undergrowth with weird apparitions. A fox barked and night-birds chattered amongst the branches.

Each soughing bough, every flickering leaf was alive with eerie menace. As they came to the foot of the moor they drew rein and dismounted. A wind-driven flurry of rain lashed their faces, wrapping their cloaks close around them.

Laurence urged his companion on in a tremulous voice. 'You are on your own from here. You'll need to go afoot to yonder spot.' He pointed dramatically to the gibbet standing stark against the lowering sky. A something hung there, chains rattling, wisps of clothing flapping in the blustery wind.

Jonstone gave a nervous laugh. 'I'll not be long. I'll shake that – that thing – by its bony hand and be ten guineas richer.'

He trudged up the slope, slipping in the mud-churned track. Slopping through puddles that spattered his boots, he concentrated on keeping his footing, whisking his cloak away from the tangling brambles. He paused for breath part way up; the wind and rain had eased. He glanced up at the twisting skeleton then back at the horses, restless in the cold night air. Of his companion he could only see the outline of a huddled figure, the paleness of his face indistinct in the dark. He hesitated, thought he saw an irritated motion of the others head, turned and stumbled on. A fresh drift of rain stung his cheeks as he took the last steps. Nervously he reached out to the corpse hanging before him.

With a spasmodic jerk its arms moved jangling, stretching towards him. The bones leaped alive in a frenzied hiccupping dance. A voice wailed above the whirling wind and rattling chains:

'I'm cold and I'm dreary; I'm wet and I'm weary but soon I'll be near ye.' The thing hurled itself from its post, enfolding him, its arms clasping him in a grim embrace. The grinning skull nodded on his shoulder. With a squeal of petrified horror Jonstone scrabbled himself free. He slithered and slid down the path, mindless of brambles, mud and puddles. Pushing Laurence to one side he sprang to his saddle and galloped away.

Laurence sat in the mud, retrieved his fallen hat and began to smile. The smile built to a chuckle, the chuckle to a laugh until he lay in helpless mirth. From behind the gibbet emerged a dark figure, from the bushes close by a slighter one, clothed in gown and hood. Both were in high good humour. Long Ned bent down to remove the slender ropes from the motionless skeleton and laid it reverently aside. Rhose joined him, a hand round his waist and pressed her lips to his in a smiling kiss. She gave him a gentle punch.

'That was never Grindred, he's been down these six months.' She said as they hurried down the path to heave the still helpless Josiah to his feet.

'No. 'Twas an old drinking companion, poor soul – caught but riding a horse that was never his. Mind he'd not object to such treatment for he enjoyed a good jest as well as any man.'

Lawrence had recovered enough to shake the highwayman's hand. 'That's a good firm, lively, grip, better than friend Jonstone swore to. That was capital, Ned. I'll wager he'll not stop this side of the Ribble.'

'Less Jenny Greenteeth get him!' Rhose set them all off laughing again.

Ned brought out their two hidden horse. 'As for a wager, have you my winnings, Josiah?'

'Indeed I have, Ned, and deservedly won.'

He threw a pouch to the highwayman. They stopped to watch him pour its contents into his palm. Even in the dim light they could see there was no gleam of gold.

'I'll be damned. We've been cozened. Here's no ten guineas but ten pennies!'

He cursed roundly and long, then threw back his head and roared with laughter. After an astonished moment all three were laughing, heads together before setting off into the night, arm in arm.

Chapter Ten

Revelations

Francis, Oliver Banton and Nathaniel Lloyd strolled down Chapel Walks toward St. Ann's Square. They were making their way to John Berry's next to the Long Room to buy lottery tickets for the November draw. On a hot July day, they were all feeling jaded and discontented. The cockfight had provided a welcome spell of excitement in the humdrum existence of summer in town. The Infirmary ball offered the prospect of some amusement later in the month. The Fletchers were thrilling to the prospect of Anne's wedding to the dull George Robinson, an excitement Francis did not share. And yet the bewitching sight of young Charlotte in her finery was something to look forward to. The thought brought to mind the charming little strumpet he had enjoyed at Smith's last night. He turned to his companions, but noting Oliver's moody preoccupation, held his tongue. He contented himself with a predatory quizzing of the occasional passing beauty.

Oliver could not account for his own restlessness. He was growing discontented with Frank's increasing raffish and unpredictable ways. He found Manchester little to his taste these days. There seemed to be no end to the pulling down and putting up. The town was spreading into once open fields and soon bricks and mortar would swamp orchard and meadow alike. Already some of his childhood haunts were changed.

Daubhole pool where they used to play ducks and drakes and hope to see a witch tested on the ducking stool was now in the new Infirmary grounds. No doubt this was a good thing for the town, but he was glad his family had moved out to the country. All the people, and such people! There was an underlying violence waiting to break through. Only two or three years ago food riots had broken out. Who knew what might come from the new enterprises and the dross flooding into town. He shrugged decisively – he would come less frequently to town. He could see only one reason for returning, and she was merely an innkeeper.

A cart laden with bales of wool lumbered by, forcing them under the overhang of the houses, and leaving behind a steaming heap of dung. Francis just succeeded in stepping past, wrinkling his nose at the stench. He almost collided with a ragged child scurrying out with a shovel and sack to gather in the droppings. Francis cut at the retreating figure with his cane.

'Don't be so intemperate,' Nathaniel protested, 'the poor lad's only out to earn a few coppers. Come, what say we take a walk later to Acres Field, see the militia go through their paces. I hear from my brother it's a day for manoeuvres. He's newly joined.'

'I find this weather wearisome. 'Twould be fatiguing to watch those fat burghers and pimply youths sweat through their drill. The Lord help us if they have to defend us from the Frenchies. A pack of Tories and timeservers.'

'Why man you're overzealous on that topic! You are in danger of becoming a fanatic. One might think you a Methodistical Whig.'

Francis laughed. 'Nay, no enthusiast me. I suspect I am oversensitive. Family connections you know. I wish to shake off all that history if I am to have the future I desire. Damme, I made a promise to Mama to collect some furbelow or other from Phoebe Byrom's.'

Their talk was interrupted by a cry of 'Make way! Make way!'

as a sedan chair made its way up the street. The two carriers began to labour up the slope, the pace noticeably slowing. Suddenly the leading man stumbled and fell between the shafts. The chair tipped sideways, a pole shattering as it hit the ground. The man behind crashed against the body of the chair. In a flurry of skirts the occupant sprawled in the dust. The passers-by paused aghast. The three friends were the first to the fallen man.

'A hundred guineas he's dead,' Francis exclaimed.

'Done,' Nathaniel countered.

Oliver stooped to feel the man's head and neck.

'If you try to revive him the bet's off,' Francis protested, trying to pull the other away. Oliver shrugged him off, then looked to the fallen woman who was struggling to her feet.

'Why Mistress Tinnys!' he gasped as he turned towards her. 'Are you badly hurt?'

'I think not. But what happened? The chairman, how is he?' Holding on to Oliver's arm she turned to the crowd that had gathered around.

'I doubt he's alive, ma'am,' someone said.

'And did no one else take my wager?' Francis surveyed the onlookers. A shocked murmur ran through those who had heard, but the attention was now on the second chairman kneeling by his fallen colleague.

'Is there not a medical man nearby?' he asked. 'It may be too late.'

'Mr Agar's shop is but a step away in Back Square.' Rhose then winced in pain. 'I fear I have injured my ankle,' she gasped, clutching more tightly to the young man.

'I am much distressed that this should happen, Mrs Tinnys,' the chairman was full of apology. 'I'm afraid Bob was not well when we started out but we thought it naught but bellyache. May I do anything for you, ma'am?'

'I will look to the lady, if she will permit me,' Oliver was quick to offer. 'You had best see to your friend and have this wreckage removed.'

Two of the onlookers had picked up the body and were carrying it reverentially down the street. Francis and Nathaniel followed, still vainly proffering odds on the unfortunate man's fate. Oliver turned to Rhose.

'Can you walk? Should you not consult the apothecary? I would be pleased to accompany you – nay, carry you if need be.'

Rhose laughed. 'You are very gallant.' She winced again as she tried a few steps. 'I think your arm will be sufficient. I would know of the fate of the poor man so if you would accompany me to Mr Agar's. . . .'

It was slow progress to the shop although it was only a short distance. Rhose was obviously in pain, leaning heavily upon her escort. Oliver found himself aroused by the pressure of her breast through the thin muslin of her gown and the rasp of her thigh against his. For her part she felt drawn to this apparently less than handsome, not very fashionable countryman. He was solicitous in his attention to her; she made as little of the pain and as much of the limp as she could. In this pleasurable distress they made their way, past sympathetic looks, to the apothecary's.

The body had been carried through to the compounding room and laid on the floor. Jonathan Agar was in no doubt that the man was dead and sent his apprentice Matthew for the constable. The second chairman had gone to inform Mr Travis and have the broken chair removed. Francis watched as Oliver helped Rhose to the chair by the counter, and gave him a knowing look. There were brief explanations, then the apothecary ushered the inquisitive people from the shop. Francis too left on his errand, explaining Nathaniel had already gone off to watch his brother.

Rhose began decorously to unroll her scarlet stockings. Agar watched Francis's departing back and turned to Oliver.

'Sir Francis will occasion real upset one day. He lacks discernment. Was he not recently the cause of a disturbance at the Bull's Head?' He knelt to attend to the swollen ankle. Rhose let out a squeal of pain as he pressed the spot with expert fingers.

'I heard something of that,' she said to cover her distress. 'Was

105

it not before the Main of Cocks? Was it a squabble over a wager? A woman?' She was aware of Oliver's frank appreciation of her slender leg and dainty foot. The young man reluctantly withdrew his gaze but not before he had caught the answering glint in her violet eyes.

'Indeed – indeed not. It was a foolish outburst sparked by a stranger mentioning a single name. One of your compatriots, Mr Agar, Joseph Bue. Frank was provoked yet again to inveigh against the Jacobites. 'Twas of no real significance.'

'That is not what I heard,' Rhose continued. 'Drawn swords, tankards flying, blood flowing.'

Agar rose to his feet. Rhose looked quizzically at the apothecary, a quirk of the eyebrows for his diagnosis.

'Not broken but a severe sprain. I will make you a poultice of self-heal, marigold vinegar, king's clover and rough sweet suet. You will need to rest as much as possible. A reviving cordial would be of help – lavender honey, rosemary and syrup of violets in white wine would be ideal.'

The mention of Bue had aroused Rhose's curiosity. 'A stranger you say, seeking Bue? But he died months ago. What could he have wanted?'

Agar turned as he was leaving to prepare the poultice. 'Ah, it must have been the man who sought me out at the cocking. A military man returned from India, in search of his family. I could not help him – he was leaving for somewhere near Blackburn that afternoon. Thomas I think his name was.'

Oliver became solicitous. 'You need to take care, Mistress Tinnys. There may be no bones broken yet a sprain should not be neglected. Agar's advice should be obeyed.'

'Oh, come now Mr Banton. I have an inn to keep. I am no delicate society lady but one who must work to earn her bread.'

They were interrupted by the return of the apothecary. She immediately resumed their former conversation. 'This stranger, Mr Agar – ah!' she gasped as he lifted her foot to apply the compress and bind it on. 'Did he say why he sought Mr Bue? I am intrigued.'

'Not in so many words. He was expecting to hear news, a message or some such. I recommended he try to see Dr Hall, he was with Bue at the last. I know nothing more. Now,' his voice took on a professional tone, 'that should ease the swelling. Rest as well as you are able and I will attend you in a day's time. Let us see how you take the weight.'

Rhose stood up with great care, but at once reached for Oliver as her ankle gave way. She sank back in the chair. 'I fear I must rest for a while. I am more shaken than I thought. But I should not complain with that poor man lying there. We must do something for his family if he has one.'

'Do not concern yourself,' Oliver replied. 'I shall speak to Travis. For now we must get you home. If you will allow me I have my gig at the Bull's Head I shall be honoured to drive you back to your inn.'

'I should be most grateful Mr Banton. You have been a true gentleman.' Her smile carried more than mere thanks. Feeling much encouraged he bowed and hurried out, almost colliding with Matthew and the constable. Agar ushered them into the back room. When he returned Rhose was standing with only a little effort.

'A fortunate accident, Jonathan. I would speak with you in private.'

Agar smiled at her little play-acting. 'I suspected your injury was not so distressing as it appeared. I will help you up the stairs where we will not be overheard. I will arrange matters with the constable, then you may take the cordial while we speak.'

Once in the apothecary's room Rhose settled on a chaise longue, enjoying a peaceful moment before Agar joined her.

'Now Rhose, what business have you with me? I trust you know that I wish to free myself from those entanglements I had recently.'

Rhose sipped the cordial, then sat forward, her voice firm and determined. 'I am fully aware of your ambitions, but you cannot easily cast off all your old connections. One of Alice Rylance's girls has stupidly got herself pregnant. It is an embarrassment to all – she must be rid of it.'

'I told you I have done with all that. I will have no more dealings with such low life.'

Rhose gave a mocking laugh. 'There was a time when you had
no such scruples. It suited you well to treat "such low life" for
the itch, the pox, whatever. Nor were you reluctant to purge a
lass of an unwanted lodger.'

'Enough. I knew you still carried on your trade with those ill-
fortuned women against my advice. And now Smith and the
so-called "Servant's Gazetteer". Is it not time you dropped such
practice? They sail too near the wind for you to be safe in their
wake.'

'Needs must when the devil drives, Jonathan. These are difficult times for a poor widow.' Agar's scornful laugh cut in. 'You
may scoff. I would fain move on and up had I your resources.
How would it be if your society clients learned of your former
practices?' There was steel in her voice.

Before he could answer they heard Oliver Banton calling
from the shop. Agar gave way. 'Very well, I shall see what may
be done. But this must be the last time. Do not press me further
or there are tales I could tell.' He helped her to the stairs. 'Now
a convincing limp for your swain?' The tension between them
eased. She smiled as she hobbled uneasily and painfully down
to the shop.

When the gig drew up at the Ring o' Bells, the story, with many
embellishments, had preceded them. A delegation awaited:
Mary was in histrionic tears; Nell Royle and Alice Rylance
hovered, two crows hungry to pick at the gossip. Oliver was
allowed to assist the invalid indoors, but then she was snatched
from his fond grasp. Rhose waved away the importunate hands
turned and gravely thanked her rescuer. He left the inn happy
at the memory of Mistress Tinnys' melting smile.

Laurence bustled over to offer his condolences and deep
sympathy adding: 'I had hoped we could discuss business with
you,' he indicated a group at a corner table, 'but another time,

another time. I trust you are not badly hurt. If there is anything, anything at all, which I may do, you need only to call on my name . . . anything.'

'You are most genteel, Mr Laurence. I believe all I require at the moment is rest. These good ladies will grant me their attention, I have no doubt.' With a gracious nod and a helping arm she climbed the stairs.

In her private sitting room the two older women were agog to hear details of the tragedy, of the attentiveness of the young 'gentleman' and of Agar's response. They soon dismissed the dead chairman, but were relieved that the apothecary was still willing to assist, albeit with reluctance. Rhose was more interested in the news of the 'military stranger' and Joseph Bue. She knew that the two women would be only too eager to gossip over old times so she casually mentioned the incident at the Bull's Head.

'Ah!' Nell seized on the subject at once. 'It's always been a troublesome place. Why, back in '45 it's where the Jacobites drummed up for volunteers, that sergeant and his strumpet.'

'Mind he was a handsome man, that Prince Charlie,' Alice had a dreamy look in her eye. 'I saw him ride through, and back again.'

'Hm, too Frenchified for my taste,' Nell grumbled. She turned to Rhose, 'Did you not get to see him? A bonny lass like you would have caught his eye from what I heard.'

'You forget I was not here then. All I saw was a ragged rabble trailing through Lancaster. But tell me more, was Bue a rebel? Did he carry arms for the Pretender?'

'He would have done but he was too young, thin and scrawny – and his father would not let him. That's why he was so bitter and fanatical ever since. 'Twas no surprise to me he went the way he did.'

'He sat a horse like a true king.' Alice was lost in her own thoughts.

'What Bue?'

'No – the Prince.' Alice roused herself, 'You know he came twice.'

'Yes, coming and going,' Rhose laughed.

'No he came first in '44,' Alice insisted.

'Go on, that's just a tale.'

Alice was indignant. 'It is not. He did stay with the Mosleys at Ancoats Hall. He visited the Bull's Head itself. I'm sure of it.'

'Twaddle.'

'Now then Nell, you always say that. But there was lots of talk of it up at the Hall for months after. You talked before of bonny lasses. Lady Mosley's maid, Mary Miller, was the bonniest I've seen – and the Prince right fancied her.'

'So you say.'

'Well, she was sent away by Christmas – what do you say to that? And what about Eliza Diggle! She recognized him when he came with his army. She said she'd seen him at the inn before when he rode over from Ancoats to read the London papers, and she was sworn to secrecy.'

'Who is Eliza?' Rhose asked.

Nell butted in. 'Her father kept the Bull's Head but he never talked of any royal visit.'

'Nor would he after '45. He wouldn't want his head on the Exchange. But the Prince was in Manchester in October '44, and that's that. I was told in confidence. Ask Eliza if you don't believe me.'

This seemed to bring the conversation to an end despite Martha's mutterings. There was a knock at the door and Mary came in for instructions for the evening meal. Rhose took the opportunity to send the two gossips on their way. She held Mary back.

'We must get a message to Ned as soon as we can. He is well to keep out of the way but now we need to meet. I have news for him.'

Chapter Eleven

The Infirmary Ball

Charlotte sat by her window listening to the sounds of the house. Frank and the other men had risen early and she had woken to the clip of horses crossing the stable yard as they left for a gallop. The Robinsons' party had arrived the day before. Tonight was the Infirmary Ball.

The women finished at breakfast and left alone, Charlotte and Anne talked of the coming entertainment.

'You must not worry, Charlotte. There will be lots of young men to admire you. You won't be left sitting alone. William Jones will have competition. Indeed John Robinson watched you with more than a little interest last night, don't you know.'

Charlotte blushed. 'Please don't tease me Anne. I'm sure I will appear a country girl amongst all the ladies of Manchester. I'm fifteen next week, I'm too young to be admired.'

'If we'd lived in a town you might have been brought out last year, it's quite the accepted thing. But Papa was adamant you had to be kept secret. You've been treated well for a poor relation. After all who really knows where you come from? La, I believe Mama still hesitates to parade you in public.' She cast an arched look at the younger girl.

'Oh, Anne, I'm sure I don't wish to be paraded anywhere. It is

111

all so disturbing. I need a quiet distraction, my head is spinning.'

'Very well, my dear ninny, how you do take things to heart. Come, let us take a turn in the garden. George and the others can join us when they return. We must calm those delicate nerves of yours.'

So saying she wrapped a shawl round her shoulders and stepped on to the terrace with Charlotte close behind.

Lady Elisabeth and Sara Robinson watched the girls from the windows of the Great Hall. 'Charlotte is becoming a beauty, Elisabeth. George tells me that John has talked of naught else since they arrived.'

'Indeed, Sara, though Geoffrey was determined she should be kept secluded. I think perhaps she is too innocent as a result. Anne has done her best to teach her the social niceties and we shall be there to act as chaperones. I must tell you, Sara, that Francis has been showing too much interest in her. Thank goodness, with Sir Geoffrey's death, he has come to realize that a wife with a splendid portion is more to his taste, in fact is an essential. Perhaps I worry in vain?'

'Surely you do. You were so kind to raise her as one of your own family. No unfortunate child could have had a better home. Will you look to marry her soon?'

'Yes, though I shall miss her with Anne gone too. Sir Geoffrey has made provision for her, a modest portion. We will meet one of the prospects this evening. The Joneses are wealthy bankers and tea-men in Manchester. You must let me have your opinion. The youngest son is already an admirer.'

'Of course, and we will do all we can to help. Edward would aid in negotiations if you wish it. He is sorry to miss the ball but business interests are pressing.'

'Thank you, my dear. You have both been so kind. Shall we join the girls? The garden is at its best now. The roses are beginning to bloom and the fragrance hangs in the air on a still morning like today.'

So the day passed. The men returned and joined the ladies.

Dinner was taken early at two o'clock and then the frenzy began. The servants flew between rooms helping them all to dress. While the men donned powder gowns to attend to their wigs the ladies primped and painted. Lady Elisabeth came into Charlotte's room, stood still, admiring the young woman before her. The violet gown wonderfully set off her dark gold curls and pale complexion. The new cuffs were of the finest lace enhancing the delicate wrists and slender fingers.

'You look lovely my dear. You just need a final ornament; a jewel will set off the whole assembly perfectly. I have brought you a present. It was your mother's, a token from your father. It was her wish you should have it on your fifteenth birthday. It will grace you as it did her.'

Charlotte turned and watched in her mirror as an enamelled white rose on a golden chain was fastened around her throat, to lie perfectly in her decolletage.

'Oh, it's lovely! It's exquisite! So like the white roses in the garden. Thank you so much. I shall treasure it for my mother and for you Lady Elisabeth.'

Elisabeth looked at the rose and thought of its history. It was such a long time ago that the original gift was given. What harm could fall if Charlotte were to wear it now?

'Come now, we must go. The others are waiting.'

The ladies were soon settled in the Robinsons' coach and four. The gentlemen rode escort as the party descended on Manchester.

Rhose Tinnys had arrived at the Infirmary gardens early in the day. The pavilions where the food would be served already stood in a rank at the far side of the field. As she crossed towards them she saw with delight the transformation that was taking place for that evening's charity ball. No longer the plain lawns she remembered from her occasional visits with Agar. The walk by the House was lined with flambeaux and trees in tubs. Next to the walk the Infirmary lake, still and tranquil, would mirror the unfolding scenes. Already small platforms were tethered in the water holding fireworks for the evening's finale. The orchestra would take its place on the dais being constructed on the far side of the water. A matting floor, still in piles, would be laid for the dancing. As promised by the medical staff the sound of music would not be allowed to disturb the patients. Soon she was engaged in organizing her refreshments, cold meats and salats, jellies and confits. Her other tent would be serving liquor; here it would be cordials and punch.

The gates opened at six o'clock, and Rhose strolled down to the lake to watch the guests make their entrances. The surgeons and physicians, led by Dr Charles White, were amongst the first to arrive, enormously proud of the new Infirmary. As promised in the advertisement the evening was to follow the form of those in Ranelagh, the Chelsea pleasure garden: a promenade, a musical entertainment, supper and dancing. She saw the Fletcher party arrive and begin their promenade along the walk, chatting to friends. To see and be seen, she knew, was the main part of the event, the ladies in extravagant evening dress escorted by men-folk equally well clad; elaborate waistcoats, the latest in wigs and carrying hats. Rhose envied them, she longed to stroll the ground. She knew she would draw envious glances as she laughed with her escort. Her eyes were drawn to the scarlet uniforms of the First Regiment of Foot Guards who together with the local militia added an extra touch of drama here and there. An elegant captain, or even a major, would be the perfect foil for her own dramatic appearance. Soon the walks would be crowded and latecomers forced to parade in the field. Rhose hurried back to her tent, where Martha was putting the final touches to the display of refreshments before returning to the inn.

Elizabeth and Sara, too, surveyed the slowly moving crowd, all enjoying the stroll in the warm evening air. Here on the edge of town it was hard to imagine you were not in the country.

'Have you seen Beppy and Phoebe Byrom yet?'

'No, but I've seen the Mosleys and their grand party. Perhaps we will be able to speak to them later. Sir Oswald sold the land for the Infirmary, you know. It seems all Manchester's high soci-

ety is here in force. The Heywoods, the Booths, the Minshalls –
I can see them all. The Egertons of Heaton Hall are over there
by the lake. The Phillips and the Birleys, as I said, have invited
us to share their box. The Duke of Bridgewater from Worsley
Hall will not be attending. Gone to take the waters in Bath, it is
said.'

Soon it would be time for the concert and then supper. The
older ladies were anxious to arrive early at the card tables to
gain a good view of the dancers so they could continue to chap-
eron their charges. Lady Elisabeth hoped to secure a table with
Mrs Jones to open the evening.

Charlotte, Anne and George walked a little behind the rest of
the party. Anne explained who was who, and commented on
their ensembles. Francis, they had to admit, was in the van of
fashion and turning many of the young ladies' heads as they
passed. He did not return the compliment, feeling it unlikely
that any of them would be to his taste. The next London season
was the venue for his search for a wife of fortune and consequence. Nevertheless he was not unaware of the covert glances
and preened himself as he strolled along.

'I'm so glad I've found you all. The crowd is growing by the
minute. I hope they haven't sold too many tickets or the dancing will be an impossible crush.'

'Will! How lovely to see you. George, do you remember
William Jones, we met him last winter at the Preston
Assemblies.'

'Of course, how goes business, Jones? Is banking prospering?'

'It certainly is. Manchester is exploding. There are houses
planned for those fields over there. The Infirmary will soon be
surrounded, and there's already talk of expanding here, a new
Asylum, perhaps a Bath House. How's your new venture into
the cotton trade progressing?'

'Really, George, Will, you're not here to talk business. You're
here to admire and entertain us,' Anne expostulated. 'We would
hear talk of our lovely appearance, and have none of your "grey
goods".'

'Well, Anne, I for one won't find that difficult,' said Will, 'Never have I had more charming companions to illuminate an evening. "How happy I would be with either, were t'other dear charmer away",' he hummed.

'You look wonderful, the lavender dress is most becoming,' he whispered as he fell in beside Charlotte and looked down on her upturned face. 'I hope you will allow me to escort you to supper and grant me the first dance.'

A blush spread across Charlotte's cheeks. 'I'm so sorry, John, George's cousin, is to be my first partner, but you may be pleased to escort me to supper and I'll dance the second minuet with you.'

Will bowed and thanked her. He stayed by her side, glancing over at John who was walking with Francis. He'd met the dark-haired cousin in Preston. A pleasant enough youth, a younger son destined for the wool trade with a wealthy uncle in Dewsbury. He felt able to dismiss him as a serious rival. He'd talked to his father of his feelings for Miss Fletcher. They had agreed that his mother would speak to Lady Fletcher concerning Charlotte's prospects. A marriage into the gentry would do the bank no harm, in fact quite the contrary. Will was elated at his parents' reaction. He offered his arm to Charlotte, and pressed his hand over hers when she accepted. Looking up at him, she smiled, and then looked away, the ardent nature of his gaze disconcerting and exciting her at the same time.

Slowly the crowd moved over towards the orchestra where chairs had been placed for the concert. The ladies sat whilst the men stood to the rear. The front row was reserved for the Mosleys; Lady Mosley was to govern the activities. At a motion from her fan the music swelled and a hush fell over the field. The orchestra, which had been augmented for the occasion, manfully played popular pieces. The audience clapped politely and were rewarded with an encore. Lady Mosley quickly rose and led the way to supper. The grand parties had their own boxes but the rest were served in the pavilions. As Will had predicted it was indeed a crush.

In the tents the refreshments had been laid out on a series of tables garlanded with flowers. From a discreet vantage point Rhose was directing her assistants with assured command. Nodding to acquaintances as they passed, she kept a careful eye on the whole. The serving wenches in homespun gowns and white linen caps were soon the favourites of the young bucks hurrying to gather delicacies for their female companions. Rhose smiled to herself, sure in the anticipation of an excellent night's work and tomorrow's profits. She gave her last instructions to Jenny and prepared to return to the Ring o' Bells. She paused to allow the Fletcher party pass to a private box, exchanging polite greetings. Frank's voice cut through the feminine pleasantries.

'This may be Manchester's idea of a "ridotto al fresco" but I'm sure it can't compare with Ranelagh. There are too many shopkeepers here for one thing. And it's hardly the Mode, it's antiquity to perfection! If you'll excuse me ladies, I shall join my friends. We are planning our strategy for the races in October.'

'Francis, you will do no such thing. I wish to congratulate Lady Mosley on the success of the evening, and hope to introduce you all. Then I expect you to escort Mrs Robinson and myself to the card tables. After that you are free to do as you will.'

'Very well, Mama, as you wish.'

'Don't be such a prig, Francis. We're all having a lovely time and I can't wait for the dancing to start. Look at Charlotte so eager to be the "Belle of the Ball", do not spoil it for her.'

'Oh, nothing could spoil it, Anne.' Charlotte did not notice the sarcasm in the words. 'I could just sit and watch and I'd be thrilled. There are so many lovely clothes and interesting people – and such wonderful company.' At the last she looked at Will Jones and felt her heart flutter as he returned her gaze. The slight breathlessness was a new sensation for her, leaving her slightly giddy.

'Lady Fletcher, do come in. I had hoped to speak to you. I was so sorry to hear of your loss.' Lady Mosley extended her hand in greeting.

'Thank you. We have come to express our delight at the success of this evening's event. May I present my family.'

Soon the introductions were over and desultory conversation followed. Sir Oswald drew Lady Fletcher aside. 'I was saddened by Sir Geoffrey's demise. Old friends can never be replaced. Is this the child's first season? I know that Geoffrey was anxious to keep her secluded. She is very like her mother, a beautiful girl. I remember her well. It was hardly surprising she caught his eye. Was it his gift, the necklace Charlotte wears?'

'Indeed, I saw no harm. . . .'

'No, don't tell me. It is best I don't know. She can wear it with pleasure; the history would only be a burden to her. Ah, I see my wife is looking for me. Excuse me, it is time to start the dancing.'

The music for the first minuet began. The Mosleys led the dancers to the floor. John came to claim Charlotte and together with Anne and George they joined the throng. Francis strolled over to Will.

'We'd best escort our respective mothers to cards. Bezique and whist can't wait even if our affairs must. I gather your parent is to discuss Charlotte's prospects with mama. I should warn you, she's a cold piece. Don't let her demure looks fool you, though she's pretty enough.'

'I find her most charming and she will suit me admirably. Your comments are unwarranted and offensive. Let us settle our mothers before the second minuet as I'd not miss my turn about the floor with Charlotte.'

Lady Elisabeth and Sara Robinson had already started for the card pavilion and encountered Harriet Jones on the way. Their sons had an easy task and secured them a prominent table with a fine view of the dance floor.

With a 'Good Luck, ladies,' Francis bowed and withdrew. He stood and watched Charlotte dancing happily. Damn the girl! She'd never smiled at him like that. Why did she rouse his ardour? He felt her fear whenever he came near, yet it only served to rouse him more. The sooner she was married to Jones the better. As for himself, a wife at Greenwood Lea might slake his passions. Frank turned angrily away and went to join his friends on the edge of the field. Francis told John they were invited, by the Mosleys, to a shooting party on the moors above Colne on the twelfth of August, Moorgame Day. Francis admitted it had been worth accommodating his mother. The bucks regaled each other with tall tales, indulged in a little gaming and fondled the serving girls. Jenny Driver, prominent among the barmaids, kept them well supplied with drink. For Frank, the open prospect of lechery promised a diverting evening after all.

Charlotte's evening was the most wonderful she had ever known. As Will escorted her on to the floor she again felt that surge of happiness. Several young men had approached her during supper and asked for a dance. At Anne's insistence she had accepted one or two. But she knew this was the partner she wanted to be with, and gladly agreed to dance with Will again. The evening whirled by, minuets merging into country dances. Daylight started to fade and candles and flambeaux were lit, reflecting in the water.

'Will it soon be time for the fireworks?' Charlotte asked as they left the floor.

'Indeed it will. Would you like me to bring you an ice? I think after all the dancing it would be good to cool down a little.'

'What a lovely idea! Let's sit with George and Anne.' After escorting her to their table, the men left in their search for ices.

'You look very happy Charlotte. I see you are very far from averse to Mr Jones's attention.'

'Oh, he's so kind and pleasing to be with. I've never had such welcome attention from anyone. Would you think me stupid if I told you I'd like to meet him more often?'

'Of course not, I'm sure the feeling is mutual. I wouldn't be surprised if he came courting at Greenwood Lea before long. I think Mama has taken a fancy to him so don't worry. And she's been talking to his mother all evening. Of course, his family, unlike George's, is not well connected, so much more suited to one of your station. And they've enough money for you to have a house in the town.'

The men returned with the ices. Soon a drum roll by the military band interrupted their conversation. The fireworks were about to start. The audience, now corralled back from the lake by white ropes, waited with eager anticipation.

A flight of skyrockets launched the display with a burst of coloured plumes above the spectators. Then a formation of Roman candles shot bright velvet stars high into the air. Revolving suns, rainbow candles, wheels and fountains followed in rapid succession. They were interspersed with more bouquets of rockets cascading gold and silver rain. Fountains of fire, like trees, lit up the lake. A slow shower of gold leaves and blossoms struck each platform and continued to sparkle. This grove of shimmering trees mirrored dramatically in the water was the grand finale. Suddenly it was over and darkness descended.

Charlotte turned to her companion, her face full of wonder at the spectacle they had just witnessed.

'Well, my dear, did you enjoy that! A novelty for you no doubt, I can't say I was too impressed.'

'Frank! Where's Will? He was here a minute ago.'

'I sent him off to ready the coach. Told him the ladies would catch cold and that I would escort you. Rushed off at once, anything to please, don't you know.'

'Where are the others?'

'On their way as well. George and John in charge. Told them I'd find you and join them. Still we have time to tarry a while, how about a dance for me.'

'The dancing is over. I don't understand what you mean.'

'Come, Charlotte, a turn around the floor in my arms, is that too much to ask?'

The crowd was surging round them intent now on going home. Charlotte was pushed against Francis who fastened his arms around her in a steely grip. It was worse than that nightmare she remembered on the stairs, only now there was no Hannah to rescue her – in the midst of the crowd she was alone. Frank pulled her to him and began to kiss the back of her neck as she struggled to break free. Charlotte felt she would swoon, the smell of alcohol overpowering her.

'No, no,' she gasped. 'Please stop what you are doing.' Tears began to flow. 'I'm your sister, it isn't right.'

'You're not my true sister as you well know. I'm tired of watching you flirt with other men. Would you be pushing Will away?' Francis put his hand behind her head and pulled her face to him, kissing her violently. Charlotte was terrified.

'Stop, stop! I implore you. Let me go home. I won't tell Mama or Anne.'

Suddenly Francis drew back.

'Well, well, Frank, it seems you've found yourself a pretty morsel. Is there plenty to go round, or is this one all for yourself?' Charlotte felt another hand engage her waist and was spun round to face a young man she had never seen before.

'No, just a maid I came across in the crush, Nat. Acquaintance of my sister's, so you'd better leave her alone, or she'll be telling tales. I'll take her back to her party and then join you at Smiths. I hear he has new doxies willing to play a game or two.'

After an ironic bow to Charlotte and shaking hands with Francis, Nathaniel Lloyd was lost in the crowd. Holding Charlotte by the elbow, Francis propelled her towards the line of waiting coaches. Will who was watching for them coming, rushed to greet them. One look at Charlotte's face told him of her distress.

'She was accosted in the crowd when we were separated. I chased him off soon enough but it gave her a fright. All's well now and she'll soon be home.'

'Come my dear,' Lady Elisabeth hurried over and put her arms around the sobbing girl. 'Help me get her into the coach, Sara. Anne wrap the shawls around her, she's had a dreadful shock. I hold you responsible for this Francis. No doubt you weren't taking enough care of her. Coachman away as soon as you can.'

Charlotte was bundled into the coach. Francis mounted his horse and rode off into Manchester. John made to follow but George reminded him they must escort the ladies. The party set off for home leaving Will to watch helplessly. He didn't blame Francis. He blamed himself. If he had stayed with Charlotte no harm could have come to her. He would lay down his life to protect her. He vowed never again should she suffer if it was in his power to protect her.

Chapter Twelve

A Damnable Trade

'. . . and, Lord, you should have seen the fireworks, sparkling and fizzing and banging over the lake! I've never seen such a sight.'

Jenny Driver was living it all again, perched forward on her chair. She and Rhose were in the private sitting-room of the Ring o' Bells. The morning sun was setting the dust mites dancing in the still air. Rhose, amused, was only half listening to the girl's prattling.

'It was indeed a thrilling night and a busy one for you serving wenches.'

'As for that there was much drunk – and it didn't end there after you left.' Jenny gave a satisfied giggle as she sat back, taking up a cup of chocolate with exaggerated daintiness.

Rhose laughed. 'We all had a busy time at the ball then?'

'Why we've not had such business since the cocking.' She burst into a fresh set of giggles and pushed her cup back on the table. 'You know what I mean? I reckon it was those fashionable ladies, acting all hoighty-toighty, got the young bucks so frolicsome. All those charmers with their airs and graces! All that flesh, and not to touch, gets 'em all on heat. Why, that Frank Fletcher—' She stopped, hands to mouth, eyes wide.

'Do go on, he is of no consequence to me.'

'I didn't know whether . . . I know he's one of the gentry that comes here . . . I thought perhaps—'

'Oh, come now. Don't stutter and stammer so. I know his family, that's all – as for his reputation, well!'

'It was only a bit of horseplay I suppose. I saw him fair tousling that young sister of his.'

'Anne, you mean?'

'No, t'other one – the young one – the prettier one. She didn't seem to take to it. It came to naught at all events. But it fair heated him up. Why he had Molly and Phanny together!' She squealed with delight.

'That is enough. I have no wish to know such Sugar Lane tittle-tattle, enough that I share an interest. Which brings me to my reason for calling you here this morning.' Rhose stood, smoothing her skirt and moved to the table, collecting the cups and plates of the breakfast they had shared. 'I have thought it time you took more part in the arrangements at the house. Alice grows older, less – reliable.'

Jenny sat straighter in her chair, preened and began to speak but was silenced by Rhose standing over her.

'You are young, attractive and, despite your giggling ways have a sound head. You can have a wicked tongue' – the other began to protest – 'but you also know when to keep silent. I have watched you over the last months and I am pleased with your progress.'

'I thank you, Mistress Tinnys. I'm sure I always do my best and no one's ever complained of me – in or out of bed. Oh, there I go again! I do try to curb my tongue and I'll try harder. I know how delicate certain matters can be. I swear I would satisfy in how you might use me. As for Alice Rylance, I'm truly grateful for all she's done for me but. . . .' She left the sentence in mid-air.

'Here will be your first test. I am being brought two young-sters. I would have you take their measure, see their suitability and introduce them to the niceties of the trade. Not precipitous, with care and some gentility. Do this well and there could be much in the future. I am putting trust in you, Jenny Driver.'

'Thank you again, I'll not betray that trust, I swear.'

Before any more could be said there was a knock at the door and Mary pushed in. 'That man Smith is downstairs along with two childer – bonny little things under the dirt. Shall they come up now?' She cast a quizzical look at Jenny in obvious doubt as to the propriety of her being there at that hour.

'Send them up', Rhose said, 'and please take away the breakfast things.'

Moments later Smith arrived with a courtly bow to Rhose and a mocking inclination to Jenny. There was no doubting that the young girls he ushered in were straight from the country. From identical faces identical blue eyes stared out blankly at a frightening world. They wore simple shifts above sturdy legs with stubbly bare feet, rough broken-nailed hands hung by their sides.

'As like as two peas in a pod,' Jenny exclaimed in delight. Grime had been scrubbed carelessly from their faces, arms and legs but still matted their long honey-coloured hair.

'What do you think, are they not beauties?' Smith beamed a self-satisfied smile. 'Just thirteen years old, dewy fresh from the farm, innocent as the day is long – and the night longer.'

Rhose silenced him with one look and knelt before the children. Her voice was low and kindly.

'Now, dears, how come you here? Do your ma and pa know you've come?'

'Undoubtedly. Do you believe I would—' Smith's protest was cut short by a wave of Rhose's hand. Jenny quietly circled the group, studying the newcomers intently. The girls exchanged glances, clasped hands and one prodded the other. In one long exhaled breath they gabbled.

'Pa's poorly, Mam's right moithered with six of us an' we'se th'oldest so we'se got to get brass an' this nice man,' they gave a sketchy curtsey to Smith who responded with a satisfied smirk, 'give Pa a whole guinea an' he says . . .' they stumbled, searching for the words. One sister prodded the other again and whispered. Parrot fashion they went on, 'says we "may be brought up t'trade in't big town".'

Spent, they sighed and lapsed into silence. Two pairs of unblinking eyes fixed in wary hope on Rhose's smiling face. She patted their arms, stood, turning toward Smith:

'Thirteen, you say? And genuine twins? Untouched?'

'I've the father's sworn statement and I paid hard cash. He'd heard of the *Gazetteer* you see, out Rawtenstall way. Pitiful it was to see those poor bairns, anything I can do. . . !'

'Save me the hypocrisy, Mr Smith. Well, what do you think Mistress Driver?'

Smith's grin widened as he watched the young woman encircle the girls for a second time. They huddled closer together, frightened by all the attention. Jenny bent to them as she dropped her polished manner.

'Tha's no need to be afeared,' her voice, too, was gentle as she stroked their backs in turn. 'Auntie Jenny'll tek care o'thee. Cans't tell me tha names?'

'I's Sarah and she's Etta.' The bolder of the twins replied, the other simply held hands and stared.

'They're gradely names for such bonny lasses.' She picked something from the tangled locks and popped it between finger and thumb. 'Tha's lively heads of hair at any rate.' She grimaced across at Rhose. Tenderly she cupped each face in her hand, pressing open their mouths. 'Good teeth,' she muttered, but turned away from the stink of their breath. Carefully she felt along each little body, arms, legs, belly, smiling and chattering all the while.

Rhose glanced at Smith whose sardonic look had changed to one of professional approval. Jenny stood, arms around the twins.

'They'll do – sound bones, sturdy limbs. A good wash, a bit of fattening up and pretty dresses will do the trick. I know many will pay good guineas for a romp with this pretty pair.'

'Well now,' Smith stepped forward, rubbing hands together, 'you and I should talk business, Mistress Tinnys.'

Before she could reply there was a knock and Mary's head appeared round the door. 'There's excise men downstairs. You'd best come.'

'What do they want? They're wont to give us a warning of a visit. Treat them as usual, I will be down directly.'

Rhose smile at Smith whose sallow features had grown even paler. 'Why, surely you have nothing to fear? All ship-shape at the Coffee House?'

Jenny suppressed a giggle, the twins stood silent, one picking her nose, the other twisting a coil of hair.

'Down the stairs, quietly along the corridor, and you should be able to get out the back without meeting – anyone.' Without a word he slipped out of the room.

'Jenny, you did well. And the children – Sarah and Etta – I believe you will be happy with your new family. You stay here with Aunty Jenny for a while. Would you like a cordial? Though I doubt not you are used to something rather stronger.'

There were bemused nods as they were led to the settle and Rhose hurried downstairs.

As she entered the main room, Mary gave a significant nod towards the back to show that Peter Smith had indeed slipped away. At the centre table Molineux and Tobin sat, legs spread, tankards at their elbows. They shuffled to their feet when they saw Rhose.

'Now what may I do for you gentlemen?' She waved them back to their seats. 'You checked for dutied goods not two weeks gone. Surely it is not time again?'

Molineux showed some embarrassment: 'No ma'am, indeed not and that is not what we are here for.'

'We've had information – good information,' Tobin strode forward, hand clasped to sword, 'there's new men about. Brandy, we've heard, lace, we've heard, tea and coffee, all being brought up river, o'er land, whate'er way can be. There's duty not paid. It's a hanging matter for any that does it, or any that aids them what does.'

'Really, Mr Tobin, there's no need to grow fierce with me.'

Rhose looked him square in the face, hands on hips. 'Have you ever known me ought but honest? Do you think I harbour smugglers in my cellars – or, mayhap, under my skirts?' With this she hiked her skirt over her ankles then flounced it down with a rustle of petticoats.

Molineux, chuckling, drew his colleague back. 'Nay, forgive my partner, Mrs Tinnys, we've been fair trounced by them above us for not putting a stop to this trade. Pray do not be alarmed, our search is but a formality.'

Tobin muttered some kind of apology and returned to the table to down the rest of his drink.

'Why, surely! It is a damnable trade when we are in the midst of war. Yet like all poor traders, I find the taxes burdensome. 'Tis hard to make an honest living in these hard times. The inn is yours. I'll get the lad to see you to the cellars.'

She went to the back to call Elias. The boy appeared from the back brushing straw from his coat. He was about to say something but stopped when he saw the two men. At a word from Rhose he led them down through the trap door. Mary returned to join Rhose behind the long counter. They whisked away boxes, which clinked as they walked. Two went inside a lidded settle, a tattered rug thrown over. Down the corridor, a panel under the stairs was prized open, and more packed inside to nestle with tightly packed bundles. They worked quickly and silently with well-practised ease. Martha bustled in from the kitchen, nodding reassuringly.

'All's well back there,' she whispered. 'not a thing to be seen that shouldn't be.' Hurrying back she let out a strangled scream, the ladle she was carrying flew through the air to clatter against the wall.

'Martha, my beauty, do you not recognize your old friend? Come give us a kiss.'

A dusty, dishevelled figure stood in the doorway, slouch hat over his eyes, black kerchief round his neck, boots caked with dirt. Long Ned spun the flustered cook round as he strode into the corridor.

Mary scurried away to the front while Rhose put out a warning hand. 'There's excise men here,' she said, but was silenced by
a quick, hard kiss.

Ned gave a short laugh. 'I'll not be stopping then. This town's
not healthy for me. I've others at my heels. My horse is saddled
and ready.' He took the stairs two at a time, calling down softly:
'I've things to fetch then I'll not trouble you further.'

'Hold! There are—' Rhose got no further. Squeals and a muffled,
'Deuce take me' revealed that he and the girls had met. Shrugging,
with a quick glance round, she joined Mary back in the bar.

The cellar door crashed back. Elias emerged grinning, dust-
ing off his breeches. He winked, 'I reckon I've showed 'em
everything.'

Tobin came up behind him, puffing and brushing dirty
strands of cobwebs from his face.

'You young blackguard! It was no accident you knocked down
those sacks. I'll learn you – gallows bait!' Tobin aimed a blow at
the lad, who skipped lightly out of reach and disappeared into
the kitchen. The excise man chased after just as Ned came
bounding down the stairs, a sack in hand.

'Hey! You! Stop!' Tobin reached for his sword, blocking the
stair foot. Ned vaulted the banister, swinging the sack full in the
other's chest. He went down with a crash as the highwayman
raced to the kitchen. Molyneux, shouting, rushed across the
room to try to intercept him. Mary, in melodramatic fright,
screamed, threw up her apron knocking over a chair as she did
so. Chair and man collided, collapsing to the floor together.
Meantime, Rhose, in an apparent attempt to help Tobin,
succeeded only in tangling him with jacket and sword and effec-
tively blocking the passage.

It was at this moment that Jenny appeared at the top of the
stairs, the two girls clinging to her skirts, both crying and mewl-
ing like frightened kittens. The cacophony died down as men,
women, and furniture untangled. The silence that followed was
broken by the sound of hoofbeats clattering across cobbles and
away. Immediately it all restarted: officers protesting, Rhose

129

and Mary solicitous in apology, renewed wailing from the stairs. It was Martha who brought calm. From the kitchen door, her voice carried over the hubbub.

'Shall I be starting on today's dishes? The man's away so you might as well settle yourselves down, there's nought to be done now. I only hope he's not taken much!'

She turned on her heel and with a swagger returned to her own domain. Rhose summoned Jenny and the girls and they came down to join the others at the centre table. Tobin was for pursuing the fugitive but Molineux, with Rhose concurring, persuaded him otherwise. Another tankard was the convincing argument.

Jenny appeared anxious and flustered. 'My, Mistress Tinnys, who was that man? He fair gave me and the bairns a fright – with that mask and all.' She turned to the twins who were sobbing most convincingly.

'Nay, don't be afeard. It was nobbut a lot of noise and be sure these kind gentlemen are officers o' the law. They'll see no harm can come to thee,' Jenny reassured them.

'Ah, Mr Tobin, Mr Molineux,' Rhose took up the cue, 'you see how frightened these poor children were, why they're still shivering. As for that brutish fellow, he must have climbed in through a window, I only trust he has not stolen much from me.'

The two excise men were now more taken with the young women and the whimpering children than any remaining duty. Rhose wrapped protective arms around the twins.

'Such a fright for the poor bairns only freshly come from the country and I dare hold that Miss Driver is not so calm as she pretends.'

Jenny duly gave a delicate yet provocative shudder, which did not go unnoticed.

'Do you think you could be so kind as to conduct them through town? It will be so trying for the little ones.'

'Well . . . we do have our official duties to perform, other inns to inspect,' was Molineux's reluctant response.

Tobin, openly leering at the three, put in: 'Oh, come now

Walter, it would be unkind not to see these young ones through the streets. Surely it's our duty as – officers of the crown – and gentlemen, to see they are safe delivered.'

Jenny fluttered nervously, pushing forward the twins. 'Think how fearful my young charges are after the brutal appearance of that dreadful man. My, they still shiver, look!'

Prompted by a gentle nudge the girls trembled as they clung to their new 'auntie'.

'And, no doubt, when we return to Sugar Lane, there will be the opportunity to show our gratitude. . . .'

Molineux was at once won over and, with Rhose's blessing, the trio set out under the assiduous protection of the excise officers.

'Let us know what has been taken,' were Molineux's parting words. 'We'll apprehend the knave, yet!'

As the door closed, Mary and Rhose breathed a companionable sigh of relief. 'Mary, I shall retire to my sitting-room. After this morning's adventures I need time for peace and quiet.'

'What if Mr Banton should call? He has been most constant in his attentions since escorting you home those weeks ago.'

'Ah, I would not refuse him. For all others please preserve my peace. Oh, Mary, how turbulent life can be!'

131

Chapter Thirteen

Holywell House

Now he had high hopes of meeting Lady Fletcher and his lost darling. The horse climbed the steep track leading over Anglezarke Moor to the next valley. Pausing to rest at the summit he looked back, the hills fell away in waves to where a blue haze hung over Manchester. Up here the air was clear and the only sound the song of a mistlethrush in the woods below. The track led down into another valley leading, eventually to Blackburn. Soon he would reach a junction with a packhorse trail that climbed over to Tockholes. He remembered these hills so well as he often accompanied the chapmen, ponies and drivers when he was young. With luck he could enter the grounds unseen and somehow arrange a meeting with Lady Fletcher – or ride up to the front door if he felt bold. He would decide later. The walk to the Healing Well by the house was well known to the locals and that, he concluded, was the one to be favoured.

Soon he was riding down the trail with beech woods above. A hedge on the top of the left bank marked the edge of the Robinson lands. The horse stepped carefully down the steep paved track with cross stones helping to provide a grip. Now in woodland the air was warmer and the light appeared pale green under the branches. Shafts of sunlight lit up glades here and there. A far cry, Thomas thought, from the dusty plains and harsh colours of the Indian landscape he had grown to love. Down in the trees it was hard to believe the open barren moor lay so near above. An ancient stone bridge crossed a small stream and Thomas could hear a mill at work some way off to his right.

A string of ponies heavily laden with packs appeared on the trail below, the drivers calling to each other. Thomas guided his horse under the trees above the way and watched as the men and animals passed beneath him. He thought he recognized one of the drivers but now wasn't the time to renew old acquaintances. As they passed on out of view he descended to a junction, where a bridge crossed a fast flowing river. The walk to the well began on the near side. Thomas remembered a steep climb into the open and then a descent down to the Hall. The open land was meadowland but there could be labourers about. Still cautious, he decided to go on foot. Dismounting, Thomas led the animal into a thicket of hazel and bramble and tethered it out of sight. It was early afternoon so it would be light for several hours. Taking out some bread and cheese from his saddle-bag, he lay on the ground watching the light filtering through the trees. How beautiful it was, he'd forgotten the peace and tranquillity of these woods.

Much had happened since his return. Bue's death had been the first blow, his parents' death the second. Lying now in the bright sunshine, he recalled his talk with Dr Hall in the chilly corridor of the new Infirmary. Bue had passed the secret on his deathbed in the hope that the girl might be reunited with her true family. He had seemed so near the end of his quest for Mary's child. He chafed at being constantly thwarted. Then at Greenwood Lea disappointment again, the family were away. A little golden persuasion revealed they were staying with the Robinsons of Holywell House, the daughter Anne's prospective relations. He knew it well, less than two hours ride from his family's farm. Now he was here, soon to see Charlotte at last. He rose to his feet and began what he hoped would be his final journey. Deciding to follow the stream and cut through the woods above the house, he whistled softly to himself happy that he would soon be reunited with the girl he last saw as a babe in arms.

Holywell House lay in a sheltered hollow below the moors; a long drive connected the property to the road. The house was hidden behind a belt of ancient trees and only the fine gateposts announced to the outside world that anyone dwelt there. There had been habitation on the site since the Middle Ages, and pilgrimages were then made to the 'Holy Spring' that gave the house its name. The ancient terrace, which led to the spring, was now part of the garden. At the far end, the water still flowed through a carved stone lion's head into the well and was attributed with healing properties for the eyes. By agreement with the Robinsons, local people still came to visit.

'I think we should walk in the garden, you can admire my new Snowy Mespilus which I lately had from Telford's of York, though it will be next April before we can admire the flowers again.' Edmund Robinson was known for his passion, gardening. 'We must take advantage of such a fine day. Come, the roses are in full bloom.' The Fletchers and Robinsons dutifully followed him through an arch into the enclosed garden. The ladies dressed in their flowered summer silks, their faces hidden from the sun under Bergere hats. Discarding their coats the men sported fine white linen shirts under their waistcoats.

'These red roses are the emblem of Lancashire and those striped red and white are known as the "York and Lancaster" after Henry Tudor. A fitting symbol for the wedding of Anne and George don't you think, as he will inherit some of the family's Yorkshire interests. Then we've Maiden's Blush, Blush Provence, Red Damask, now that's the apothecary's rose. . . .'

Sara and Lady Elizabeth followed him across the grassy plat that lay within the enclosed garden. At the foot of walls covered with honeysuckles and espaliered fruit trees were beds full of flowering shrubs.

'This Provence rose is said to have a hundred petals. We've missed this cinnamon rose, it flowers in May; Rose de Mai is its other name. That came from Perfects nursery in Pontefract. It's hard to keep the season going but this Late White Cluster is autumn flowering, a real treasure and so sweetly scented.'

The younger members of the family were falling back, knowing that next would be the vegetable garden then the orchard with various apples, apricots and cherries.

'Let us move on to the kitchen garden. My new Belgian pear, Glou Morceau, has set well this year. I trained it on the wall. . . .'

'Let us move on to the well,' whispered Anne, 'la, I cannot abide those pears again. We'll get our skirts wet on the long grass in the orchard and those willows on the far side of the stream always make me sneeze at this time of year.'

As Edmund led his wife and Lady Elisabeth past the fishpond at the end of the plat into the kitchen garden the others mounted steps that led on to the upper lawn, the terrace leading to the well. A sheer grassy slope led up from the lawn to the woods behind, an area known by Edmund as 'the wilderness.'

'What a wonderful view from here,' exclaimed Charlotte. 'I can see right down the valley and to the moors beyond. It makes the house and garden seem like an oasis in the desert, there are no other dwellings in sight.'

'More like a cabin in the American wilderness with savages your only neighbours,' countered Francis. 'Let us walk to the spring.'

As they crossed the grass the sound of running water soon reached them. In an angle of the far wall of the property the famous carved lion head was spouting water into a deep stone basin, the famous well.

'Just behind the top of the wall there is the tank supplying the main spring. There are no less than five springs feeding into it. It's always cold, John and I used to swim in it when we were younger. Perhaps if you ladies weren't here we'd avail ourselves of it on a hot day like today.'

'Don't let us prevent you, George. Charlotte and I can join

your parents in the orchard, but don't forget we are to visit Longworth Hall this afternoon.'

'Quite right, Anne. However inviting the idea, we must soon return to the house. Shall I escort you to see the tank? Take my hand, as the steps are steep. Allow me Charlotte,' John spoke quickly offering his arm.

'Oh, thank you, this is such an adventure. Why the water looks black, the trees are shading it from the sun. No wonder it's cold.'

'Nor a place to be at night, I warrant. One of our uncles was forced to shelter in the lea of the wall one snowy night not knowing how near he was to the house. He swore in the morning he had been kept company by ghostly figures long dead.'

'What a horrible story! You and John are still determined to frighten us, just like when we were children. Let's go back into the sunshine, it must be nearly time to go.'

'Oh Anne, look at the patterns of light under the trees, the wood looks so inviting.

'Perhaps you'd like to walk there, Charlotte?' Francis suggested. 'Edmund was telling me how he has started to build a grotto a little way up the stream. I'm sure there is time to explore before we must leave.'

'Do you think so Frank, I'm really not sure. . . ?'

'Of course, and we won't be out of view of the house.

'Will you come too John?'

'I had better return. Edmund has put me in charge of the travel arrangements. I need to see the coach is ready.'

Anne, George and John descended the steps and with a wave of the hand and a 'Don't be long', they started for the house.

Francis escorted Charlotte into the woods. 'You look charming today.'

'Thank you Frank, but don't you think we should return?'

'No, come, we only need to walk a short way up the stream. Edmund tells me the site is enchanting, a mossy bower within the trees.'

A faint path could be seen crossing the deep green grass

ahead; dappled with sunlight it looked very inviting. Francis strode ahead, and after a moments' hesitation Charlotte felt obliged to follow. At the top of the rise the path descended into a deep bowl nurturing a mixture of shrubs and trees, an artifice devised by man. Near the floor a mighty oak dominated all and a pile of rocks was cut into the slope as if a cave.

'This is the place,' called Francis as he descended. 'It's magnificent, come and see. A stream rises from within, we can sit and rest before we return.' Charlotte was captivated; the scene resembled some romantic idyll. The rivulet crossed below her to vanish once again into the hillside on its journey to the well. Entranced, she carefully made her way to the oak, expecting at any minute to see Lords and Ladies people the grove.

'I'm so glad I came, nothing could be more beautiful.'

'I'm so glad you came too.' Francis was at her side. 'I think we have some unfinished business. This time there is no Nathaniel Lloyd to interrupt us.'

Charlotte found herself pinned to the tree, the weight of his body preventing any movement. Francis's hand was over her mouth and she realized his other hand caressed her breasts. Quivering with terror she began to cry.

'Tears will do you no good. I have dreamed long of this.' He crushed his lips on hers. Lifting her skirt, his hand was soon stroking her naked thigh, and she felt the bark of the tree pressing into her. Released from his hand she bit his lip and managed to cry out for help.

'A noble try, but there is none to hear. Come let me introduce you to my column, you shall pleasure me now.'

Charlotte felt Frank undoing the buttons on his breeches as he covered her breasts with kisses. She beat her hands on his back and cried out again in a final despair.

As Thomas reached the last rise above the house he heard a cry coming from the trees on his left. At first he thought it was a bird, but then it came again, more urgent this time. He moved back into the trees following the direction of the sound.

Suddenly he was standing on the edge of a descent and below in its depth a man and woman were struggling. He had no doubt what was happening, he had seen too many drunken soldiers behave like this with Indian maidens. Without a second thought he ran down and pulled the man away from his victim. The girl pulled at her skirts and gathered her bodice together, sobbing.

Thomas stared at the man – he remembered him from the inn. Well, they could have the fight now here in the woods. Francis took the moment to recover his breath, his breeches half undone. He too recalled their previous encounter.

'I see I am going to have to teach you a lesson after all.'

'The pleasure will be all mine. A man who tries to rape a girl is no man to me.'

Francis cursed the luck that meant he had left his sword in the house; still his opponent looked an easy target. In a frantic rage, Francis threw himself on top of the intruder thrashing him left and right. Thomas remained calm; years of soldiering had prepared him for such an encounter. Fighting in a temper always led to mistakes and he could make the most of that. Blow followed blow and Thomas forced Francis to the floor. Looking up for a moment he caught site of the girl cowering by the tree; his eye was drawn to the trinket round her neck, a white enamelled rose. He had seen it before! It was the token the Prince had given his sister, Mary. My God, the girl must be Charlotte. He called out her name.

'Charlotte, is it you at last? I have searched long for you. I am your uncle, Thomas. I am so glad—'

His voice was silenced as Francis brought a rock down on the back of his head. In the minute that Thomas's attention was diverted, Francis had risen and grabbed a stone from the pile by the grotto. Charlotte took one look at the stricken man and fled.

Francis let her go. The man might be mortally wounded or not, but he must hide him without delay. Soon he had dragged the body out of the glade and into the depths of the wood behind. A fallen tree proved the perfect solution. Pushing the body under the branches Francis knew it would not be visible until the autumn, if then. Wild animals might do their worst, and if he was alive? Well, who would believe his story? After washing in the stream and rearranging his clothing, Francis set off after Charlotte.

'I knew you should not have let them go further. This really is too much. We shall leave without them. John summon the coach.'

Edmund Robinson was most displeased. The visit to Longworth Hall had been specially arranged and he would brook no change to his plan. The coach drew up at the door. Edmund and George helped Sara, Lady Elisabeth and Anne inside. Edmund joined them. The two younger men mounted their horses and followed the coach and four towards the south.

Charlotte ran across the lawns back to the house. Flinging open the door she fell exhausted into Hannah's arms.

'Miss Charlotte what on earth has happened?'

'Please, where is Mama?' Charlotte was white with terror.

'They've left. They were very angry that you were not here.'

'Get my cloak and ask Rob to bring the carriage to the door. I must go home this very instant.'

Hannah looked at Charlotte's dishevelled state and knew at once what had happened. Without a word of argument she went to find Rob and within minutes they were on the road to Greenwood Lea.

Chapter Fourteen

The Road to Damnation

The coach rocked along the lanes to Greenwood Lea, Rob whipping the horses with unaccustomed frenzy. The Robinsons' second best coach was old and worn and Charlotte felt every rut in the road as a further blow to her person. The girls were tossed about inside, clinging to the sides to avoid being thrown to the floor. Finally skidding down the track to the house the horses drew up in a lather outside the front door. Without waiting to be helped down, Charlotte rushed inside and up the stairs to her room where she flung herself sobbing on the bed.

Where was Frank now, she wondered in terror? Would he follow her here alone or would Lady Elisabeth be with him? Who was the man in the woods? Had she dreamt that he said he was her uncle? So many questions and no answers! This morning had been so delightful; yet now her world had turned upside down. Overcome with horror at the events of the day, the girl collapsed completely and laid shivering, eyes wide as silent tears coursed down her cheeks.

Downstairs Hannah and Rob were making plans. Quietly opening the door to the housekeeper's room, Rigby and Clegg were to be seen dozing after their usual evening porter. Closing the door again Hannah turned to Rob.

'Now's our chance, they're both sleeping soundly and Miss Charlotte's too upset to hear what we do. You gather as much silver and trinkets as you can down here. I'll go pack my things and see what I can find upstairs. The mistress has taken her best jewels with her. Miss Anne is careless and I know where she hides her keys. We should be able to take a tidy amount to set us up.'

'You're right lass, we could hardly want for more. We'll take the coach and horses, they'll add to the profit when we've no more use of them. I might even marry you, now you've got a dowry.'

'Get away with you Rob; the quicker we are gone from here the better. The Fletchers will be following us if Frank hasn't told a tale to explain our absence. He's plenty to lie about from the state of the young lady above. It's one thing showing me his maypole, quite another with Miss Charlotte. It seems however she was rescued at the last moment. I wonder who that can have been? Still I must fly upstairs and you go treasure hunting.'

Hannah hurried to her bedroom and gathered together her few possessions. At last she would be able to buy some new clothes instead of having others' cast-offs. Perhaps she'd take a dress or two from below and some lace trimmings. The Fletchers were not bad masters, still there were opportunities now for the likes of her and Rob. Towns were expanding and given some cash and a little luck they could prosper. She'd heard all about the chances in London, they could soon vanish once they reached the capital. With the coach and horses they would be ahead of the hue and cry.

She rushed to Anne's room; as she thought she was able to find a necklace and some bracelets. She also helped herself to a fine yellow silk gown and petticoat together with a handsome brown velvet cloak. She stuffed them into her bundle and returned to the landing. The door to Charlotte's room was open. The girl stood there pale and trembling, her stained bedraggled dress telling of her encounter in the woods.

'Hannah, what are you doing? Why are you still wearing your

cloak? Will you please help me change?'

'I'm sorry Miss, Rob and I are off to Manchester. We're running away to be married. We can't stay in service here and be together.'

'No, no, you can't leave me here alone. Suppose Frank comes and finds me again.' She broke into uncontrollable sobbing once more.

'We can't stay. Miss. We must seize our chance, I'm sorry. I mean you no harm but we must leave at once.'

'Then take me with you. I won't stay. I know Mrs Rigby and Clegg are below but they will be in their usual state by now and won't be able to help me if I need them. They will believe what ever Frank tells them, they durst not do otherwise. I must go with you. I can send word to mama when I'm in Manchester.'

'Where can you stay? How will you explain to your friends why you are there? Your reputation will be ruined. Sir Francis would deny everything. You should stay here, he won't try again.'

'Please help me Hannah. I cannot endure he should find me here alone. I must come with you.'

'Well you could stay with my mother, though it is a humble house. You could send word to your mama from there.'

'Yes, yes anything not to face him again.'

'Well, you need to change. Here, put on this brown dress and petticoat of mine, we're much the same size. Your oldest shoes and some black stockings will let you pass as a serving girl like me. We can take a cloak from the kitchen, there's always a couple hanging by the back door.'

'Thank you Hannah, I'm so grateful. . . .'

'Be quick then. I'll go and tell Rob we're ready to leave.'

Rob was angry. 'We must make a quick escape, not take the girl to your mother. We'll be in extra danger if they think we've kidnapped her into the bargain. Get in the coach – we can leave without her.'

Rob picked up his haul. Suddenly the door to the house-keeper's room swung open and Clegg stumbled out.

'Is that you Robert, what's all this commotion. What be you doing in the house? It's no place for you. Has Hannah let you in?'

As the pair turned to face him, Charlotte came hurrying down the stairs into the Great Hall.

'Miss Charlotte, what are you doing?' Mrs Rigby woken by the noise had emerged. 'Oh my goodness, you're wearing Hannah's old dress. What is going on?'

Charlotte stopped at the bottom of the stairs, and looked at them all with bewilderment. Her hands repeatedly straightened the unfamiliar coarse skirt. She still trembled and her eyes were red from weeping. Before another word was spoken, Hannah grabbed her hand and half dragged her across the hall and out through the front door. Clegg and Mrs Rigby stared as Rob, offering them a low bow, followed the girls then banged the door shut. When they opened the door a minute later all that could be seen was the rear of a coach as it pulled out of the yard.

'Those scoundrels! I thought them better than most. Come Clegg; let us see what they have taken. There will be a reckoning soon. As to Miss Charlotte, I can't begin to explain that.'

By early evening the coach was sedately entering Manchester; Rob knew better than to call attention to the party by some reckless driving. He was determined not to linger any longer than needs be. John Seddon would ask no questions about the coach in the stable at the back of the Hare and Hound and would be glad to swap some ready cash for a pair of silver candlesticks. He was notoriously mean in his dealings but Rob was in no position to argue. The money would take care of the road tolls and inns along the way. As he drew up in the shadows at the back of the inn he called to Hannah over his shoulder.

'Make haste, take her to your mother's and leave her. I've business with Seddon and I need to tend the horses. You'd best be back within the hour or I may leave without you.'

As he watched the two girls hurrying along the lane he realized he was beginning to have second thoughts about marriage. He was not inclined to a wife who would not do as she was told.

Yes if Hannah wasn't back he'd leave without her. If she were –
well, a few more warm nights wouldn't come amiss. Rob swung
himself down and went in search of John Seddon.

Hannah pushed open the door to her mother's; all was quiet.
Charlotte followed and stared at the room, the like of which she
had never seen. Cramped and low ceilinged, an open hearth at
one end had a cooking pot hanging from a hook. A small table
and two chairs together with a rough cupboard filled the rest of
the space. Hannah looked through an open doorway into a back
scullery. Finding no one she ran up the open stairs in one corner
leading to the first floor.

'No one home! She must be out attending to a birth. Now
what shall we do?'

Before Charlotte could answer a small plump woman
appeared at the doorway.

'Looking for your ma, are you? You've missed her. Gone to
Sugar Lane, one of Alice Rylance's girls needed her. Don't expect
she'll be long; it's not a place she'd want to linger. Your ma's not
fond of leaping houses. Only gone as a favour to Alice, 'cos they
both grew up in Paradise Court.'

Her mission accomplished the dame vanished as quickly as
she'd appeared.

'That was Sarah Blinkhorn, lives next door. Nothing moves
around here without Sarah knowing. Come on, it's close by. Be
quick, I don't want to miss Rob.'

Without further ado Hannah hurried up the street with
Charlotte trailing after. The dirty streets were unlike the ones
near the Market Place, the ground was filthy and the smell
was overpowering to one of Charlotte's disposition. She
thought she was going to be sick. Hannah stopped and looked
at the houses. Deciding which was the one she sought she
entered a low doorway. With trepidation, Charlotte followed.
The room was dark and smoky, small like Hannah's mother's,
a counter at one end acted as a bar. Several men were standing around supping ale.

'Well, well, what have we here. Some new nuns you haven't shown to us, Alice?'

'What a pair of pullets, I'll take them both. How much mother!'

Alice came in through a curtained door on the side of the room; the premises were two houses knocked together.

'Why Hannah, what are you doing here? Your mother is upstairs, come through and you can talk to her. Who've you got with you? Brought me a dell? She looks as if she'd clean up pretty, and then she'd fetch plenty from her upright man.'

'No, we must talk in private.'

'Come through then. Bring the green goose with you, I don't want her sullied before I've prepared her for the nunnery.'

To a chorus of catcalls the two girls followed Alice through the curtain. Another identical room met their eyes. Here several girls in loose-bodied gowns vaunted themselves to the newcomers.

'Not now, my dears, 'tis only Hannah come to see her mother. Take her upstairs, Jenny. You'd better take the other one too. I think I could find a use for her. Now I'll bring a couple of customers in. The sight of those two has caused a stir – which you can no doubt satisfy.'

As Alice returned to lewd comments from the men, a girl Hannah knew led them up a flight of rickety stairs and then up another. Charlotte was overcome with shame. She had no idea what was being said, though the men reminded her of Frank and the terror in the woods.

'Hannah's here to see you, Widow Brascie,' Jenny called outside one of the doors on the second floor. 'Shall she come in?'

'I've finished here. I'll be out shortly, just wait there.'

Within a minute or two Hannah's mother appeared in the dark corridor.

'Is this room free, Jenny?' she said indicating a door opposite.

'Yes, I'll tell Alice where you are so she won't send anyone up.'

They entered the room and Jenny went downstairs.

'What brings you here, Hannah? I've told you I don't want you coming to places like this. There better be a good reason. And who's this?'

' 'Tis Charlotte Fletcher! She needed to leave Greenwood Lea – it's a sorry story.'

'I'm sorry, Miss Charlotte, I didn't recognisze you. What has happened?'

'It was at Holywell Ho—'

The door burst open. A woman in a state of undress flew into the room followed by a raggedy man in the act of unbuckling his belt, both were laughing.

'Oh, Alice didn't say the room was took. Come on Jack, we'd best use next door.'

'I'll come when you like, Phanny. Why don't I take the lot of you? The girls look tempting. The old crone can watch the door to prevent more interruptions.'

Widow Brascie drew herself up and grabbed hold of Phannys' shoulders, turning her round. 'Out! Out of here, Phanny Heap! We want none of you or your knocker in here.'

Quickly she pushed them out. Jack falling over in the corridor, his breeches round his ankles. Phanny fell on top amid lascivious comments, grabbing and more laughter.

Alice Rylance appeared on the corridor. 'Get up you two! Into the room at the end there!'

As the two moved on she advanced to the open door. 'Jenny told me you needed privacy. You'd better come into my sitting-room. We can talk there.'

'I can't stay,' interrupted Hannah.' Rob told me he wouldn't wait long. We're for London to be married. You can see Charlotte safe home, Ma. I'll send word when I know where I'm staying.'

Without waiting for a reply, Hannah ran down the stairs and was lost from view.

'Let her go Mary. Let's get us a dish of tea.' Alice reached for Charlotte's hand. 'Come, my dear, this must all be distressing for you. A quiet sup will help calm your nerves and we'll discuss what to do.'

The 'sitting-room', tucked away at the back on the first floor, was little better than the other rooms. A fire was burning fitfully in the grate. A pale female urchin was pouring water from a kettle hung in the fireplace into a cream teapot decorated with flowers. Charlotte, noticing the flowers, was reminded of home, all the rest was a nightmare.

'Take the chair by the fire, child. You'll soon warm up. Here's a dish of tea that'll help.'

'Oh, please I want my mother. I know she will come and take me from this dreadful place. I can't understand. . . .'

'Yes, yes, just rest now.' Turning round Alice shook her head. 'The girl's mad with worry.'

'I think we must send word at once,' Widow Brascie said anxiously, 'I don't know what Hannah was thinking of. Bringing a child like Miss Charlotte to a place like this. Why she ever brought her from Greenwood Lea at all, I can't imagine.'

'Hannah understands, I begged her not to leave me alone at Greenwood Lea: not after what had happened. I couldn't stay. No one to help, no one to stop him.'

'Well, I suppose what's done is done. The sooner we get you home the better. Your mother must be ill with worry.'

'We can send word tonight. Joan Heywood is going there to help with the washing as she does every week. She can take a letter with her.'

'No Alice, I think I might go myself. I don't like what Hannah has done and I expect there's more to this than we know. Why are they off to London I ask? Who is the man she is so terrified of?'

Charlotte sipped the bitter tea as she stared into the fire, the conversation unheard. Her reverie was interrupted by a sharp knock on the door, which opened to reveal Rhose Tinnys.

'Rhose, what brings you here?'

'I met Hannah in the street, running to John Seddon's. She wouldn't stop but I gathered she has left Charlotte Fletcher here. I thought I could possibly help.'

'Oh, Mistress Tinnys,' Charlotte cried,' I'm so pleased to see you. I remember how kind you were when you came with Mr Agar.'

Widow Brascie broke in, 'Charlotte must be returned home, Mistress Tinnys. The family knows you, like me. Perhaps you would help me arrange it?'

'Of course, Charlotte can come to the Ring o' Bells meanwhile. This is no place for such a young tender girl.'

'You reassure me. I was indeed loath to leave her here.' Mary Brascie cast a glance at Alice Rylance. 'I am engaged for a delivery in Salford tomorrow and was expected this evening. I can go now in good heart.'

'Certainly, you need have no fears. I shall take care of her myself. Off you go. I shall let you know when all is attended to.'

Widow Brascie crossed the room to Charlotte, bending over her she spoke softly, 'Take care, my dear child. I brought you into this world hoping you would have a happy life. Forget what you have seen here. It's not for the likes of you. Perhaps it would be best not to tell your mama where Hannah brought you. I wish you a safe journey home.'

With a nod to Alice and Rhose she left.

'Alice can I have a word? Don't worry Charlotte I'm just stepping outside the door, then we will be off home.'

The two women retired to the corridor, gently closing the door.

'What do you mean – taking her to the Ring o' Bells,' Alice demanded angrily. 'She'd be a great attraction here! We could sell her to the highest bidder. None of our clients would know who she is.'

'Don't be a fool, Alice. News would get out you had a dell. It would be sure to attract clients from Smith's eager to be the upright man. Several there might recognize her. My way is best. We might expect a reward from the family with the right tale.'

'No! What you say may be true but we could still pass her on. Several leaping houses in Liverpool would pay us a good finder's fee, more than any reward the Fletchers can offer.'

'You are a fool Alice! Rob and Hannah stole from the family. There'll be a hue and cry all over the county. If we get involved

like you suggest and then caught it'll be a hanging, or transportation at least. I'm taking her. If anyone asks you never saw
her. Is that clear?'

'Yes. It's your business, but I still think—'

'Enough!' Rhose opened the door. 'Come along Charlotte. I'll
escort you to my home and you can rest there.'

Rhose put her arm around Charlotte's shoulders and helped
her to the door. Alice stood back to let them pass. Rhose opened
a door, which led not to a bedroom but to a flight of stairs. Soon
they were in the back lane. It was getting dark, as clinging to
Rhose's arm, Charlotte was led through the quiet streets to the
Ring o' Bells.

To Charlotte Rhose's sitting-room seemed paradise; cosy and
warm, she felt safe at last.

'Thank you, Mistress Tinnys. I will tell mama how kind you
have been to me. I am so relieved to be going home.'

'What had happened to take you to Sugar Lane? I cannot
imagine circumstances that would place you in such danger.'

The relief was too much and with much sobbing Charlotte
poured out the whole story to her sympathetic listener.

'Did you say your rescuer said he was your uncle Thomas?'

'Yes he did. I don't understand. My mother died when I was
small and I have heard nothing of her family. The Fletchers took
her in before I was born. Mistress Brascie told me she delivered
me. So much strange information has been given me. What can
it mean?'

'Do you have no memory of your mother?'

'No, nothing, though mama, Lady Fletcher, told me I look very
like her when she gave me the necklace; a token given to her by
my father. See, it is very beautiful.'

Rhose stared entranced at the jewel, the white enamelled
rose Charlotte drew from beneath her gown. This was the girl
she sought; the Jacobite symbol the final confirmation. Here
before her stood Bonnie Prince Charlie's daughter. The Stuart
heiress to the British throne!

'I know you want to return home, Charlotte, but I think it would be best if you stayed with me awhile.'

'Why? Surely I am safe now?'

'I'm afraid not. Francis will be looking for you. Hannah and Rob stole from the house and the word is out that you were a willing partner. They have left Manchester and until they are found there will be no one to confirm your story. If Frank finds you, he will see you meet with an accident to stop you telling your mother what happened. You can send a note to your mother telling her you are safe. I will deliver it myself. You will stay in hiding until the servants are found. I have a comfortable room in the attic where you can stay and I will wait on you myself. It really is for the best, my dear child.'

Charlotte made little protest. Overcome with exhaustion and deeply perplexed by the day's events she meekly agreed to Rhose's proposal. She penned a short note to her mother before ascending the stairs to bed and a fitful sleep. Rhose smiled to herself as she turned the note over in her hand. Deciding against throwing it into the fire, she finally buried it amongst her other papers. The girl could make her fortune. The Fletchers would pay to have her back. No, Frank would not want their Jacobite connections known. Better to suggest he paid her to keep quiet. He wouldn't want anything to disturb the coming nuptials or his chance to enter London society. The Jacobites might pay too. This girl was indeed a treasure. When Ned arrived they could make sure all would be in place for the next stage of the game.

Chapter Fifteen

A Black Enamelled Bowl

Breakfast at Holywell was taken early the day after the return from Longworth. Lady Elisabeth and Anne were too distracted by Charlotte's sudden departure to lie abed. When Francis had eventually joined the party he had told them that Charlotte had returned to Greenwood Lea unwilling to meet more new company.

'She is ever a timorous thing, you know,' he had explained with disdain. 'Too much excitement and novelty has upset her nerves.'

As she had Hannah and Rob to accompany her, the family considered her precipitate action a discourtesy, but were willing to excuse one so young. Sara Robinson reassured her friends that the girl would be taken good care of at home. No doubt the Infirmary Ball and the preparations for the coming wedding had indeed been overpowering for a delicate constitution. She would soon calm down in her accustomed surroundings. Lady Elisabeth had been consoled yet Frank's nervous manner raised suspicions she could not suppress. After a restless night of anxiety, these suspicions had deepened and she had awaited her son's appearance with misgiving, not understanding the disap-

151

pearance. Charlotte had been so blithely happy walking in the garden. Anne for her part mused on what could have passed between her brother and Charlotte when they had been left alone in the wilderness.

When Francis strolled down, in his Indian nightgown, a hail of questions met him. Edward and his sons had already ridden out on the estate so Frank faced the female assembly alone. He protested that he could not put his mind to anything until he had had his first cup of chocolate.

'Zounds, all this pother over a silly chit of a thing,' he said as he threw himself on to a daybed by the curtained window. His mother gasped in protest, but Francis persisted: 'I doubt not that that hussy Hannah had some part in the girl's departure. They've always been too thick together. Lud, Ma, I think you too indulgent with the servants – and Charlotte. Well, she's 'twixt and between, ain't she?'

Anne rose from the breakfast table, indignant. 'Why, brother, that is an unwarranted slur. Charlotte has always been my little sister. And you showed partiality to her in a hundred ways. I know she may not be blood kin but she has ever been one of the family. Father would have reprimanded you severely for your impropriety.' She flounced out of the room with a brief curtsey to her mother and hostess. Elisabeth could not hide her discomfort over the exchange and Sara hastened to heal the breach.

'Now, come Francis, you do seem overly censorious. After all she is only fifteen. I know how your mother and father have treated her with the tenderest care and brought her up as a true lady.' She turned to Lady Elisabeth. 'I am certain it is nothing but childish whim. No doubt she was overcome by all the attention and activity over the last weeks. Also,' she paused, searching for the right words, 'who knows how the death of your dear husband may have touched her – more than she has yet shown.'

The repeated mention of Sir Geoffrey had a deep effect on his widow. She sat motionless in her chair while silent tears began to trickle down her cheeks. Francis hurried from his lounging to comfort his mother. He knelt by her and put an arm tenderly round her shoulder. Sara, taken aback by her own thoughtlessness, rang for her maid.

'There, Ma,' Frank spoke quietly and sincerely, 'it has been a hard and busy time since – since father died. You have borne up so well and taken so much upon yourself. All this fuss and bother, you need rest and quiet, not the upset of more worries. Will you go to your room? Mrs Robinson's maid will attend you. Leave matters to me. I am convinced this Charlotte business may have a happy outcome. Do not concern yourself any further.' He helped his mother from the chair into the arms of the lady's maid who led her out of the room.

'I fear your mama has not allowed herself time to mourn,' Mrs Robinson said when she and Francis were alone. 'I have suspected as much since you arrived. She has a heavy burden to bear. Anne is settled, and happily so I trust. For Charlotte, who knows? As for you, young man. . . .' She looked him squarely in the face; there was accusation in her voice.

'Oh, I know. I'm the scapegrace of the family. I am aware of the gossip and I accept I am no saint, but I have my own way to make in the world.' Sara began to speak but Francis waved her to silence. 'I was ever a disappointment to father. I could share neither his politics nor his concern for the estate. My interests lie elsewhere. I say I have my own way to make and, by god, I'll make it. Now, if you will forgive me I'll go see to mama. She at least needs me.' With a courteously extravagant bow he left the room.

This brief calm was shattered by an urgent message for the family to return at once to Greenwood Lea. There followed a flurry of activity. Anne, flinging on a light cloak, rushed downstairs. Francis dressed hurriedly then escorted his mother in some disarray from her room. A carriage was speedily got ready. As soon as he had seen his mother and sister safely inside, Francis spurred his horse on to the road.

At Greenwood Lea the upheaval had subsided, to be followed by an expectant and uneasy calm. The old butler wandered bemused from room to room, stopping in each to sit by the door looking around in wonder. He was overly fond of the 'little orphan biddy' as he called her and now was lost in uncomprehending despair. Mrs Rigby had taken firm control, checking and re-checking all the household goods. She had even ventured into the private sanctity of the wine cellar. She waxed righteously indignant on uppity servants who had not known their place. She could not understand what had led that sweet child to throw in her lot with them. Though, she confided to the cook, there was more to this than appeared on the surface. She believed the young master had something to answer for, the way he had played up to that flaunting baggage, Hannah.

It was in the midst of one of these tirades that the 'young master' returned. Leaping from his steaming horse he stormed into the house demanding to know what the deuce was the furore. His mother and sister were half dead with worry, his future relatives rudely discommoded and all because of a damn ridiculous young girl's fantastic imaginings. He stopped in mid-curse when he caught the housekeeper's puzzled expression. He realized that whatever was amiss it was not the revelation of the incident at Holywell but something else. He coughed apologetically and waited. Mrs Rigby was the only member of the household able to intimidate him.

The story poured from the housekeeper's lips, prompted at times by the butler who had shuffled to meet his master. How Charlotte, sobbing and hysterical, had been ushered away by that 'baggage'. How there had been such a whirl that she had not known where to turn. And, really, she couldn't have eyes everywhere. And that Rob hustling about the house like an indoor man when he was nobbut a stable lad. And how was she to know what—

With a weary motion Francis managed to stop the flow of words and turned to Clegg for his account. The butler was brief and circumspect. 'I hardly know what to say, Sir Francis. The young mistress—' He was interrupted by a scornful sniff from

Mrs Rigby and a muttered 'mistress indeed'.

'I shall always look upon her as a true little lady,' Clegg was on his dignity, 'and I shall thank you, Mistress Rigby, to keep your opinions to yourself.'

'Yes, yes,' said Francis, 'but what did Charlotte say, what precisely have the three of them done?'

'Why, sir, little miss never said a word the whole time she was here. Crying and shivering she was as though in fear of her very life, poor little biddy.'

'And well she might, knowing what those two were getting up to. I'll not say she was party to it but she went off with them so what else is there to believe?'

'Party to what, Mrs Rigby? Deuce take it I want a straight story before ma and sis arrive.'

Clegg spoke up. 'Well, sir, they – that is Hannah and Rob, because I cannot believe that Miss Charlotte had aught to do with it—'

' 'S blood, Mrs Rigby, you tell me.'

'They stole, sir. They stole these.' She handed him a sheet of paper. 'I took the liberty of checking as much as I could. And, I hope you will forgive my boldness, I've been down to the cellar because the old – Mr Clegg – was too distraught to attend to it himself.'

'Thank you. You did right.' He took the list and began to study it. The two servants were surprised at the calmness with which he had taken the news after the violence of his entrance. Indeed to Mrs Rigby he seemed to have been relieved when he heard the details. She had expected him to be furious at the losses and especially over Charlotte's involvement. He had in the past shown more than a brotherly partiality to her.

They were interrupted by the arrival of the Robinsons' carriage. Lady Elisabeth was asking questions as soon as she crossed the threshold. Francis was quick to explain what had happened, Mrs Rigby insisting on re-telling her own story. The two newcomers were appalled by the description of Charlotte's hysterical state and of her apparent complicity in the theft.

Anne would not accept that her sister would have stooped to such a thing whatever her distress. She held Rob responsible for everything and called for raising a hue and cry at once. Neither Francis nor his mother wanted the affair made public. Francis was inclined to dismiss the stolen goods as a trivial affair, more concerned as he was about the possible revelations of his own actions.

'Mama, you are overwhelmed and exhausted. You had best rest again. We need time to consider what needs to be done. Mrs Rigby, would you please see that tea is sent up to my mother's room.'

'How can Charlotte cause us so much trouble?' Anne complained. 'Clegg, would you tell the coachman he may return to Holywell.'

Clegg left the room.

'The Robinsons have been most understanding, I do not know what they may make of all this. All my hopes for the future ruined by that wretched girl! What shall we do to salvage our good name?' She flounced out of the room, in floods of tears.

The servants went about their tasks while Francis accompanied his mother up the stairs. At her bedroom door she plucked at his arm and led him in.

'I must speak to you. There are things you should know but they must be confidential between us.'

He saw her to a chair and perched himself none too comfortably on a padded stool at her feet. 'Is this about Charlotte, Mama? You and father would never speak of her parentage. Neither Anne nor I could tease the truth from you. We always believed her some poor cousin orphaned by a tragic accident. Anne invented a romantic tale of gypsies stealing her from some lordling's castle and leaving her at our door.'

Lady Elisabeth sighed. 'The truth is most romantic but, alas, more tragic.'

They were interrupted by the arrival of Anne carrying the tea-making requisites. With a brief word of apology she left for her own room. There was silence while Elisabeth readied the spirit lamp and Francis spooned green leaves from the caddy. When all was prepared she continued, her hands on Frank's shoulders.

'We have guarded the secret for fifteen years and I would have kept it for ever, had not this – this – disaster occurred. Even now I cannot believe that Charlotte would bring such disgrace to her family.'

'Not *her* family, Mama! I suspected she was no kin and now she has proved herself nothing but a drab, a thieving trollop.'

'Hush, Frank, you do not know what you say. Charlotte is – Charlotte may be – no. Charlotte *is* of royal blood.' She paused, as Francis stood up, shocked.

'Please, listen, be calm. Charlotte is the daughter of Mary Miller, one time maid to Lady Mosley. It was at Ancoats Hall she caught the eye of Prince Charles.'

Frank could not contain his anger. 'That damned Frenchified arch-traitor.'

She cut across her son's outburst. 'I know your views on that, but please honour mine, and your father's. We were true upholders of the Cause though never active followers. Our sympathies were and are well known as are yours. You must appreciate we dared not reveal the truth, especially to you.'

Frank strode about the room seemingly too small to contain his rage. 'The truth! What truth? A whoring maid's bastard child fobbed off with some bullcock story.'

'Francis, mind your language. The poor mother is dead, shortly after Charlotte's birth. We took them in full knowledge of their predicament and vowed to take care of the child as if she were our own. It was a sacred vow your father honoured to his grave, as shall I.'

Francis stopped before his mother, speaking reasonably and softly. 'But, Mother, cannot you see this cannot be true. Was Charlotte not fifteen but two weeks ago? She cannot be the Pretender's child. He had not set foot in this country in June of '45. He was still in France when the brat was spawned.' He stepped back triumphant then hesitated. 'Unless. . . ?'

'Yes, the legend is true. Prince Charles was here in '44, secretly. It was then that he fell in love with a pretty young maid at the Mosleys' house.'

'Bedded a willing wh— hussy, you mean. Oh, can't you see, Ma, how she put upon you. 'Twas likely a stable boy or some flunky and she passed the babe off as a royal "love child". All these years!'

'All these years, yes. You did not know Mary. She was a sweet trusting thing of an honourable family. She would not, she could not, lie. Besides she had the Prince's very own token to pass on to her child so that she might not be repudiated.'

'Ah! Stolen by that same flunky. More foolishness. How could you be fooled by such trickery? If you want more proof, the thieving baggage has shown her true colours. Sweet fifteen, a runaway, lickspittle to robbers and harlots! I warrant it's Rob she's off with, not Hannah.'

'Enough!' Elisabeth stood. With a fierce thrust she pushed her son back down on to the stool. She was trembling with a mixture of anger and fear. 'You go too far. Whatever may have happened here I have no doubt of Mary's honesty and Charlotte's innocence. I do not forget that the last we knew of the girl at Holywell was she was alone with you. What was it made her flee from that place?'

Francis avoided his mother's eyes. 'How am I supposed to know what prompts the mind of a foolish child? A child you now tell me might be – might be, I say – the offspring of a peasant and a popinjay?'

Suddenly Lady Elisabeth collapsed, falling into her chair, head in her hands, sobbing. 'Oh, Francis, what are we to do? None of this must come out. Think of the scandal – your sister's wedding – the Robinsons. And what of Charlotte herself?'

Francis kneeling by her chair offered her tea. 'Mama, calm, calm. I am sorry I became so overheated. Forgive me. You know how I hate and fear all this Jacobite nonsense connected with our name. If only father had been more discreet and broken with his connections in '45. We must now do what we can to protect the family. Who knows of Charlotte's supposed parentage?'

'Only Bue was in the secret and he is dead. Perhaps Dr Hall, but he is secure. No one else outside this room.'

'Then Anne must be kept in ignorance and all could be safe.'

'Although—'

'Yes?'

'Mary had a brother, Thomas. He was sent to India after the rebellion. He wrote that he was to return this year, but we have heard nothing from him.'

Francis started at the name. 'Nor ever will' he muttered.

'What did you say?'

'I merely wished we would not – hear from him, I mean. Charlotte does not suspect?'

'How should she? Apart from the token I gave her on her birthday. The letters are all destroyed.'

'Letters? What letters?'

'Thomas, Mary's brother, wrote to Bue, who passed them to us. I burnt them at your father's dying request.'

'Damn, Mama, what can you and father have been thinking of?' Francis could contain his rage no longer. 'You could have brought us all to ruin with your obsession. George is, and always was, the true heir to the English throne. I mean to rise in the county and beyond. If your actions become known, however misguided, I'll be finished.' He strode across the room and picked up a black glazed bowl standing on the mantle shelf and thrust it towards his mother. 'How many of these atrocities were made? They mark you all as traitors. No doubt you still gaze at this inscription – "May All True Gentlemen have a True Steward and may the Tenant be ready when the Steward comes". I've heard it often enough when secret visitors came from Downham, Browsholme, Townley and the rest to toast Prince Charles. Well, it shall end in this house!' So saying, he raised the bowl and smashed it in the fireplace. True gentlemen now toast King George, and I am proud to be one of them!'

As the bowl broke, memories came flooding back to Elisabeth.

She was once again in the room with Geoffrey, pale and gasping, the last brief clasp of a cold hand. Long before that another cold hand, Mary that sickly waif-like figure, once so pretty and full of life, thrusting the small warm bundle into her arms. So many memories, so much death and tragedy over the years and now this. . . .

'Mother!' Francis caught her as she swooned from her chair. 'Anne, Mrs Rigby, come quickly!'

He held the unconscious body close to his chest, lifted her gently and laid her on the bed. Anne in dishabille hurried in with the housekeeper close on her heels.

'Oh, Francis, what have you done now?' Anne cried.

In shocked disdain he snapped, '*I*, nothing. See to your duty and I will to mine.' He pushed past roughly and sprang down the stairs calling for his horse. He had to hunt the fugitives down. Thank God he had disposed of the uncle. Had he known then he would have made quite certain of him. Now he had to find Charlotte – and silence her.

The ride to Manchester through the warm summer breeze gave him time to plan. He determined to go about the search cautiously. It would not do to stir up questions or provoke rumours. There was to be no mention of the wretched girl, but a hunt for the absconded servants in a borrowed coach. And best not to detail the stolen goods – he did not want the constables involved yet. He fell to cursing the whole tribe of servants who couldn't keep their hands to themselves and women who couldn't keep their legs together.

His first call, to Hannah's mother, did nothing to cool his temper. A drunken hag appeared who, too far gone in liquor to make any sense of his enquiries, gave him senseless answers. Wasteful hours were spent touring the taverns, inns and coffee houses with the same enquiries and eliciting the same responses. Seemingly the servants and coach had passed through the town like smoke in the night, stopping nowhere, seen by no one. Not believing this he reluctantly realized that the veil of secrecy was not to be broken. His blustering quick temper had earned him a bad reputation in the town and he felt there was more sympathy for the fleeing couple than for his loss. Even the normally accommodating Mrs Tinnys was curt in her dismissal. At last, on the London road, the turnpike keeper was willing to admit that a coach had gone through early that morning. It carried a smart young lady in a yellow dress and a surly groom'. So, Frank thought, they had driven south and the immediate emergency was over.

He returned to Greenwood Lea to find John Robinson waiting anxiously for news of the missing girl – and of the family's carriage. Frank was pleased to find his mother recovered somewhat and equally anxious to hear of the fugitives. Francis reported briefly on the frustrations of the mornings search and a rapid conference ended with the two young men determined on the journey to London.

Late that night, in the woods above the Holy Well, Seth Bradley, together with his nephew, was pursuing his nocturnal business. It had been poor poaching; a lone rabbit hung from his belt. His dog, swift and silent, nosed through the undergrowth, stopped and pawed beneath a fallen tree. Seth hurried forward, under the branches lay the body of a man.

Chapter Sixteen

Pursuit!

After three days' hard riding and no sign of their quarry, Frank was growing tired of his companion's tales of the welcome awaiting them from his aristocratic relations. Although the younger, John Robinson was more familiar with London society. He took great delight in his family connections, especially his cousin Christopher Bland. If he was to be believed, Kit Bland was the victor of three duels, the darling of titled ladies, feted at Westminster and *persona grata* at court. Indeed for his like no door was closed, high or low.

It was a great relief for his ear, his post horse and his backside, when Frank spied the outskirts of London creeping across the fields. How much had changed in the few years since he last visited. Already Cavendish Square was mostly filled with houses but with sheep still grazing. John reined in at Hanover Square with a flourish. The fine four-storey mansion was scarcely ten years old. Liveried servants ushered them into the spacious entrance hall where they ascended gracious stairs to be greeted by a bluff Sir Matthew and a gushing Lady Eleanor. Frank took in the handsome portraits, the new mahogany furniture and was exceedingly impressed by the chinoiserie style of the mirrors: here was something for a pattern for a remodelled

Greenwood Lea. The old people seemed over-fond of young John and, over tea in the sunny drawing room, asked for news of their northern kin. There was much discussion of the coming nuptials and Frank was uncomfortably aware of a cautious prying into the suitability of this new provincial connection. Both John and Frank were quick to allay any fears that might arise over the reasons for their hasty journey. Sir Matthew was at once aroused to wrath over the iniquities of the age. Fumbling for his favourite magazine, he bellowed out, 'Perjury, forgery, adultery, sodomy and homicide are so frequent as hardly to attract notice.' He would have gone further had his wife not calmed him with a second dish of tea.

Francis soon found himself accepted in the settled routine of a busy sociable household. It was unfortunate that the season was almost ended and many of the best families had already left town. He was promised however that he would be able to attend the last rout of the Duchess of Northumberland, undoubtedly the most fashionable hostess and rumoured to be close to the Prince of Wales.

The Right Honourable Christopher Bland arrived the second day and proved to be all that John had promised. Elegant in his severe cut-away coat and tight breeches, silver-buckled, he quizzed Frank with a critical eye.

'Why, most welcome Sir Francis. How fares the bleak north?'

'Fair, my lord, fair.'

'Ha! A wit! 'Tis an error to think all be chawbacon outside the Bills.'

'The Bills?'

'Aye, the Bills of Mortality – London in all its splendour and sprawl! But come, you shall see as much as time warrants, I'll see to that. Yet, ain't you here on some hunting errand?'

'Indeed, my lord.'

'Stuff, no lords, no titles – me name's Kit to those I care for.'

'And mine Frank. You are most kind. We are indeed on the hunt, for vermin, low thieving vermin.'

163

'Ah, this sounds a tale to be savoured. What say we adjourn to Slaughter's and plot over coffee?'

They took chairs to the coffee house, Kit pointing out buildings going up on Leicester Fields, one of which his family was to lease. Slaughter's was crowded in the afternoon with elderly men, conning the newspapers and bursting into indignant exclamations. 'Horrid periwig bores', Kit called them and ushered his new friends to one of the private rooms upstairs. Frank relaxed, basking in the feeling of belonging, of being where he ought to be. He compared, with a shudder, the comfort and elegance of London's coffee houses with Smith's and others in Manchester. When they had been served he recounted the tale of the servants' robbery and flight. He mentioned only casually that a more refined young girl might accompany them. John would have added more but he was silenced by Frank's warning glance. Until he could catch and silence her, Frank wanted Charlotte's name kept out of things. Kit was intrigued and promised that Rob and Hannah might soon be tracked down. He knew a thief taker, lately in the employ of the magistrate. If anyone could find news of the stolen carriage and its occupants, it was Jemmy Twitchet. He could set the search afoot that very evening. In the meanwhile he would be delighted to show them around the town.

There followed a week of drinking, carousing and whoring. The most memorable was a visit to Ranelagh. This proved finally to Frank how pitiful had been the Infirmary Ball in its attempt to emulate the capital. The warm summer evening brought the fashionable – those still in town – to the gardens after the crowds gathered for the music had left. The Rotunda lived up to all Frank's expectations. Pillars festooned with flowers rose up to the roof surrounded with forty-seven boxes with side-tables. Kit issued dire warnings against the miserly food served there, wafer thin ham and inexorable chicken. Though even he was moved to praise the blue-sky ceiling and the twenty-eight chandeliers. With the candles flickering a sunset glow suffused the amphitheatre – 'In truth and beauty, elegance and grandeur it was not equalled in Europe'. Beyond the Rotunda, dark alleys radiated, shunned by the cautious, they were renowned as the haunt of footpads and cutpurses.

A daytime ride to the City brought Frank back to a different reality. The decayed heads still spiked on the Exchange reminded him all to clearly of the '45 and the fate of Jacobite sympathizers. There was continued gossip of the fate of Earl Ferrers, hanged but two months previously for the murder of his steward. Kit took great pleasure in recounting the spectacle of the occasion: the Earl all in white, the three hour procession to Tyburn, the white cap Ferrers had donned before the noose. It showed that no one was immune from the law, whatever their standing. Francis thought uneasily of the body in the wood.

It was a relief when there came news of 'Rob from the North' seeking to fence quality stuff. Most nights, Twitchett reported, he might be found at the notorious Cock Inn in Bow Street. That night Kit appeared in a dark enveloping cloak and slouch hat looking more a highwayman than Long Ned, laughed Frank. He and John were arrayed in leather jerkins and moleskin trousers – 'A canting crew out on a jag', Kit retorted. They pushed their way through the jostling crowd filling the narrow lanes around Covent Garden, thrusting aside the importuning of draggled women and poxy boys. The 'Right Honourable' displayed knowledge of curses and oaths that silenced all protests. The tavern, formerly the haunt of the well-born Mohoks Club, was a filthy den of sweat and stink. Frank thought he had never seen such a gathering of degenerate pockmarked faces, scars, hooks, peg-legs and blowsy women. At the dirt-encrusted window a gang of stylish flash blades lounged in indolent affectation. A noisome crowd in the centre was gaming, rallying and catcalling each play. And among them all well-muscled drabs circulated with tankards and glasses, snarling back at the chaffing, beating off drunken groping. There was no sign of Rob.

'Through the door at the back,' Twitchett whispered from the shadows. There in a snug, thick with smoke, Rob was sitting at a table, a scrawny girl on his knee, nibbling his ear. As soon as he saw the three enter, he sprang up, tossing the girl to the floor. Before he could move further Frank was on him, fingers at his throat.

'Where is she? What the devil have you done with them both?'

The room sank into silence, the girl's squeals of protest halted, as all eyes and ears turned to the newcomers. Rob wrenched the hands away, grinning into Frank's face.

'I left the silly baggage back on the road. I'm not for tying up with a useless simpering jade. See what I can get now.' He hauled the girl back up to him with a smacking kiss. In one movement Frank thrust the woman away and grabbed Rob by the ear, hauling him half across the table. Kit put out a warning hand, too late. A knife flashed upwards ripping into Frank's side. He fell back as Kit's sword flashed out. Rob dropped the weapon, hands clutching his bleeding face. The girl let out a fiendish screech and sprang at Frank. John desperately flung himself between them; her nails scraped deep gashes into his cheek. By now there was uproar. Through the glimmer of the room's torches daggers flashed, cudgels appeared.

'Back to back, lads and no quarter.' Kit's voice cut through the harsh clamour. He seized a flambeau and dashed it around the threatening circle.

'Here, see what you can do with that!' He thrust the flaming torch into Frank's hand.

John was frantically struggling with the virago. He held her two wrists in his hand, his other scrabbling at her head as she spat and bit, her legs wrapped around him. Frank slammed the torch into her back. She screamed and fell away, beating at her scorched hair.

The hubbub settled into a concerted low growl, the combatants warily sizing up the others. The three friends stood back to back, three swords circling; the torch thrust forward, casting a harsh glow over the hunched bodies circling them. Frank crashed the table over, kicking it hard against those nearest him. Two men went down as others sprang aside. A burly giant swung a club but was felled by the lunge of a sword before it could land. John let out a great whoop; Frank, feeling the surge of fighting blood, howled a curse and swinging the flambeau with one hand, lashed out left and right with his blade. Grabbing a fallen stool, John smashed down more bodies. More calmly Kit parried and thrust at any who attacked. Freeing himself from his cloak, he swirled it around two toughs, heaving them backwards into the milling crowd. A flying cudgel found its mark, John collapsed, sword falling from his numbed arm. Frank grasped him and held him upright. A cut from his sword sliced the ear of a wall-eyed brute. Blood was seeping from Kit's sleeve, but now, armed with swords in both hands he cleared a space before him.

'Getting warm, don't you think?' he muttered. 'I fear your bird has flown. I hazard 'tis time we do the. same.' With the most blood-curdling cry yet, he charged forward. Those nearest shied away, pushing the rest back. Frank with John hanging from him followed in his wake. At the street door Frank, with a twist of the wrist cut a torch from the wall, flinging it back into the room. They reached the open air to hear a cry of 'The Watch! The Watch!'

They slowed their shambling run when they spotted lanterns approaching. There were four watchmen, armed and hurrying. They looked curiously at the bedraggled trio. Frank greeted them with a cheery, 'Evening gentlemen. There's a deuce of a row coming from that low tavern. Would you not look to it? Why, 'twould frighten decent people from your handsome city if it were not curbed.'

With a surly growl of acquiescence the four men hurried towards 'The Cock'. A dull glow from the open door silhouetted figures stumbling out into the darkness.

'Why, friends! Damn me, I've not had such a night's entertainment this twelve month!' Kit put his arm around the two of them. 'Was that not a knife that cully pulled on you, Frank? Are you bad hurt?'

'Nay, as they say in my part of the country, nobbut a scratch, thanks to the jerkin.'

167

'And you, cos, how fares it with you? Egad, you'll carry those pussy scars awhile, young John. By Christ, that bitch had sharp claws. You near went down, too.'

'Recovered now, I vow,' John chuckled, rubbing his injured arm. 'Just a bump, but I'll not be two handed for a while.'

'Ah now, two hands! I know a place where two sweet hands will make you a man again. What say you both to a sally to Mother Cocksedge – she lives close by, right next to Sir John Fielding, don't you know! Is this the blind magistrate? The night is yet young and that – entertainment – has put me in the mood for more agreeable activity.'

'But,' Frank protested, taking the other's arm from his shoulder, 'you're wounded, too. I saw blood.'

'Nobbut a scratch, me boy, nobbut a scratch!' His laugh lingered as they stepped on into the night.

Two nights later Frank was attending a different function. He had been duly impressed when put down at Northumberland House, the finest mansion on the Strand. Even more when he strolled among the throng at Baroness Percy's last rout of the season. There must have been over a hundred and fifty of the best people milling around the main rooms and seemingly lost in the immensity of the gallery. He was admiring the vista, the gilding of the walls and ceilings, and the pictures: here a Del Sarto, a Rembrandt and so many other Dutch masters. A tap on his arm interrupted his reverie.

'Sir Francis Fletcher is it not? I am happy to see you.'

He turned to find himself face to face with his hostess. The Duchess, painted, powdered and perfumed, was magnificently dressed in golden flowered brocade with a velvet patch, *à la grecque*, on her cheek.

'Your Ladyship!' He bowed ceremoniously.

'I am always delighted to welcome fascinating young men to my entertainments. Especially one, whom, Kit tells me, enjoys the rough and tumble of our nightlife. An interesting encounter with an alley cat, I believe.'

'It is my pleasure your ladyship. And yes, a beastly cat, indeed, Ma'am.'

'You should take care. Our – felines,' she hesitated on the word, 'can be diseased I believe.'

She did not wait for a reply but, indicating the guests, continued, 'I am afraid you come rather late to my receptions, there are only a few of note here. You must return when there is a fuller company. I shall give orders that you should be admitted whenever you may call. But for now, I must attend to my guests.' She was soon lost in the swirl of bodies. So, Frank thought, the story is abroad. Kit had brought him here with a reputation already established. No doubt he had given a lurid but circumspect account of their night-time adventures. He had been aware of the buzz of conversation as he moved around the room, and noted the admiring glances flashing from feminine eyes. Gad, there was any number of fine fillies here, if he couldn't make a good match in this company he deserved to rot forever in the backwaters of rural Lancashire. He settled down to circulate, to talk, to flirt, and to impress. It was, after all, his last night in the capital.

The following day he was to horse early, carrying letters and packages to his soon-to-be relatives and his own family. John Robinson was staying behind, nursing his still bruised and numb shoulder, but with a promise to return for the races as soon as he could mount a horse. He assured Frank he would not miss Vulcan's victory for the world. Frank left London with mixed feelings. They had failed in their pursuit. Rob had disappeared completely in the city's impenetrable stews. Where the two girls were, God alone knew. Charlotte must be found. No hint of the scandal must come out; his whole future depended on that. And what a future! With the interest of the Robinsons and the Blands and the open invitation of the Duchess of Northumberland, what could he not do? A commission in the Guards, a seat in Parliament, anything was possible. As for a suitable marriage, he had already made discreet enquiries. Yes, he thought as he spurred his horse on the road, nothing could stop him now.

Chapter Seventeen

Plots!

Rhose lay quietly musing, careful not to disturb the sleeping man by her side. Her first problem was Charlotte. She had been hidden in the attic for two weeks now. Her terror of Francis still played on her mind so that she willingly accepted her incarceration. This could not last, Rhose understood, but what could be done? A movement from her lover disturbed her preoccupation. He stirred, turned and laid a hand gently on her stomach. She squirmed around to put her arms about his smooth slender torso. He raised himself on one elbow and brushed the dark hair tenderly back from her face. Slowly he kissed her eyes, her cheek, her mouth. She pressed closer to him, lost in the growing intensity of the kisses and her awareness of the strength of his body. He pulled away and held her face in his two strong hands, peering deep into her eyes.

'Ah, Rhose, there's bird lime on those sweet lips.'

'And honey on that tongue,' she smiled in reply.

'No, my love, the honey is in your soft white flesh; ambrosia is at your delicious breast.'

His lips began again to nuzzle her body, delicate nibbles at breast and nipple. She arched backwards, moaning as his hand whispered along her stomach, slowly, rhythmically.

'Oliver,' she breathed, 'oh, no more for now.'

'Ah, yes precious love, it is not yet light. Night's pleasures chase away the day. I long to lose myself in your lush charms once more.'

His tongue, urgent, licked, tasted and explored her belly while restless fingers played along the soft flesh of her inner thighs. She seized hold of his hair, pulling his head up to stare into his hazel eyes.

'Enough, I said, monster. You wear me out.' Lazily she shook him gently, easing herself away from his questing hands. 'I must return to my own room. You are a guest, a visiting traveller at my inn,' she pushed him playfully but firmly back, 'The proprieties must be kept, else I lose all respect with the servants and reputation among my fellows.'

Oliver Banton rolled on to his back and laughed quietly. 'If this is the welcome for travellers at the Ring o' Bells it will soon surpass all other inns in the kingdom.'

Rhose, standing naked by the bed, bridled and blazed at him, 'You think me nothing but a cheap whore, some trull to be tumbled by whoever calls!' A blow from the back of her hand rocked his head sideways. She whipped the sheets from under him, rolling him face-down to the floor. The sheet was flung on to his back as a foot cracked into his side.

'Out, damn you, out! I believed you to be other than the – the – cock-sure coxcombs you run with, else I'd not have shared your bed,' Rhose cried with anger as she hastily shrugged on her nightdress. 'All those sweet words were only sweeteners for a leap. I thought better of you, Oliver Banton, I did.'

'Rhose, please! I could bite off my tongue. Forgive me, it was but a jest.' He rolled over; clasping her foot he kissed each toe with reverence.

'Do not be angry. Don't go, I would love you all the day, every night would kiss and play, if with me you'd only stay.'

'Ah,' she said, releasing herself from his grip. 'You would win me with a song. Well, I have one older than that: "Sigh no more, ladies, men were deceivers ever".' She laughed. 'Come, get up. I forgive you. But I must go. I hear movement, Mary will be down shortly.'

Oliver scrambled to his feet, gathering the sheet around him. 'Rhose, Rhose, there is no deceit in me. Would that you could leave this life. I could offer you one more worthy.'

Rhose paused as she pulled a shawl around her shoulders. The smile died. She looked down on him with a frown.

'To be your kept woman? For that is what it would mean. I told you once before I have a living to earn and I mean to earn it. You have proved a most gentle,' her tone softened, 'gentleman, and I honour you for it. But you must know our lives are so far apart although,' a smile, 'our bodies may be so very close.' She leant forward to give him a hard swift kiss then slipped from the room.

She did not at once go to dress but mounted the stairs to the attic. She was concerned that Charlotte, after two weeks kept close, was becoming restless. Luckily the absconding pair had disappeared into the stews of London. Their pursuers had, by all accounts, failed to track them down. Even young Fletcher had returned empty-handed. She also knew that he would not rest until he found her. How much longer, she wondered, could the girl be hidden? Already too many people were in the secret, Alice forever pestering for profit from such marketable young flesh. Rhose shook her head, dismissing such a thought.

Pausing in the doorway of the attic bedroom, she looked down on the sweet face just stirring into wakefulness, the rose token clasped in her hand like some lucky talisman. Trusting eyes blinked open, meeting her gaze.

'Oh, Mistress Tinnys, good morning.'

'Charlotte, please, I tell you, you must call me Rhose. Can you not look upon me as an elder sister by now?' She sat on the edge of the bed, reaching out to the still sleepy girl. 'Would you welcome a dish of chocolate to break your fast? You must regain your strength, you know. You were languishing for days when you first came.'

Charlotte sat up, the borrowed too-large nightdress slipping from one slender shoulder. Rhose thought how pretty yet vulnerable she was. Already the promise of full womanhood suffused the fifteen-year-old.

'Have you had word from my mo— Lady Elisabeth, or Anne? I so long to see them again, to – to – try and explain – but Frank. . . .'

Her eyes filled with tears, her hands rose to cover her face letting the necklace fall. Rhose put her arms around the trembling body.

'Hush, child, do not fret so. You are safe here. I will not let Sir Francis, or the constables, near you.'

'Oh no,' she flung her arms around the older woman burying her head against her neck, 'cannot you tell them? I had nothing to do with the silver and the other things. I simply wanted to escape from – from—'

Rhose took the tear-stained face in her hands, looking deep into the troubled eyes. 'My dear child! I tell you as I told you before, you will be treated the same as Hannah or Rob. Sir Francis claims you guilty of robbery. If caught it will mean transportation or worse. And if Frank – Sir Francis, should find you first, I fear he would not let you speak. Or you would not be believed over his denials.'

'But Lady Elisabeth would believe me. I know she would, and Anne. Cannot I speak to them?'

'Alas, I fear their minds have been poisoned against you by the one you fear. Lady Elisabeth has been prostrate since . . . since the robbery and Agar is sent for.'

The girl flung herself full length on the bed, her body wracked with sobs. Rhose reached over, stroking the tumbled hair.

'Hush. Hush. You have good friends here. You need not be afraid while in my care. I have an idea to secure your safety with the help of someone you know. How would you like to go on a journey?'

The sobs weakened and, under the caressing hand, Charlotte relaxed. She turned around to look up at Rhose as she continued:

'I may be able to arrange for you to leave Manchester until the danger is passed.'

A look of alarm crossed the girl's face. 'Leave here? Leave you? But where would I go? Who. . . ?'

'It is not settled yet. I need to talk to an acquaintance, a friend – one we may both trust. In any event you cannot hide here forever. Sir Francis continues his search and there must soon be rumours.'

She felt the girl stiffen. The small hands were once more around her neck.

'Oh, please, please, Rhose.'

'Do not fret, little one. Rhose Tinnys is not one to be outplayed by a foppish boy.' With the slim body pressed against her own, the older woman scooped up the token. 'I'll keep this safe, child, you would not want to lose it.'

Rhose hummed as she descended the stairs, then recognized the air as the one Oliver had misquoted earlier. She laughed aloud as she held up the jewel and hurried to dress. It was two hours before she had time again on her own. Oliver and two other travellers had breakfasted and gone on their way. Oliver, with some reluctance, had wished her a formal farewell. Rhose was aware that this had not allayed Mary's suspicions. She had more than once remarked on Mr Banton's frequent visits since Rhose's accident. Nor did she fail this morning to comment on his unexpected overnight stay. Rhose dismissed all this with light disdain, chivvying the maid into her duties of readying the inn.

After checking the cellars and their hidden contraband, Rhose could settle at last to her paperwork. She looked over the latest entries for the 'Gazette'. Here were two boys, thirteen and fourteen, who looked likely prospects, but Peter Smith would have an eye to those for his special rooms. There were more requests for cooks, and she thanked heaven for Martha. She sighed as she sifted through the innocent enquiries for positions 'with good families', and the less innocent for 'willing YOUNG serving maids'. Perhaps it would be well to be rid of this kind of work? As she had imagined it was paying well, but she felt like the tightrope walker she had seen at the Exchange, or the

174

Italian who had tossed knives in the air: three, four, five, one slip and. . . !

She found she could not concentrate on the accounts. Her mind kept drifting back to that strong supple body and the warmth of the bed. Oliver's rootling filled her with a languorous pleasure – different from the rough thrusting vigour of her high-wayman. A shiver of remembered ecstasy ran through her. She shook her dark hair loose to clear her thoughts. Guiltily she brought to mind her husband. Poor William was dead only months and already forgotten. Yet, as she had told Oliver, she had a living to make, and not an easy one.

The business of the day did not let up. The Chester coach disgorged a party of merchants come to meet with fustian and Manchester cloth makers. Later some packmen arrived, piling their bundles and packages in the yard while they piled them-selves inside. Mary, Rhose and Elias were run off their feet filling tankards, plates and glasses. The long trudge over the moors had left the men's appetites seemingly insatiable. Early evening was a quieter time until the inn filled with a rowdy mob of serious drinkers. They were joined in a short time by a riotous flurry of young gentry visiting town to taste the 'low life'. Among them were the familiar figures of Sir James Falkner and Robert Johnson. Soon an argument ensued as to the relative merits of Levi Whitehead, the Bramham pedestrian and one George Guest of Birmingham. Tempers became frayed as claims of race hobbling and claims that 'there'd never be a fair race north of the Dee' rent the air. Things began to look ugly. Mary quietly seized a weighted stick from behind the counter, Rhose hurried from the taproom, Elias at her heels.

'There'll be a few broken heads,' muttered one of a group of Brindley's canal diggers.

'Now there's one way to settle this,' a commanding drawl came from the street door. Everyone turned towards the newcomer. Long Ned strode into the room, his riding coat covered in muck and dust. He carried saddle-bags slung over his shoulder, a riding crop in his hand.

'Why don't you of the "fancy" arrange a match between the two of them? That would settle all wagers.'

'Now that, my fine fellow, is a capital proposal.' A large jovial character slapped him on the shoulder, to be smothered in a cloud of dust. His coughing raised a general laugh. 'What say you, Jemmy?'

Sir James nodded. 'And I know just the cove to arrange it. He'll be drinking at the Three Tuns if I know his habit.' There was a chorus of shouts and cheers and a general move to the door. With a cry of 'Fifty guineas on Levi' Robert Johnson led out a laughing, jostling crew trading wagers as they went.

Only Sir James stayed behind to have a quiet word with Rhose. 'Do you know where Agar is?'

'He has been tending Lady Fletcher but I've had word he'll be back in town tomorrow.'

'Excellent, I have need of his services. I thank you Mistress Tinnys.'

Then he too scurried after the departing mob.

'Well, Rhose, are ye not pleased to see me?' Ned clasped Rhose around the waist swinging her around. Those left in the inn raised a cheer.

'Well, you got rid of half my custom which I'll not thank you for. And you stink like a shotten herring. Away with you to the yard and swill that dirt off or you'll get no drink tonight . . . or anything else for that matter,' she added under her breath. Hanging his head in mock shame, his shoulders drooped as he ambled out the back with slow deliberation. The room settled down again, now in a merrier mood. Satisfied, Rhose went upstairs to await her highwayman.

Ned soon appeared, hair still dripping, shirt open to the waist. Flinging the saddle-bags to the floor, he seized Rhose in the hug of a bear. Their mouths closed in long fierce kisses before she broke away, gasping, 'Let me get my breath, Ned. You leave me for weeks on end then walk in as though you had never gone. Who knows what—'

'Now, pippin, don't play the coquette with me. Look, I've

brought you a peace offering.' So saying he picked up the bags and produced a necklace of matched emeralds. 'This will grace that pretty neck far more than it did the scared fat harridan I lifted it off.' He fastened it around Rhose's neck, bending to kiss it as he did so. His hands crept down inside her bodice. Rhose broke free and crossed the room to admire the gems in her mirror.

'Ned, 'tis lovely – but will it be safe to wear abroad?'

'Why, yes love! The sad matron was as Welsh as they come, nary a word of English. I doubt she had been out of the principality before – and never will again. I could hardly make her understand it was her jewels I was after and not her cunny!' He laughed and reached towards her again.

'No, Ned, we have serious things to discuss and urgently. I too have a jewel: the Fletcher runaway.'

'What? Here? I heard of that on the road. A rum business, I thought they'd fled to London. But the child – a sweet innocent thing to take up with such as them.'

'Indeed. Sweet, she is, and so innocent. But no thief, and not a Fletcher.'

'Not?'

'A Stuart, by my life.'

'A Stuart? What mean you, a Stuart?' Ned perched on the table, pulling Rhose against him.

'Listen, and listen well.' She pulled affectionately at his ear. 'You know the story of the young Pretender staying secretly with the Mosleys in '44?'

'Aye, I've often heard Alice and others drag it out. As Martha says, "nobbut a yarn".'

'A true yarn! I had it all again from Alice and she knew all the servants at Ancoats Hall. And there's the letter, don't forget the letter.'

'What letter?'

Rhose bounced away from him, fumbled in a drawer and drew out a piece of paper. Ned stared down at his filthy boots as though seeing them for the first time. He tried to ease one off against the other.

'The letter you prigged from the post boys the reason you left town in such a hurry. I said it would be a treasure, and it is. It tells of a soldier back from India, a girl child hidden and fifteen years old. And written to Bue! Remember he died defending a lost cause? The Jacobite cause!'

Rhose knelt and began to pull the boot from his foot.

'You flummox me, pippin. Slow down, this is too deep for my simple mind.'

Rhose continued, though her patience was becoming tried. 'Item. Prince Charles was at the Mosleys' in October '44, and he had an eye for the maidens, specially, according to Alice, the maids. Item: a lady's maid, Mary – Alice knew her – left at Christmas with no reason given. Item: A soldier called Thomas . . .' Rhose rocked back on her heels as the boot came free.

'Just tell me the end of the tale, precious, please.'

'Oh, pew, these stockings are for the midden.' She tossed it aside with a look of disgust, bending to the other foot. 'Very well! Charlotte came to me in great distress, fleeing from the clutches of that scoundrel Frank Fletcher. She was fifteen in June. She has a white enamelled rose given, so Lady Fletcher told her, to her mother from her father.'

'I still . . . haaa!' He breathed a contented sigh as the boot and stocking followed the other. Rhose stood, brushing mud and dirt from her front and hands.

'Oh, Ned, I lose patience. Charlotte told me that a stranger saved her from Frank's groping. He said he was her uncle, Thomas! Now do you see? Everything fits. The Fletchers had Jacobite leanings so who better to succour the Prince's love child.'

'Charlotte is the Prince's bastard?'

'I know she is his. I feel it in my bones. The letter, the Jacobite rose, the uncle, they are proof enough, Ned. Ned, I'm sure Frank knows. If he should find her she'd not survive. Alice was for putting her to work or selling her to the highest bidder.'

'Nay, I'll not have that.' Ned was on his feet. 'I've naught against Alice's trade or her hen house, but I'd not have such a babe sacrificed to the pox or worse.'

'Ned, for one of your profession you have a soft heart. But you've not seen the babe recently, have you? She's a comely young woman now, ripe for the picking. But you're right, that's not for her, there's much more to be made from her.'

'Enough, Rhose. I've been patient and I'll hear the rest, but we've other business first.'

Catching Rhose round the waist he pulled her to him. His kisses stopped her protests as he carried her to the bedroom.

Chapter Eighteen

A Machiavel in Petticoats

Next morning Ned held Rhose close, his arms crossed over her breasts, warm in her bed.

'Well, Rhose, let me hear what you propose.'

'Why, are you not satisfied yet?' She pressed herself against him.

Ned laughed. 'Nay, lass, a night with you would satisfy any man. I was thinking rather of the child upstairs. What do you intend with her? I've been puzzling my brains as to how we might profit from her.'

Rhose pulled away, turning to face him.

'There are two plans that I see. First, Sir Francis is over-eager to make his way in the fashionable and political world. You know how he grows violent at the very mention of Jacobitism. How would it be for him if it were known that the Pretender's own daughter was reared in the same house? That he had carnal knowledge of her?'

The highwayman surged up from the bedclothes, grabbing Rhose. 'He – what? I'll swing for him myself.'

'Hush, calm, my love! He did not, but only thanks to the mysterious Thomas. No, it was enough for the story to be put about and his future would be bleak indeed. Now, what might he not pay or do for silence?'

'You'll not sell her to *him*?' The highwayman pulled back releasing Rhose.

'Please, Ned, credit my own kind heart – would I do so to one like her? No, she will be – shall we say – kept well apart, safe from him and from discovery.'

'How? I like it not. What if she should talk to others? What if he were to track her down?'

'Fear nothing. She is ignorant of her pedigree, knows nothing. She is in such mortal terror of Frank, and of prison, she will not talk. My plan is simple. Jonathan Agar will soon go journeying again. She will go with him. Now my love,' he started to protest, 'such service did me no harm. Agar is as trustworthy a gentleman as one could find. As it happens this very evening has presented a golden opportunity which I shall take up with the apothecary.'

'Why, pippin, you are a Machiavel in petticoats. I'll not ask how you'll persuade him not to peach to the Fletchers. More secrets I suppose, but can you manage the young buck?'

Rhose coloured with surprise. 'How did you. . . ? Oh! I see, you mean Sir Francis. I shall have no trouble there I can assure you.'

Ned relaxed back on the pillows. 'And what of the second plan? You said there were two.'

'Now that is more difficult, and needs someone to undergo a hazardous journey.'

'Ah, this, my dear Rhose, is where I smell action for Ned.'

Rhose knelt up beside him and began to stroke his hair. 'What say you to a trip to France?' she tweaked his hair and whispered into his ear.

'But we are at war.'

'That's not stopped you from enjoying French brandy or helping yourself to French lace. If someone could reach the Pretender, if he knew of Charlotte's existence, his heir, who knows what advantages might arise.'

'So, I am to take the child to France now – be shipwrecked or end prisoner in a stinking French gaol. This is a fine nonsense, Rhose.'

'Not a nonsense! See this is Charlotte's necklace. It will guarantee your reception at the Stuart court, 'tis a love token given by the Prince to the child's mother. We will be amply rewarded for the news of an heir. See – here it goes into your pocket.'

'Stay,' he held her hand. 'This trinket – it could get me hanged. I'm to risk all on this bauble?'

'There's no risk!'

'So you say. It's not you facing a hangman! – or worse the bottom of the sea. What guarantee have I that even if I get to France I'll get to the court?'

'Fie, Ned, I never took you for a coward.'

'No, nor ever was I. Nor am I a fool!'

Rhose twisted away but not before dropping the rose into his pocket. 'I think you will go, Ned.'

'And why would that be?'

'Because I ask you.'

'You can usually twist me into anything, but this? This? I won't agree – and I'm no coward. I'm taking this token to France, so you want, but what to bring back?'

'A father's gratitude expressed in gold.'

'Ha,' he laughed in scorn.

'But there is no heir to the Stuart cause. They will pay handsomely for knowledge of Charlotte's whereabouts.'

'I dislike this politicking. I'll take no part in this whatever you think!'

'Mistress! Mistress!' Mary's voice came up the stairs.

'I shall have to go down and see to the inn. I'll soon be back. Just clear away those stinking clothes whilst I'm gone.' She kicked angrily at the heap of cast-off garments as she pulled on her petticoat.

'I'd not been out of those for three days. And I'd not been into one of these for much longer!' Ned lunged from the bed, hands fumbling beneath her garb. Rhose boxed his ears then backed away, leaving him hanging half out of bed.

'Mistress Tinnys!'

'I thought you sated after the night.' Rhose glared at him. 'I do have to go. We will finish this later.'

His laughter followed her down the stairs as Ned dressed quickly. Taking the trinket out of his pocket, he studied it thoughtfully, tossed it in the air, and returned it to his pocket. Then he strode from the inn.

Later that morning Rhose hurried down the Dark Passage on her way to see Jonathan Agar. She had left Charlotte sitting for her portrait. Ned had gone to see the Seddons seeking news of a passage to Liverpool. She felt elated. If all went as she planned, a new life beckoned. Opening the door to the shop, she could barely refrain from singing Oliver's song.

'Rhose, come in, how good to see you.' Agar offered her the chair she had sunk into those weeks ago. 'You are fully recovered, I trust? I heard from Matthew that you were seeking me. I have to thank you for my new clients. Sir James Falkner was full of your praise. He trusts that my Transcendental Golden Electuary is a sovereign remedy for the pox – which it is. He wishes me to visit him at the family estate at Guilden Sutton. An excellent connection to be sure. This will be my entry into Chester society. I am leaving tomorrow. Matthew is nearly trained and will watch my business here for a week or two. Who knows, if all goes well I may set up in Chester itself.'

'Excellent news indeed, Jonathan. You deserve to prosper and I am pleased to be of some assistance. I would beg a small favour in return. I have a maid, who needs care and protection who needs to be kept out of sight, or out of Manchester. It would be well if you could take her as your assistant.'

'I follow you not. A maid? Who – a drudge – or a virgin? Why hidden from sight?'

'A virgin – a true virgin. Charlotte Fletcher!'

'Charlotte! You are mad. The whole county is looking for her, even though the tale is that she fled to London. Why have you hidden her?' He paused in thought. 'No, I'll not take her. The girl must be sent home at once. Her mother is distraught with worry. I have advised her to take the waters at Harrogate Spa in the hope it will bring her some relief.'

'I must advise you to do no such thing. The girl is as innocent as a lamb, but you must believe she will be found guilty. I found her in Sugar Lane and rescued her before any ill could befall her. She must be kept secret until Hannah and Rob have been taken and can prove her innocence. It will be in their own interests to do so.'

'What you say may be true, but I still would return her to her family immediately.'

Rhose stood and looked the other squarely in the face. Her tone was harsh. 'I'm afraid I can't allow that, Jonathan. You will oblige me or the whole world will know of your connections with Sugar Lane. Then where will your county practise be? Fled away and you in disgrace with it.'

'It was a bad day when I met you, Rhose Tinnys. I had thought when we worked together we might have become better acquainted. My fancy for you has allowed me to oblige you in the past. Now that comes back to haunt me! Very well, I will do as you say – there's some truth in the girl's predicament. I own that Sir Francis seems set on blackening her name.'

'Thank you kindly, Jonathan. We have meant much to each other and now I am in your debt. Charlotte must be moved at once. I have heard gossip. She rides she tells me, so she can accompany you on a pony.'

'I have one in the stable. Matthew uses it. It will suffice, 'tis a quiet gentle chestnut.'

'I will send her round with Mary at once so you can instruct her before your journey tomorrow. She can hide here tonight.'

'It would seem I have no choice but it pleases me not.'

'I will bid you farewell. I hope your society connection prospers, and your assistant proves quiescent. I am sure she will.'

'Farewell, Rhose. I know not what this endeavour will bring. I suspect there is more to this than you allow. I will guard her safe till I return to Manchester. After that I make no promises.'

Rhose turned and left the shop. The apothecary stood angry and bemused. The woman was impossible yet he was still doing her bidding. Were his aspirations to be blighted when all seemed set for success? A pox on Sugar Lane!

Sir Francis himself was entering Peter Smith's coffee house as Rhose left Agar's shop. His search for Charlotte in London had proved fruitless, though he and John had enjoyed the ladies of the town by way of consolation. Back home he began to wonder if indeed Hannah and Charlotte had ever left Manchester. Could the coach on the toll road have been a trick, to throw pursuers off the scent?

'Smith, a word with you in private if you please.'

'Why certainly, Sir Francis, would you please to come upstairs?'

'I've come to seek your help,' Francis continued as they entered Smith's sitting room. 'In the matter of my missing sister.'

'Aye, we've all wondered the truth of what happened. She seemed such an innocent thing.'

'Let that be. I'm wondering if they've slipped back around here. There was no trace of the girls in London. Would you do me the kindness of enquiring of your chapmen for news? They get to hear secrets in their travels I've no doubt. I'll see they are well rewarded for their trouble and there's a bonus for the man that can bring me information.'

'I'll do that for you willingly. I have heard tell of a hidden girl but it was naught but gossip. I took no notice of it. There's always tales when something like this happens. Still I'll see what I can find out. Would you care for a drop of Canary wine? I've a new shipment just arrived you might care to sample.'

'Well, thank ye, most gracious. I hope to hear from you soon on the other matter.'

'Indeed, Sir Francis, you may rely on me.'

Frank left Smith's with a lighter step. Perhaps the tales of the hidden girl were true. Could it be Charlotte? Or Hannah perhaps? Either way he'd find her and silence her. There was no going back now. It would be too dangerous to take her back to Greenwood Lea. He could never trust her not to tell what happened. And if his mother's tale of her birth were true it would be a catastrophe for his ambitions. No, there was no other way; she must be disposed of. He hesitated as to what to do next. Another tour of the taverns might produce better results than on the night of the flight. The chink of gold might refresh memories. He determined on a visit to the Ring o' Bells; he still had an itch for the handsome widow Tinnys.

Frank swung in through the door only to bump into the woman herself.

'Why, Mistress Tinnys, my apologies.' He swept off his hat in an elaborate reverence. 'I had but thought of you, then there as by magic you appear before me! I swear it is witchcraft.'

'Indeed, Sir Francis, I might almost say the same, for you had been in my thoughts but recently.'

'You flatter me, ma'am. I believed your interest lay elsewhere. However if I may be of service – any service – you need but ask.'

Rhose's reply was brusque as she led him through the public room.

'I wished to speak to you on matters of business. I think my proposition would be of mutual benefit.'

Rhose saw with relief that Mary was back about her duties. She turned to the serving girl. 'Is your errand complete?'

'Yes, madam.'

'Then bring up the best French brandy to the visitors' room. Or would you prefer a Canary freshly arrived, Sir Francis?'

'Frank chuckled. 'I have already tasted the Canary – it is more like canary droppings however "fresh" it may be.'

He followed her up the stairs.

'A commodious room,' he commented at the door of the large sitting room. The furniture spoke of a past century, dark oak and heavily carved.

'Indeed, one I normally reserve for travellers or important business. Please to take a chair, I'll be with you in a moment.'

Frank settled into a leather-backed carver at the head of the table. The brandy and glasses arrived. He was pouring a generous dram when Rhose returned, a fine embroidered shawl in her arms. She sat opposite at the other end of the table, hands demurely draped over the shawl.

'Your health, Mistress Tinnys! Will you not join me?'

'I would rather not, Sir Francis. A personal rule – not to drink while on business.'

'Ah, now to that.'

'I'll straight to the point. You recently had a loss, financial and personal.'

'You know well. You were somewhat curt in response to my enquiries. I still search. I still offer a reward. I will catch those damnable thieves.'

'As for the theft, I know nothing. As for the flight of your – do you still call her sister?'

Frank banged his glass on the table. Rhose continued, unhurried.

'Before we speak, let me tell you I know all. Who Charlotte really is. Who her father was.'

'Devil take you woman.' Frank rose then sank back into the chair. 'Witchcraft this surely is. You can know nothing; there is nothing to know. The baggage is nothing but a common thieving trollop, fated for a hangman's rope. What do I care what you fancy?'

'Fancy you say! The girl is the Pretender's child, the Jacobite heir to the throne perchance. A bastard offspring of a bastard claimant harboured by *your* family, brought up in *your* house, honoured by *your* worthy father and cherished by your fond mother – why almost bedded by *your* fine self!'

The chair crashed over as the man sprang to his feet, glasses shattering on the floor. He charged round the table, stopping short as he stared – a pistol had appeared from beneath the shawl. It was levelled firmly at his forehead.

'There is nothing to be gained by violence, Sir Francis. I said we have business, and we have. It will be of benefit to us both, I assure you. Let us discuss the matter calmly.'

'Bitch!' he turned and righted his chair. Seated he conjured a condescending smile.

'Why, who would believe you, a common tavern wench, when I deny it all?'

'No tavern wench, sirrah. I'm a respectable widow with respectable connections. And, what is more, with proofs, letters, a love token rose and, do not forget, the girl herself.'

'You have her here?' He was again on his feet. The pistol waved him to his chair.

'What simple booby do you think I am. She is safe, well out of your reach, to be produced whenever I wish it.'

'I still have little to fear. What harm could mere tittle-tattle have on my reputation and standing?'

'Such as it is in this town, I own little. But there is your sister. When is the marriage, pray? Are the Robinsons privy to the family secret? Would their proud Protestant relations welcome such a connection? Or your political ambitions, how would they fare?'

Frank glowered, but shrugged his shoulders in contemptuous dismissal.

'And your mother? I hear she is far from well. I would do nothing to hurt her tender nature but is she aware of all that occurred at Holywell?'

This was too much for Frank. He was white with fury, fists clenched before him on the table. His eyes glistening he pitched forward. 'If you breathe one word of that . . . if you damage mama in any way, I'll spit you like a turkey cock, come what may.'

Rhose shrank into her chair. The pistol raised, deadly.

'I have too much respect for Lady Elisabeth, though none for you with your goatish rutting. Now listen. The price of my silence, of Charlotte's continued absence, can be negotiated between us two. No one else will know, nor need any of the truth ever be known.'

'How much?' The words were rasped out.

'Really, Sir Francis, you can hardly expect a tradesman's bargain with a bill of sale. This is something you need to consider at leisure. I myself have yet to decide how best we might serve each other.'

'I see. You intend to bleed me like some apothecary's leech, drop by drop, 'til I can give no more.'

'Come, how would that serve either of us? There is more to this than mere money as you must comprehend. I suggest we meet again to come to such arrangement as may suit. What say you?'

'You're a damnable impudent scheming strumpet. It would seem you have me.'

He stood as she did, pistol now held loosely at her side. He made for the door, passing before her as she stood back. With a lithe twist of his body, his sword was in his hand striking her weapon to the floor. She gasped as she backed into the wall, the sword point at her throat.

'Or do I have you?' He grinned over the blade, tipping it at her chin.

She did not flinch, her eyes flashing defiance. 'Harm me and I shall be avenged, be sure of that.' Her voice was a mere whisper of venom.

'And you, you witch, beware of me! Our business is indeed not yet done.'

He sheathed his sword and flung open the door. As he left she called to him, 'What of Thomas?'

He stopped and turned on the stairs. Rhose stood above him, one hand resting on the banister the other idly swinging the pistol. 'Where is Uncle Thomas?'

Cursing, he stumbled out of the building.

Seth Bradley sighed as he trudged back to his cottage as dusk fell over the valley. It had been near three weeks since he had stumbled on the body in the woods. Then he had thought the blood-caked wound was mortal. Glad he was that he had not left the poor soul, but wondered how much longer he and his Betsy would have to nurse the stranger. One more mouth to feed – and Maria Makin to pay! She was a good woman for all her strange ways, versed in nature's law by her mother and her mother before that.

He bent through the logs doorway to find Maria by the makeshift bed next the fire. She was feeding her sickly patient a noxious looking draught.

'Thou must take it, foul though it is. Black hellebore root is dangerous for those who know not what they do, but I must use it.' She turned towards Seth, sadness in her face. 'I fear he is near death. He's fought long but his strength is waning.'

The two sat with the dying man and as the light failed, the light also left the stranger's eyes.

Chapter Nineteen

To Liverpool

Agar left his shop at sun-up together with his new assistant. To his relief he decided that only an intimate relative would recognize the girl now dressed in a servant's habit. She mounted the pony and with eyes downcast followed him out of Manchester. Traders carrying produce to the town by boat could be heard laughing on the river below the Chester road. If they had stopped at Throstle's Nest they would have seen the *Baccus* below them in the lock, but they rode on unaware.

Ned, with his fellow passenger Laurence, had walked along the Chester road at dawn; there was little traffic so early in the morning. Over the far side of the river the trees of Ordsall Clough could be seen raising their tops above the swirling mists that lay over the water. A slight chill caused the travellers to draw their cloaks tight around them. They were to join the boat at the first lock out of Manchester, Throstle's Nest. The Seddons had warned Twigg that the excise men were keeping watch on the Quay at the bottom of Water Street. Soon they reached the rendezvous and climbed down the steps to the lock. The fields adjoining the river were covered in dew and the two men stamped their feet, looking anxiously towards Manchester. Slowly the mist began to rise as the sun warmed the air. A

Mersey flat, the craft peculiar to the local waters, hove into view, its dark red sail piercing the lingering vapours. Skilfully it was steered across to the lock-side, avoiding the pull of the river cascading over the weir.

'Good to see you, Twigg,' called Laurence. 'Can we help?'

'Aye, grab the rope. We'll tie up while you climb aboard.'

The men, their luggage stowed below by a small boy, jumped on as Twigg opened the lock gates. Sam Harper steered the flat. The gates were closed and the mechanism that emptied the lock engaged. The flat emerged the other side, held by the rope to the bank whilst the lower gates were closed.

'They need to employ lock-keepers but you'll soon get used to the system. Mode Wheel, Calamanco, we'll pass several more before we come to Runcorn. The wind is with us today so we should have no need of the bankhauliers to pull us along.'

'Bankhauliers? What are they?' queried Laurence.

'Strong men we use to run along the bank heaving the boat by the rope. It's a tricky job when the bank's wet or steep. It takes away from the profits of the trip so we're always glad of a fair wind. Let's be off.'

The river curved steeply away to the right.

'Hey, watch the bank, Sam, we're heading straight for it,' shouted Ned to the helmsman in the stern.

Twigg laughed. 'It's the current, we must steer close to the bank where the water's deepest or we'll be grounded on the far side. She's stout built on purpose, there's always the risk of a grounding when the water's shallow. We've no cargo on this trip so we should be drawing plenty of water. Just leave it to us.'

Ned tried to relax as he sat and watched the scenery. He'd rather have a horse under him than water, but soon he found the gliding motion a pleasant change. The sunny banks were now brilliant green, studded with buttercups and daisies. The grounds on the starboard side belonged to Trafford Park. There were fine stands of trees, some reaching down to the water. Then the square tower of a church, with cottages nestling below, made another pleasant sight.

'Look ahead. That must be the Barton Aqueduct the canal diggers were talking of in the Ring o' Bells. It's extraordinary – those three immense stone arches. I've heard it called Brindley's "Castle in the air". The canal that crosses it will add to the Duke of Bridgewater's riches.'

'That's as may be but he'll take trade from us. No doubt about it. He plans to run the canal to Runcorn,' grumbled Twigg. 'Lower the sail!'

The boy, called Titus, pulled down the sail, ran to the windlass on the foredeck and helped Sam quickly lower the mast onto the deck. Ned and Laurence ducked low, much to the hilarity of the crew, as the boat passed under the low stone bridge that crossed the river. Sheepishly Ned and Laurence sat up again.

So the journey passed – locks, ferries, cottages, willows, woodlands all entranced the eye, then were gone. Small communities on the riverbank were ignored, as Twigg was anxious to reach Runcorn that night. Beyond Irlam the water meadows lay on either side as they came to the confluence with the Mersey, though the Irwell seemed the larger river. The men could feel the flat twist and rock as the two currents came together. Whirlpools opened before them and the hull banged into them. Then they were away again on a faster stream.

'We'll stop at the inn at Hollins Green for a bite to eat and sup some ale. But you must be sharp.'

Then on they went. At the meeting of small streams, groups of anglers lined the banks and Ned could see shoals of fish glistening through the clear waters, green weeds moving with the current.

'Next stream's the Bollin, it's known as one of the best for catches of fish and eels.' The river made large sweeps and curves, sometimes seeming to come back, so they imagined they were returning to Manchester.

Yet the passing of the sun told them they were heading west towards Liverpool, that it was late afternoon when they passed Bank Quay and Warrington. One final loop of the river then the course began to widen as they sailed down the approach to Runcorn.

'We've missed the tide tonight. We'll tie up above the lock and enter the Mersey on the early tide. Time to stretch our legs and get something to eat. Titus will cook the grub and fetch some ale. Take a walk, enjoy the view.' Twigg was in jovial mood; an uneventful journey had reached a safe harbour for the night.

Ned and Laurence walked over to the edge to view the river below. It was a beautiful summer evening. The broad sweep of the river glinted golden as it flowed to the sea. As they watched, the vast expanse of sands and water was lit by a burst of colour when the sun's crimson disc sank below the western horizon.

'A fine sight, Ned. Where will that river take you soon, I wonder? I hear passage to France is needed. I'll not ask why. I can arrange it so long as you can pay. First to the Isle of Man, then with the help of the Guernsey privateers, across to Brittany. Then it will be up to you. I hear there are a couple of escaped Frenchies waiting to cross to Man. Maybe you can join up with them and they will aid you in France.'

'Rhose, no doubt, told you I had plans which could take me in that direction. But I've a mind to visit a friend in Flint. I'm on a promise of right royal entertainment from a lady I met recently. I've no fancy for a French gaol as I told Rhose. The Welsh hills are a far better prospect.'

'You're a rascal and no mistake. No doubt Mistress Tinnys knows naught of that offer. I'll not enlighten her, though I may take my chance while you're gone.'

Ned laughed. 'Rhose always welcomes attention, so there'll be no hard feelings from me if you try your luck.'

'I'm here to see some Liverpool merchants, our "investors" you might say. I shall be staying at the Ship on James Street. If you want to contact me send word to the landlord, Davy White. He'll see you straight if I've gone. I'm to Chester for the races, then back to Manchester.'

The men strolled back to the flat. After their meal, Twigg and his crew retired; they would be entering the lock two hours after midnight. Ned and Laurence watched as other flats drew up nearby, listening to the sounds of men relaxing after their work ceased. Somewhere a flute began to play. Wrapping themselves in their cloaks they joined the others on the deck and tried to sleep.

It was dark as they descended through the lock. The water was alive with boats, produce for market, rock salt for the works next to the docks, woollens and worsteds. Laurence gazed intently over the river.

'The whole of the North of England is sending goods out of Liverpool. Trade looked grim last year with the French sending a squadron into the Irish Sea. No ships could sail for weeks, but the English frigates saw them off in February. Now business is booming again with the Isle of Man. Unfortunately the customs are becoming better organized to deal with the trade. It's a thorn in their side. I wonder how long our profits will last? Take note, Ned, that's Eastham on the Cheshire bank. You can take a coach to Chester from there, there's a ferry from Liverpool. It's how I'll go to the races – or you to Flint.'

'Ah,' Twigg growled. 'Let's get safe to Liverpool first. Some of these captains are cullys when it's dark.'

Dawn saw them approaching the waterfront. Liverpool's two docks were packed with ships. Others lined the pier that protected the quays from the winds off the Irish Sea. Twigg drew up at a wharf; the area was crowded with cramped houses and inns, seamen's haunts of vice and profligacy.

Laurence said his goodbyes and slipped into the crowd on the quay.

'We're off to Ma Murphy's on Bridge street. It's right by the water. We get good treatment. Susannah Taylor, Twigg's woman, is barmaid,' Harper assured Ned. 'Been here since she scarpered from Manchester last winter. Titus always stays with the flat. Ain't got no folks, hid on a schooner from the West Indies and landed up at Murphy's. He's a useful lad. Keeps us warned if the pressgangs are about. Don't want to end up serving His Majesty's Navy, Ned.'

Ned shuddered at the thought. 'Give me the open road any day, too many dangers in a seaport. I'll take my gear to Murphy's then I'm off to arrange a passage to Wales, by horse this time. I'll see you later maybe.'

'Don't worry about the gear, Titus will see to it.'

Ned acknowledged the favour then he too clambered up to the quayside.

For Ned the visit to Liverpool was astonishing. Never before had he seen so many tall ships lined up along a quay unloading cargo; their masts overlapping into the distance like a forest of branches in winter. Ned decided to stroll out along the mole joining a fine assembly taking the air and admiring the view. Strange tongues could be heard mingling with the local hubbub. As he stared at the decks new sights seemed to meet his eye at every turn. Men of colour were unloading bales of cotton fibre; Ned remembered Twigg's remarks about Liverpool's wealth coming from the triangular trade. Twigg had served on the runs to Africa taking goods from the North. Collecting slaves and elephant's teeth in exchange, they ran across the Atlantic to return to Liverpool with sugar and cotton. Ned thanked providence that he was no seaman. His thoughts turned to his Welsh conquest as he looked out across the Mersey to the land on the opposite bank, somewhere in that direction lay the Welsh mountains. As he turned at the end of the pier he took in the fine perspective of the Liverpool waterfront.

'Good day sir! Is it not a wonderful prospect? I did not expect to meet another Manchester man taking in the view.'

Ned found himself looking at a tall young man, whose face seemed familiar. Yes, he'd seen him at the Ring o' Bells. One of the young bucks that Rhose liked to encourage.

'You have the advantage, sir.'

'William Jones at your service, I believe we met at the cocking.'

'Ay, yes. What brings you to Liverpool, William Jones? I'd have thought the races in Chester were more to your taste.'

'I'm here on family business. We're still tea men as well as bankers. I'm organizing a cargo for my father. But, I'faith, I'll take any excuse to visit Liverpool. There's such entertainment as we know not in Manchester – the Assembly Room at the Tower, now their own Ranelagh gardens, best of all, the playhouse in Drury Lane. The play – aye, there's the life!'

'Why, man, I'd not think one of your standing would take to such fripperies.'

'Fripperies, sir! I'll have you know there's nothing else in all life to match the life of the theatre. "All the world's a stage,

> And all the men and women merely players:
> They have their exits and their entrances;
> And one man in his time plays many parts. . . ." '

He struck a dramatic attitude, declaiming to the unheeded waters.

Ned laughed out loud. 'Well, good luck to you and your fancy. I must away, I have business to attend to.'

'No, stay! There was a reason for my accosting you. No doubt you heard of the disappearance of Charlotte Fletcher? It's why I accosted you. Do you have knowledge of what happened? Your contacts on the road – have they reported where she might be?'

'What is your interest in the young lady that you should risk talking to the likes of me? It'll bring you a bad reputation, Mr Jones.'

'I think you may be able to assist me. Charlotte would never have run away without cause and as for stealing, never. She would have come to me if she could, something dreadful must have occurred. Anne, her sister, hinted as much before she was whisked off to Harrogate. It doesn't make sense; why would they go to Yorkshire with Charlotte vanished? Francis is behind this somehow, I know he is.'

'Well, there's something we have in common, a dislike of Sir Francis Fletcher. I consider myself an honest rogue. Sir Francis is a dishonest flash man if ever there was one. Shall we walk back to the quay? I may have something of interest to tell you.'

Ned regarded his companion with a degree of compassion. It

was evident the youth was devoted to Charlotte. Ned had been unhappy with Rhose's proposal from the start. He still felt uneasy about Charlotte's fate. He feared Rhose would let Francis have her if the money was right. And what did he want with a trip to the Stuart court? It was nonsense. His livelihood had taught him that his quick wit had got him out of many scrapes, but France was different. An Englishman caught there in the time of war would be hanged. No, he was right, this game was not for him. Rhose knew him well – he had a soft heart. The girl should be back with her family. Will Jones was the answer. He'd see Sir Francis could not harm her, especially after he'd heard what Ned had to say.

'Let's retire to my tavern. Don't worry, I'm not going to rob you,' Ned laughed as he saw the worried look on the other's face. 'As a token of my good faith, take a look at this.' Ned drew out a packet and carefully unwrapped the jewel.

William gasped as he gazed at the enamelled rose he had last seen at the ball. He grabbed Ned by the arm.

'How. . . ? What does this mean? Where is she?'

'Come, we'll to Ma Murphy's. I'll explain all and then . . . we'll find her.'

Susannah slapped two foaming mugs of ale onto the table then vanished into the crowd. Ned was seated with his companion in an alcove at the rear of Ma Murphy's. Talking quietly he knew they were unlikely to be overheard.

'Drink your ale and still your questions 'til I've finished. I'll tell you all I know about the lady in question.'

Ned embarked on the tale of Charlotte's supposed history. He spared Will none of the details of Frank's actions in the woods. Nor held back from revealing the plans to blackmail Sir Francis and obtain money from the Stuarts whilst Charlotte remained out of sight. He paused as he noticed Susannah hovering around their table.

'Here, wench, more ale,' he called. She left with a toss of her head.

'Travelling to the Jacobite court is not for the likes of a Lancashire highwayman. This token could be proof of nothing. I'd rather see the wench safe with you.'

'You have amazed me, sir! I know not what to say. My abhorrence of Frank Fletcher is confirmed a thousand fold. For the rest, it matters not to me. And yet . . . whatever her true pedigree Charlotte has been raised a Fletcher, and none question that. Her mother and sister, for that is how they behave, love her truly. Her father, yes we may call him that, has left her a portion as dowry. My family were happy to arrange a marriage between us. None of this need to change. We must find her at once and I will return her to her mother at Greenwood Lea. We can explain her flight. I will be her protector till we are married. Then all will be forgotten.'

'Very noble, but Charlotte is not aware of her heritage. How will she feel when she finds out she has no right to the Fletcher name? Your father will not allow you to be allied to a Stuart bastard.'

'He will never know,' the young man interrupted, 'neither he nor Charlotte need find out the secret. If it could be proved I might think differently. There is no proof. Charlotte's mother loved her father, there's no sin in that. The Fletchers guarded her good name. If the marriage takes place as arranged neither Mistress Tinnys nor Sir Francis can have any hold on us. No one would believe the former and the latter would not want his family name besmirched. They could approach my father, though I doubt he would yield to blackmail. I would confess and throw myself on his mercy. He could disinherit me but I'm not afraid. The world is changing, business is booming. I could make a new life for Charlotte anywhere as long as we're together.'

'Boldly spoken like a man in love! Time to find your dear one. I think it best we leave Liverpool separately. You will take the ferry to Eastham and join the coach to Chester. I have arranged for a horse and will ride over. Take lodgings at the Golden Ball on Water Street, I'll find you there. I've contacts in the district so I should have news of Agar and the party at Guilden Sutton when we meet again.'

'I will do as you say. I cannot express my gratitude enough, Ned. We will surely rescue Charlotte. Soon she will be in my arms once more.'

'Agreed. Come Mr Jones, let's be away.' Ned embraced his new conspirator, thinking of the Welsh lady that would be soon in his own arms. ' 'Til we meet again!'

Susannah Taylor watched the conspirators leave the inn separately, smiling to herself. Now she had secrets of her own, and there could be a reckoning with Rhose Tinnys where she had the upper hand.

Chapter Twenty

Proposals

Will arrived at the inn late the same afternoon. The crossing of the Mersey had been rough. The coach had been crowded and the roads appalling. He bore it all with fortitude thinking only of his mission. Next morning after enjoying a hearty breakfast, and knowing Chester well, he decided a walk through the rows would help him pass the time. A light rain had begun to fall, but the ingenious design of the two-level streets meant he could stroll safe from the weather.

'Will Jones, what a pleasure to see you. I've just come from Manchester and your father told me he had sent you off to Liverpool. Have you come for the races?'

'Oliver, good to see you, too! Yes, I finished my business with speed so I could come racing. Father does not approve of bankers gambling so your discretion would be appreciated.'

'Say no more. What say you we get away from these disagreeably dirty shops? I've finished my business with the jeweller, a token for a lady. The rain has stopped and a walk around the walls will yield more pleasant prospects.'

The two young men enjoyed the perambulation. Far away the Welsh mountains were partly covered in cloud, on the Cheshire plain Beeston Castle crowned its rock and the river Dee wound its way beneath the walls. They paused on one of the arches that afforded entrance to the city, watching the comings and goings below.

'I hear Sir James Falkner's entered the Manchester races. Has he a horse running this week, too?'

'Three, I believe. He's a party come from London to join him. He's bringing them to the Exchange this evening for the opening Assembly of the meeting. They are to stay at his town house. Why don't you accompany me there now? We may glean some tips for the betting.'

Will was just about to agree when he noticed a familiar figure on the road below. Ned, slouching below a broad brimmed hat, was riding into town.

'Sorry, Oliver, I have urgent business, but I will join you later if I can.'

Quickly he hurried back to the inn. He found Ned already seated with a pint of ale to hand.

'Why Mr Jones, I do believe, will you join me in a drink?'

'With pleasure, sir. Have you discovered the maid, is she still with the apothecary?'

'Quietly, sir, we don't want the inn to know our business. Yes, they were at Guilden Sutton. He treated Sir James Falkner, with success I'm told. And there lies the problem; they were to have been in Chester today, but the triumph of the remedy caused a change of plan. Falkner's boasting reached aristocratic friends held up at Parkgate. They are bound for Ireland but the weather prevents sailings. Seeking for entertainment they sent for Agar to administer to their pox, and their wives' vapours. We must leave at once. If the wind changes,who knows, Agar may sail for Dublin with his new patrons.'

The conspirators set off on the road to Parkgate, riding the horses at breakneck speed. They stopped at the halfway house, The Dublin Yacht, at Woodbank. Ned hoped to pick up the local gossip. The talk was of the dangerous footpads threatening travellers as they crossed the commons. A certain Andrew Ram had been robbed at pistol point in June. The owners of the coaches

and post-chaises were demanding action. Ned voiced his agreement, indicating that as a precaution he too was armed. Once
more on the road, he burst out laughing.

'Jamie Armstrong will be pleased he's causing such a stir. I
met him when I worked the Welsh side of the Dee. The Royal
Yacht that sails to Dublin, with its naval crew and cannons,
attracts aristos and gentry. Foolish of them to think, as they're
safe on the water, they'll be safe crossing the local heaths. I've
sent word to Jamie for news of Agar.'

As the road entered a copse, an armed man stood in their
path. Will reigned in his horse preparing to flee. As he strained
to turn his mount he saw that two others had taken up their
place in the rear. To his amazement he saw Ned had
dismounted.

'Good to see you, James, may I introduce my companion, the
honest William Jones. Do join us, this is the notorious Mr
Armstrong.' Retiring into the wood, Jamie produced bottles of
ale.

'I've done as you asked. The apothecary lodges at the Kings
Arms. You're in luck, the wind's too strong for anything to sail.
The town is packed; another two passengers won't be noticed.
I've warned Ben Tyson, landlord of the Beerhouse Inn, to expect
you. It's on the far side of the village at the bottom of the lane
that leads to the river. The Hole there has deep anchorage so
there'll be ships riding at anchor waiting to enter Parkgate. The
customs men are down in the village checking goods and
luggage in and out of their long room. Licensed thievery, of
course! There can't be a customs house in the land that doesn't
pillage all it handles. We're just the obvious targets for
complaint, Ned.'

Soon the road was busy. Carts, as well as coaches, were carrying passengers down to the irregular row of houses that lined
the strand. Will felt elated; somewhere below Charlotte was no
doubt among the moving scene of figures strolling in the fields
behind the dwellings.

'Come,' turning his horse Ned rode into the lane that ran

along behind the town. 'We'll visit the Beerhouse first, tend to the horses, and walk into Parkgate later. The landlord may have news of our quarry.'

'I trust this room will suffice gentlemen. With the outside stair you can come and go as you please. The town's bursting, making hay while the sun shines, eh? They are out-bidding one another for rooms at the Kings Arms where your man is staying. The young lady sleeps with the maids. She's not seen much, just the occasional walk along the shore with her master. He's out and about though, currying favours. Offers consultations in a room at the Customs House; with the wait, there's plenty of trade for hangers-on. I've heard he's now recommending a "marine plunge" as a cure for all ills!'

'A bite to eat is what we need, then a stroll into town to take the air.'

'I'll send up some grub, boiled chicken and sack whey. You'd be fighting for it in town. There's some "liberated" Cheshire cheese to follow.'

Will could hardly wait, bolting the unedifying food, cheese excepted.

The two set out on the short walk to Parkgate.

'We must approach Agar with caution. I'm sure Rhose has blackmailed him into hiding Charlotte. He's a lot to lose if he's found out. I'll speak to him first, you must stay out of sight.'

Ned worried that the young man, once he came within sight of Charlotte, would seize her by force if necessary. The interest of the military, sure to be waiting passage, was not something Ned planned to attract. Both he and Agar needed to make themselves scarce before Charlotte re-emerged as Miss Fletcher.

'Surely we can just go and fetch her away? She'll come with me; Agar needn't know anything about it 'til next morning. We can be in Chester by then.'

'A sound plan for you two maybe. No, we must take him into our plans. I'll talk to him tonight.'

Entering the inn, the noise was deafening. It was hard to

believe that so many society notables were crowded into this nondescript inn on the banks of the Dee. Travelling to Dublin by the Royal Yacht, courtesy of the Lord Lieutenant of Ireland, had gained social cachet. The *Dorset*, purpose built in 1753, was an elegant ship. Merchants, too, were among the press. Trade with Ireland flourished in both goods and people. Like ballast in the hold, workers shipped over in May for the harvests were returned home in the autumn.

'I'm seeking an apothecary', Ned leaned over the counter, 'I hear one's lodged with you.'

'Aye, can't say I've seen him this evening though. He hangs around the Earl of Gisburn.'

'The apothecary you say,' a ruddy man interrupted. 'George Norman, river pilot, at your service. He's dining on the *Dorset*. Saw them come aboard as I was leaving. I was informing the captain the winds set to change so they should all be away in the morning. You'll catch him when they come ashore.'

'Ned, Ned, do you see who's sat over in the corner. The actors I saw at the theatre in Liverpool. I shall pay my respects.'

'Aye, go on lad. No doubt they're off for a season in Dublin. No attempts to talk to the young lady, agreed?'

'Agreed.'

The evening air felt cool. Ned took a deep breath. This was his time of day, soon it would be the dark hours. Standing watching the river he could feel the wind had shifted. Under the lee of the bank he could make out groups of travellers huddling together, too poor to pay for the meanest accommodation. Every day, trapped by the weather, saw them sink further into misery. The honest poor – somehow scraping together the few pence for a passage. The dishonest poor, the Irish destitute, got a free passage paid for under the Poor Laws. Gathered at the House of Correction in Neston they were marched onto the Dublin bound ships every day, except, of course, the Royal Yacht. That was for the establishment vagabonds! The sound of oars dipping in the water drew near to the shore, animated conversation and laughter carried over the water. A longboat was beached and sailors helped the passengers onto the shore.

'Let us pray this is the last evening we spend in this infernal spot. A day's acquaintance may have rustic charm, but two weeks has become intolerable.'

'Yes, my lord, the captain assured me we will weigh anchor the morrow.'

Ned recognized Agar's voice. The party started for the inn with Agar at the rear. Quickly slipping to the inn door, with hat pulled well down, Ned accosted the apothecary.

'Excuse me, sir. Do I have the honour to speak to Mr Agar, apothecary of Manchester?'

Agar took a step back, the light from the doorway throwing the enquirer into shadow.

'I have need of your services. I know the hour is late but it is a desperate case. A young lady from a genteel family is in danger.'

Agar paused, the voice seemed familiar. 'It is late, sir, but illness does not respect the hour. Will you show me the way?'

Ned drew Agar towards the shore.

'Well, Jonathan, we meet under strange circumstances.'

'Ned! I thought it was you. Have you a message from Rhose?'

'Nay, I come of my own accord. Me thinks she has played us both as pawns in a game of her choosing. You have Charlotte with you still?'

'Yes, but I dislike it. I have the chance to accompany His Lordship to Dublin. An entry into the echelons of the highest society is for my taking. I want not to take the girl.'

'Then it seems we can help each other. I was supposed to go to France to aid Rhose's ambition, but a mighty argument put paid to her plans. It was a foolhardy notion as I told her. Now I have other plans. I met William Jones in Liverpool. His parents and the Fletchers have agreed a match between their children. He loves her truly and would return her to her family. I think it would resolve both our problems. I think Rhose would sell her to Sir Francis if the price was right, I abhor the man and his intentions. It was one of the reasons for our dispute, I forbad her to entertain the idea.'

'I am at one with you, Ned. I despise the man. You have a plan I trust.'

'You go to Dublin as you have arranged. If they were to come looking for you, you could take ship for the New World. Plenty of vessels put into Ireland before the Atlantic crossing. You could vanish there for ever.'

'Not a prospect I relish; still it's unlikely to come to that. What of you?'

'I'm to Flint on the ferry. A most attractive party has invited me to pleasure her as long as I like. Long Ned, yet again, whilst I take cover.'

'What of Rhose?'

'We had a disagreement. I'm minded to give her time to come to her senses.'

'And Charlotte Fletcher? What does she know of this?'

'Nothing as yet! William will go with you to visit her. After a touching reunion arrange for him to take her back to our lodgings where I will await them. That's all you need to know.'

'Good luck to us both. Once they are back in Manchester the hunt will be on.'

'Perhaps, perhaps not. The families may wish to keep it quiet. If not, well, the tide has turned so we'll be away tomorrow and long gone.'

The two men shook hands. Ned hurried off down the shore, Agar returned to the inn. Will was still ensconced with the actors; he looked up at Agar's approach.

'Mr Agar, I'm pleased to see you. You are alone.'

'Come let us talk Mr Jones. Please excuse my friend.'

They retired to the counter.

'I am asked to take you to the party you seek. If you will oblige me, please come to my room.'

Showing Will into a small room, Agar explained he would go above for Charlotte. Within minutes he returned and ushered her into the room.

'Will, oh Will, is it really you?' Charlotte burst into tears as she flung herself into the outstretched arms awaiting her.

'My dearest, dearest darling, thank God I have found you. You are safe. I will never let you go again.'

Agar spoke quickly: 'You must take her to your lodgings, Ned is waiting. He will explain his plan. I have tried to guard you well, Charlotte. Try not to think too ill of me. Now, away, I think we will not meet again. Good luck, and a happy life for you both.'

Charlotte was led by the hand out into the night. As soon as they were away from the houses William looked into her eyes and vowed that he would love her all his life and care for her with every breath he took. Charlotte returned his sentiments before yielding to his impassioned kisses. Breathlessly they hurried up the outside stair to meet Ned.

'I'm pleased to meet you, Miss Fletcher. I see you have accepted my friend's advances.'

The pair blushed and Charlotte looked down at the floor embarrassed. Ned laughed, 'I only jest. William will guard you 'til you are safe home. Listen carefully; I have a proposal, which I think may be safest for your future. If you return to Manchester there are no guarantees that Sir Francis may not harm Charlotte before you wed. Why not marry before you return?'

'Oh, Will could we? A clandestine marriage – so romantic, don't you think.'

'Not so fast, Miss Charlotte. There is more to my plan. Rhose told me that Smith has got his chapmen looking for a hidden girl. If you take the roads north to Scotland you may be seen and news reach Sir Francis. You don't want to be found in the wastes of the Lake Country. Pity, they changed their laws in the Isle of Man or you could have wed there. No, you, Charlotte, can travel to Dublin with Agar as arranged.'

'No, I won't leave her!'

'Gently, Will! You can travel with those actors. You can arrange a wedding there. When you return to Manchester you will be man and wife and none can threaten you. Your mothers will forgive you and they are sure to carry the day.'

'Oh, William, we could, we could! Frank would never harm me once I am your wife.'

'A splendid plan! The situation calls for boldness. I will send word to my father that I've heard of a business opportunity in Dublin; he'll trust my judgement and won't worry if I'm away awhile. That should give us plenty of time without arousing suspicion. Will you not mind sacrificing a splendid wedding, Charlotte?'

'No, it's so wonderful. Nothing matters to me except being safe with you. It's what we feel in our hearts that matters, not the fine clothes we would wear.'

'Dublin it is then! Now we'd best get some sleep.'

The two men gathered their cloaks and waited outside, as Charlotte made ready for bed.

'Keep her secret, Mr Jones, until you feel it safe to tell her. When you are married will be time enough I think. Maybe never.'

'How can I thank you? You have been a true friend to our love. I can never repay you.'

'Keep my name out of your story, that will be thanks enough. An upright man like you should have no truck with a highwayman, even one as sentimental as me. I'll go and tell Agar of the new plan.'

The tide turned. Mr Jonathan Agar and his demure assistant accompanied the Earl on a smooth crossing to Dublin; Long Ned boarded the ferry to the Flint shore. Having sent word, a carriage arrived with an eager lady who took him off into her mountain fastness. Soon William Jones and Charlotte Fletcher stood on the deck watching the Dublin Quay draw near. They had all the time in the world.

Chapter Twenty-one

The Fight at Tin Brow

Long Ned jogged thoughtfully along the Chester Road, nervous at the reception he might expect at the Ring o' Bells. Roistering with his Welsh lady had been a frolicsome interlude, but he knew in his heart no one would replace Rhose. He clattered into Deansgate, a watery sun etching the spire of St. Mary's Church. He tipped a greeting to Miles Brower standing at the gate of his hattery and received a friendly wave in response.

He brooded more on the future as he passed by Water Street. He was an adventurer; not for him the settled life in town when there was wide country to roam. Why this very night a new prospect opened, though at first he had been wary of being involved in such an organization as Josiah controlled. There were profits to be made but the risk was great; much better a brace of pistols and a fast horse than a leaky flat and drunken sailors. Still he was committed now! As he dismounted at the inn, his thoughts were interrupted by a scathing:

'So! You're creeping back then? You'd better try making up with the mistress, she's been right ill-tempered since you let out. I'd not be in your shoes.'

Martha was standing at the kitchen door, arms akimbo, her face flushed scarlet by the heat and steam of the day's cooking.

'Why Martha, as blooming and merry as ever, I see! How's about a welcoming kiss?' He whirled her round as he strode into the inn, she beating at his broad shoulders in mock offence.

At that moment Rhose pushed backwards into the kitchen, arms loaded with empty plates and dishes. Clapping her round the waist. Ned nuzzled the back of her neck. She gave a small cry then snuggled against him, forcing them both backwards towards the kitchen table. Ned released her and stepped away to admire her as she carefully put down the crockery.

'Ah, my pippin, you—'

A sharp slap across the face silenced him, a second sent his hat flying across the room. 'Rhose, pet . . .' he tried again, only to be driven in retreat as she advanced on him.

'So why are you not in France? I feared you had become a coward when Josiah turned coy. And the jewel? And the treasure, our Charlotte?'

Ned, with his back to the wall, spluttered, 'I never liked the plan. Charlotte's too sweet a girl to be bargained with. And Will—'

'Will, what Will? Don't tell me you've given her away to that banker's booby – what profit is there in that?'

'No profit, but no risk of the gallows to you or me. Nay, lass, don't you see we were getting into deep water – and I'm afeared of water.'

'You agreed, you agreed to go to France – you've thrown away our chance of riches. I'll never forgive you!'

Martha stood watching with undisguised glee as Rhose scrabbled for a weapon. A ladle descended on Ned's upflung arms. He reached to grab it as Rhose flailed again. Then it too was flying across the room as his arms went round her, mouth pressing hard in a long smothering kiss. He crushed her to him in a great bear hug, broke away and held her at arms length to gaze into her eyes.

'Ned Edwards,' her words came in gasps of half anger, half

delight, 'I should beat some sense into that thick head of yours. Off like that, sending no news, leaving me distraught – off to tumble with that trull in the Welsh mountains.'

'Who told you. . . ?'

'Told me? Told me? You great looby! No one needs tell me how you employ that weapon – of yours.'

She thrust her fist at his crotch as he twisted out of the way, still smiling. 'Then you come scuttling back here without word again. Creeping in – taking liberties – almost making me smash my livelihood – an inn full of people.' Without pausing, without turning, she called, 'Martha, that broth's about to boil over.'

That's not the only thing either,' the cook muttered as she pushed past the couple to the fire.

Ned reached into his coat pocket. 'Come, come, my pretty! Your Ned's back. I could never stay away from you – and look what I've brought you.' With that he produced a string of pearls he let play through his fingers.

'So you think you'll buy me with trinkets now?'

'Trinkets! Why these come from the finest—' He stopped, casting a wary glance at the cook, busy with the cauldron.

'Oh, come Ned, Martha's as wise to your game as she is trustworthy! She knows everything that goes on, and tells nothing: isn't that so, Martha?'

The cook turned, regarding them sternly in turn. 'What I know; I know my place. I know your place, and I know yours.' she waved a dripping spoon menacingly at the highwayman, 'and it is not in my kitchen.' With that she plunged the spoon back into the broth with such force that the fire spat back at her.

Rhose stalked from the kitchen with Ned in pursuit. Martha chuckled. 'The inn's busy, she says, and I know, but I'll wager she'll not be back down for a while yet.'

And she was right.

'I am pleased to see you home again, Sara. You look much recovered, Elisabeth. In fact you ladies seem to have blossomed in the Harrogate air.'

Edmund Robinson, his wife and Lady Elisabeth were taking a morning turn around his beloved garden.

'I think we should sit under the magnolias over beyond the pond. I have had the servants take out some seats for us. It will be pleasant in the shade this warm day. You can tell me all about your travels, while I contemplate the garden.'

Slowly they made their way under the trees. Together with the seats was a table carrying glasses, cordials and dainty biscuits.

'Well, Sara, tell me all.'

'Oh, Edmund, we had such a wonderful time and the water has so improved Elisabeth's constitution, has it not?'

'Indeed, I was so reluctant to go but I can only thank you sincerely for persuading me otherwise. I had heard of the Harrogate Spas, of course. Francis had told us how it has become the place for society to visit in the summer to take the waters. I had always been convinced that it was a dreary moor with a few houses around the edge, and the water was quite disgusting to the taste.'

'And now you know differently?'

'Yes, High Harrogate is very pleasant with excellent hotels and villas. The prospects of villages, fields and woodland are wonderful. We could even see York Minster on clear days, and that must be twenty miles at least. We could not help admiring the other visitors; the town was full of the English and Scottish nobility. And even the common people partake. They swear by the Old Sulphur Well in Low Harrogate; one of those stinking wells that first brought Harrogate to notice.

'So, Elisabeth, as you are now recovered have you decided on your next course?'

'I have. I cannot put the events after the ball out of mind. Charlotte is still my daughter and I know her character too well to believe ill of her. There must have been a terrible reason for her leaving without a word to me. Anne and Frank disagree and wish me to cease the search. They are convinced of her duplicity. At Harrogate I came to realize that Francis and Anne are wrong; however it may appear, I'm sure Charlotte is innocent of any crime. For now, Edmund, Anne and George's happiness is of the utmost importance. Your willingness to continue with the betrothal means much to me. I can never thank you enough. Charlotte can never lose her place in my heart, but Francis and Anne insist we must look to the future and there I can agree with them.'

Sara, aware of the battle Elisabeth had fought to distance herself from her children's charges, was concerned Elisabeth should not distress herself once more.

'Come, let me pour you a cordial, Elisabeth.'

'Thank you, I think Francis should be here soon. He is bringing Mr Rogerson, the lawyer to draw up the marriage settlement.'

'Yes indeed, I shall leave you ladies to your gossip. My attorney should be arriving within the hour as well. I shall return to the house to greet them. I will send Anne out to join you whilst we men attend to the business in hand.'

It was late afternoon and the lawyers had departed. The contracts had been agreed and the way was clear for the marriage to take place. As the discussion for the coming nuptials proceeded apace, Francis took the opportunity to escape.

No one saw him hurry across the plat and into the wood behind the well. He stood for a moment watching the house to see if he was followed. No, all was quiet save for the cawing of the rooks above. His anger mounted as he remembered the events that had brought him to this wood. Damn the girl! Thank goodness his mother had been persuaded to take his point of view and that Anne, afraid to lose her marriage, had supported him. Now there was Rhose Tinnys to deal with. Yet he'd not let a common innkeeper stand between him and his ambitions. His whole future depended upon his good reputation. He had worked hard to live down the lingering doubts surrounding his family's rebellious background. Anne's marriage promised well bringing with it an entry into society, everything he hoped for seemed possible. With the influence of the Robinsons in their circles a political career beckoned. Marriage to an heiress, yes, the whole of society would lie at his feet with a house in London. He felt his mood lighten.

There was the glade. It looked so innocent, the late afternoon sun casting shadows below him. Quickly he descended the bank and made for the fallen tree. He'd determined to see the body was well hidden; in his haste before he could not be sure. This was the place. He started back; the branches had been pulled away and there were signs of further disturbance. Francis searched the grounds frantically. Damnation – a pox on the Millers. The body was gone!

The rain came that night. The summer storm swept down from the moors, across Manchester, lashing the River Irwell into a boiling froth. Later it settled into a relentless drizzle belying the sunny promise of the day. It stayed mild despite the wet and the moon attempted fitfully to break through the lowering clouds.

Two men standing on the Old Bridge dragged their cloaks around for protection. They were silent as they studied the bend in the distance, waiting.

On the river only one boat moved. A flat, mast lowered, hugged the Salford shore, around the bend away from the Quay. As it passed under the bridge it swung over to the opposite bank, the Collegiate Church looming high through the mist of rain. The men crossed to the opposite parapet to watch. A lantern flashed briefly where cliff and river met: Tin Brow, waste ground, thirty-two steps from the graveyard above. A lonely spot that tonight looked harsh and menacing. The *Baccus* poled into the bank. A dark lantern revealed dim figures crowded beneath the overhang. No words were spoken, as the flat was straight away made fast. Men scuttled along the deck. Barrels and kegs were heaved over to waiting hands. In well-ordered efficiency despite the rain, chests and bundles followed. The chain of men began the trudge up the steps.

Suddenly a whistle from above was cut short. A warning shout rang out. More lanterns glimmered atop the cliff. The splash of a tea chest into the water heralded a cry of 'In the King's name'. Musket fire spat from the heights.

'By Christ, they've brought the military.' Twigg at the prow cursed long and hard. There were more splashes as the crew dived overboard, swimming for the Salford shore. On Tin Brow the tubmen dropped their burdens. Those on the steps faced troopers coming down. Scrambling through the scrub in an attempt to escape, they were hauled back or beaten with flat of sword. The rain had stopped. A glimmer of moon lit the desperate scene. Feet slipped and squelched as smugglers and soldiers alike slid down the bank. Two batmen stood astride the cargo still on the bank, swinging their six-foot staves. Recruited by Laurence for their height and strength they were not going to give in. Whirling their clubs they faced the first onslaught. A head cracked, a trooper went down. A second had the sword smashed from his hand. Then, outnumbered, the bully-boys turned to climb the brow. A shot rang out and one slithered to his death. The other lashed out his foot at a pursuer, Molineux, the excise man. Molineux hung on and the two twisted and wallowed along the slope. Grabbing at tree roots to halt his fall, the batman found himself grasping a bleached bone. A skull, breaking from the soil, grinned in his face. With a howl he flung himself backwards, he and his captor crashing onto the river path. Winded, he half rose only to be clubbed with the butt of a musket.

On the flat, Twigg was struggling to get away. He cast off forward and he was heaving on the aft line when he was challenged.

'Hold, Twigg! You can't escape.' It was Tobin the other excise officer.

'Curse you! You'll not take me. It's death either way.' He swung a long oar, downing Tobin. On the bank the sergeant of the troop took careful aim and fired. Twigg reeled back, staggering across the deck, blood seeping through his jacket.

There was a despairing cry as he tumbled backwards into the water.

The action had been sharp and violent. One man lay dead, two were wounded. The soldiers clubbed and pushed the remainder into a shambling pack. Others had escaped either up the brow or across the river. The contraband lay jumbled on the path or discarded on the deck. Someone pulled the boat back to shore and retied the bow end. Molineux limped over to his fellow officer and helped him to his feet, groaning.

'Not a bad night's work.'

'Aye, but we need to get that bastard out of the water if he's still alive. The rest are of little account.'

'The sergeant's detailed two men to see to that. It's a fair haul. The information from the 'Pool was good for once. Our masters will be pleased.'

'There's some hangings to look forward to, for sure.'

'Excuse me gentlemen.' The sergeant had approached. 'We've pulled out the boatman, Twigg. Dead. Too bad we didn't get a chance of questioning him.'

'Damn!' Tobin exploded. 'I'd have liked to get my hands on the one who organizes the gangs and gets the most profit.'

'You're right, a run from Man to Liverpool and then here takes some skill in ordering. You know,' Molineux paused in thought, 'I'd swear I saw someone on the bridge watching just before we challenged. A small round figure . . . does that sound familiar, Tobin?'

'Yes, Molineux . . . and t'other with his slouch hat is no stranger!'

There was a single candle burning low in the room at the back of the Ring o' Bells. Rhose sat by the kitchen table wrapped in blanket and shawl, cinders glowing low in the grate. Three glasses and a bottle of rum stood in front of her. She was not sure whether she had heard musket fire but she was uneasy. This was the first big run – nothing, *nothing* must go wrong. Yet the hairs on the back of her neck prickled with foreboding. She prayed Ned was alright. A peremptory knock at the door brought her to her feet. Josiah Laurence hastened in, talking as he came.

'Tragedy, Rhose, tragedy! Someone has peached, God damn them. All lost! All taken!'

'What?' Rhose backed away as the little man slumped into a chair. Without pause he reached for the bottle, poured a glass, tossed it down, followed swiftly by a second.

'Soldiers, excise men, waiting! They fired without mercy, the cowards. Who alive and who dead I do not know.'

'Where's Ned? Was he taken?'

'No, he was with me on the bridge. He's off to warn his contacts. There'll be a hue and cry all over town.'

'And the cargo?'

'Taken – it must have been. I saw it scattered over the bank, floating in the water, our money vanishing. Damn and blast, all, all gone to the devil.'

Rhose lit another candle as the first guttered out, then settled at the opposite side of the table. She poured herself a drink, handing the bottle back to Laurence.

'Thank you. I hate violence. I shudder at the thought of blood, and tonight. . . ! Well, this sees my hopes for Manchester ended.' He gulped down more of the fiery liquid, cursing as he shook his head in disbelief.

Rhose reached over and patted his hand. 'Were you seen? Could they have tracked you here?'

'I think not. The carriers knew where to stack the goods but I doubt if they will talk. Twigg alone is aware of our connection. But knowing the man, I doubt if he will survive the night. He'd rather a swift end than death at the rope.'

'But you?'

'My sojourn here is ended. Too many know my name. Any caught will gladly turn King's evidence to save their necks. But you, my dear, should be safe.'

Rhose stood and moved to the fire. She stirred the ashes to a flaring blaze. The flickering light bathed her face in a golden glow. Her shadow, lengthening across the room, seemed to loom over her companion. She turned to face him.

'I'll see the cellars are clear of such goods I have. The King's gold may bring my name to the authorities. I doubt the officers will touch me. I command some respect and they are in my debt. This, though, brings unwanted trouble. Oh, I grow weary of this town, of this life.'

Laurence stood in his turn and came to her. He took her two hands in his and looked intently into her face. 'This place never did suit me. I have influential friends along the coast and through the trade in France and Flanders. I plan to go north, Whitehaven beckons.'

Rhose started at this. He felt a shudder go through her as she dropped his hold. She leaned her hands against the mantel and stared into the fire.

'Yes, Rhose, your home town. There's much that can be done there in my special trade.' He hesitated and then again approached her. 'We have known each other but a short time but I know your spirit, your mind. It may be bold of me, the drink gives me courage perhaps, but I would have you consider joining me in my next venture. A partnership, I am a rich man Rhose . . . though a business partnership if that is all you would offer. It would benefit us both . . . and you would be going home as a lady. I promise you that.'

Rhose could hear from his tone that he had hopes of more than a business relationship. Yet she thrilled at the prospect of returning to her own north country, the familiar haunts, the song of the sea.

'Josiah, I know not what to say. I am flattered by your – proposal. I had no idea . . . but I have important affairs on hand here which I must see through. And there are others to consider.'

'Aye, Ned, I know. But he's a chancer, Rhose. He'll be caught and you'll be here again, alone. Well, my offer is heartfelt. But I cannot linger. If my name comes forward, and it will, Lancaster gaol will be my destination. Remember, clear your decks, I mean cellars, and deny all. I'm away this night. I'll see a message reaches you as to my whereabouts and it would do my heart good if I thought you would follow.'

With that he took her hand, raised it to his lips in a lingering kiss, then was gone.

Chapter Twenty-two

To the Races

Ned rode into Manchester in the midst of a roistering crowd of tinkers, their gypsy wagon driven by an aged crone hurling obscene abuse at her companions. They took it in fine part and gave as good as they got. Ned grinned but kept silent, with eyes alert for constables and revenue men. He knew there was a hue and cry for him. Josiah was safely away and he too would soon leave this town behind. It was time to move on. He had found a safe haven in the Marches and there could be rich pickings on the Welsh border. If only he could persuade the lovely Rhose to go with him. He had tried to ride out of her life, but, by God, she was in his bones. They were flint and steel, sparks flew whenever they were together. She had a brain on her, scheming hussy she could be at times. She had twice his nous – but how she could pleasure a man.

'What's tha' shitten face gurning at?' The old woman flicked her whip in his direction. A lad on a shaggy pony guffawed:

' 'Appen 'e fancies a tumble wi' thee, gammer.'

The whip cracked around his ears as he kicked the pony into a trot.

'Nay, tha's too young for me, Meg,' Ned shouted across the merriment of the crew.

By now they were passing Kersall Hall, a venerable black and white building supposedly haunted by boggarts. The whole lane was heaving with jolly racegoers. Ned felt it safe to part company.

'Good hunting lads! 'Til we meet again.'

Waving farewell, he stopped by a wayside spring to water his horse. Sitting and watching the throng, he hesitated a moment, wondering how he would find Rhose amongst all these people. He took off his hat to wipe his brow. No matter what, he was convinced that fate would bring them together. There was a destiny which could not be denied.

Oliver set out early that morning from Ashley Hall, the home of his cousin, Freddie Assheton. It was not far into Manchester, but the roads in this part of the county were notoriously poor and he wished to take his time. He needed the fresh air in his face after a long night over the cards. He could not remember how many times they had toasted the six portraits staring down at them from the walls. Six good countrymen, Jacobites all, who had had the sound good sense to resist the pretender's call. Now they were solid respectable loyal landowners, untainted by suspicion. They had brought him luck nevertheless, for he was two hundred guineas the richer today. Heigh-Ho, he called to himself, as he reined the chaise around yet another gaping pothole.

There was a breath of autumn in the air. The matched pair, on loan from Freddie, trotted quietly along and he had time to muse on his plans for the day. Mayhap at the races his two hundred would become four – or nothing. He smiled, cracking the whip in sheer good spirits. Would his luck hold with the bewitching Rhose, he wondered? Since that first happy chance meeting she had run in his blood. He could not get enough of her. He had never known anyone like her, certainly not the milk and white ninnies in his home circle. She had fire, spirit, independence, and a body that responded with a passion to match his own. He daydreamed of the nights. . . .

The chaise lurched as wheels clamped into ruts. He cursed as he leapt out to lighten the load and urge the horses on. Remounting he felt in his pocket for the token he hoped would win Rhose to his proposition. A cottage on the estate would not be to her taste, nor would his family welcome it. He knew his father would turn a blind eye but his mother had ambitions for him in the matrimonial stakes. He was not averse to being tied to a brood mare but Rhose, ah, Rhose, that was somewhat different. Chester perhaps? He conjured up pictures of a neat little town house, up from the Roodee. Evenings spent with convivial friends, his own precious inamorata elegant in the latest fashions presiding. Rhose was better than a mere tavern keeper, mixing with the riff-raff of a miserable town. He could raise her to her true position, admired and envied by the County. Why not? He flicked the horses into a trot as he passed All Port Town. Along Deansgate, the equipage attracted comments from passers-by. He was sure Dame Fortune smiled on him today as he approached the Ring o' Bells.

Rhose dressed in anticipation of the coming day. The races this year had a special excitement for this was the first meeting since 1745. Three days of holiday with the town packed with strangers come for the sport, some to watch, and some, no doubt, to take advantage of the racegoers. Winners and losers all, reflected Rhose. Sugar Lane should be busy, that was a cheery thought. Forget business, today she would relish Oliver's attentions regardless of Ned.

There had been showers overnight but now the clouds were lifting. A fine day was promised. Her pink flowered silk dress was in the style of a Brunswick sac, comfortable for travelling. The short robings of green matched the buttons; the long tight sleeves would help to keep her warm. She had intended to wear a long dark green velvet cloak with a hood but as the weather was improving she would only need her Indian shawl. Carefully dressing her hair she acknowledged how much she took pleasure in Oliver's company. Not only his physical attractions but also the tenderness he showed towards her. A day together would be a delight in contrast to the disasters that had seemed to beset her. There was no word from Agar, or Ned. When she asked if Ned had sailed for France, Laurence had dissembled. She determined to put it all from her mind. Her thoughts were interrupted by a knock on the door. Mary entered in a fluster.

'There's someone to see you, someone I'd as lief send away. She always spells trouble does Susannah Taylor.'

'You had better send her up to my sitting room. If there is going to be trouble it's best out of the ear of the customers. What can she want? I thought she was in Liverpool well out of the way.'

Rhose stood by the window watching the crowds moving towards Hunts-bank, all the world and his wife were off to Kersal Moor.

'Mistress Tinnys, no doubt you didn't expect to see me again?'

Rhose admitted to herself that she had hoped never to see Susannah again. Her former kindness had disguised how much she despised the woman, had been a ploy to get rid of her. A more troublesome resident of Sugar Lane had been hard to find. The constables, who could be persuaded to ignore the trade, drew the line when it came to Mistress Taylor.

'Have you come to return my candlesticks, Susannah? I hear you have prospered in Liverpool.'

'Aye, they set me up but it was no more than were due to me. If I'd peached you would have had a taste of the sweepings, not me.'

'I see time has not improved your temper. What is it you want of me now?'

'Well I certainly didn't expect a welcome, so I'm not disappointed. I've had a terrible piece of misfortune – could say we're both widows now, though you're legitimate so to speak.'

'I don't take your meaning. Be quick as I'm expecting company.'

'My man, the captain I spoke to you about, died doing you a favour. Now I want some recompense. You made the profit and we weren't paid.'

'Twigg, are you telling me you have been living with Twigg? I didn't know.'

'That's as may be and it don't matter. Josiah – I see you recognize that name, sweet on you he is – told us all about his connection to Rhose Tinnys. The fatal run was to have set us up. Titus escaped and came to tell me what happened. Now I want my cut.'

As their anger increased, their voices rose higher and higher.

'You can have as much as me with pleasure. Nothing!'

'Liar! You never come away with nothing. If you fell in a midden you'd come up with sweet herbs and sixpence. I know you.'

'And I know you, Susannah Taylor. You were driven out once and by God it can happen again.'

'And, by God, it's not me for the Bridewell this time. The revenue are hunting for your roaring boy – they'd pay well to know where he could be found and who rides with him.'

Rhose stepped closer, face to face. 'You watch that tongue, else you could lose it.'

'I'm not afeared of you. Then there's you and Sugar Lane – that's a secret waiting to be told—'

Rhose raised her hand but the other grasped the wrist. The two stood glaring at each other, motionless. Rhose dropped back, shaking free.

'I'm sorry about your man. Someone betrayed them, I'm sure. The military got it all. I've no doubt the regiment are enjoying their spirits. I tell you I got nothing, there was nothing to get.'

'You were always a good liar, Rhose. You can fool any man, just flash your eyes and shake your arse.'

'Watch your tongue. I've warned you.'

Susannah snapped her fingers. 'A fig for that. There's money to be had for peaching. I know what I know and that's more than a run up the river.'

'What?'

'There's a young girl – Charlotte is she called? – running around Cheshire, and who packed her off? Ned couldn't keep quiet!'

Rhose reached out but Susannh slammed a chair between them. Her voice screeched out:

'I'll tell 'em all. All I've known for years. I'll see you paraded. You for all your airs and graces, you're nothing but a flashman's trollop – a slut in silk and ribbons.'

'You bitch!'

Rhose grabbed the chair and flung it to the floor. She drove Susannah against the wall only to have her spring at her with nails clawing. Rhose pushed her away, slapping backwards and forwards in fury. The two women in a flurry of petticoats rolled across the table. Rhose freed herself from the frenzied attack with a well-aimed kick. She grabbed the other's hair and forced her head backwards, arching the body away from her to avoid Susannah's spittle. With a final push of her knee she sent the bawd sprawling across the floor. Before either could continue, the door was flung open.

'Need some help, my dear. Sounds like a catfight from below. Perhaps the lady's just leaving?' Oliver made a bow to Susannah.

'Be warned, I'll get you yet Rhose Tinnys.'

With the words ringing in her ears Rhose collapsed into Oliver's arms. Susannah took one look and with a cry of 'Still trying on your charms I see,' flounced down the stairs. From the window she could be seen hurrying towards the marketplace.

'Oh, Oliver thank you for rescuing me yet again. She's an unfortunate woman I tried to help and now wants to blackmail me for it.'

'Forget her, Rhose. No doubt she's on her way to another tavern to drown her sorrows. Don't let her spoil our day.'

Holding her at arms length Oliver admired her appearance. 'You look delicious as always. I wanted to present you with a token of my affection Rhose; something to remind you of my devotion when I am not here. I had it made in Chester to my own design.'

Oliver took out a red jewellery box. As he opened it Rhose saw the inside was lined with green watered silk. In his hand sparkled a red rose hanging from a black-ribboned neckband.

'The petals are garnets and the centre is a citrine. Small diamonds are set between each petal at the edge and all is gold. I call it a Lancashire rose, a gift for my own lovely Lancashire Rhose.'

'I am overcome, Oliver. It is the most wonderful jewel. How can I ever thank you?'

'That's easy, my dear. Come and live with me. Let us be together.'

Oliver drew Rhose to him and tied the ribbons around her neck before embracing her with a passionate kiss. 'You need not answer now; I know your reservations. Let us enjoy today. I'll go below and wait in the chaise.' With a swift kiss Oliver left Rhose to finish her toilet. The chaise waited outside the Ring o' Bells, the two sprightly black mares pawed the ground. In honour of the occasion Oliver set about adorning the carriage with yellow and green ribbons.

'Oh, Oliver how lovely, how did you guess?'

'Mary can be persuaded to help on occasions like this. Come, let me help you up then I can enjoy the pleasure of watching other men envy me my companion.'

Francis Fletcher rode out from Greenwood Lea full of great expectation for the day. He kicked the hack he was riding into a jarring trot, its skinny flanks a tremor between his knees. It was unfortunate Emperor had cast a shoe and he was forced onto this old mare. George and John had gone on ahead to take Vulcan to the course, while Edmund was conducting the ladies in the coach. No matter, Frank knew he would soon be astride his stallion, then he would show the Cheshire upstarts what a gentleman could do. Riding was a sport for true blood; he had nothing but contempt for those who trusted their mounts to mere hireling jockeys. Though Falkner he thought, maliciously, had little choice in the matter. Even he had had to entrust his own thoroughbred to the new stable lad in preparation for today. The boy knew he risked being thrashed within an inch of his life if Vulcan was not in top trim. The ostler and those at the Bull's Head, where he was stabled for the night, had too much respect for horseflesh to allow any harm. Too much respect for the Fletcher temper as well, he thought grimly.

He eased up on the nag, its weariness feeding through the reins to his sensitive touch. There was no need to push the old thing, time enough to reach Kersal Moor for his meeting with that troublesome madam. Absent-minded he switched his riding crop against the horse's rump. A whinny and a startled jolt brought him to his senses. Of all animals, this was the breed he most admired; he would not mistreat the slowest dobbin. He calmed the horse with a stroke of the neck and swore at the bitch whose very image had made him forget his riding skill. He would fain lay his whip across the gloating face of the baggage, Rhose Tinnys. How to deal with her this very day was the immediate problem.

The race meeting would be too public for the beating he would wish on her. She knew too much, could tell too much. His dark mood seemed to convey itself to his mount as she broke into a canter. Women – sluts, trollops – stood in his way to success. He could, he would, ride them down as easily as he spurred over a fallen branch. Rhose's silence must first be bought. After, she must be made to speak but only to him, to tell the whereabouts of that little prick-teaser, Charlotte. Once found there must be no hesitation. And once she was dealt with Rhose would be no danger – or a danger to be snuffed out. He relaxed again certain in the knowledge that such petticoat problems could be overcome.

Nevertheless, as he rode confidently into Manchester a worry stirred in the back of his mind. What became of the body? Where was Thomas Miller?

The lane to the course ran from Hunts-bank over the Irk. Packed with vehicles of all sorts, Oliver competed with them and pedestrians, all hurrying in the same direction. List sellers, proclaiming the virtue of their correct card of runners vied with other salesmen lining the causeway. As the chaise moved slowly, Rhose was able to admire Strangeways Hall, home of the Reynolds. Standing in its park, the house was beautifully situated below hanging woods. The way ahead lead straight to Kersal heights. Oliver said it was once a Roman road. Rhose imagined it could never have seen a greater crowd. Frequently the chaise came to a halt as the crush of people surged around. Oliver called greetings to friends who passed them on their horses, bowing graciously to his companion. Slowly they arrived at the lane that led down to the course.

'Mrs Tinnys! Oohoo! Mrs Tinnys!' Rhose turned at the piping sound of her name. Waving excitedly in a fine carriage were two identical figures, cheeks rouged, hair powdered and piled high.

'Why, Sarah and Etta!' Rhose scarcely had time to return the greeting before they were ordered to sit down in their seats by the elderly, bewhiskered gentleman who accompanied them. Well, well, she mused, they have soon been accommodated.

'We must leave the chaise here. The lane is too rough to take carriages.' Oliver helped Rhose down and paid a boy to guard the conveyance. 'Hold my arm, Blackfield Lane is so sandy, I want not to rescue you from a broken ankle again,' Oliver laughed.

Rhose clung tight as she sank into the soft yellow sand at every step. And so the lurching laughing throng arrived at the course. Rhose was stunned by the sight before her. On the right as they emerged was a line of beggars with outstretched hands. Rhose recognized several as the professional mendicants who plagued the marketplace. Old soldiers, lepers, pauper families, were all hoping to make a profit from a day at the races. The meadow to the left had been transformed into an outdoor gaming field with refreshments being hawked among the stalls.

'Find the pea,' called the man nearby as he pushed the thimbles across the ground. 'Throw the dice!' Cries went up all over the ground.

'We are in time for the first race. We'll make for the slope above the course. We can see the meeting best from there.'

Rhose gasped as the crowd before her parted and a knot of six horses rushed past with flying hoofs. The crowd roared them on, Rhose deafened by the noise.

'Come on Vulcan!' 'Faster Moscoe!' As soon as the beasts had passed the crowd closed in again over the course.

'I'm sorry, I should have explained. We must have missed the bell for the start of the race warning the crowd to clear the course. They will be round again soon – four times round the track is the length and it's the best of three heats for three-year-olds. Quick, let's get to the height.' Oliver and Rhose, laughing, half ran to the sandy mount then turned to survey the scene. The horses raced on until cries in the distance announced a winner. The crowd calmed down, bands began to play, many settled to picnic on the grass.

'Oliver, I wondered where you were,' James Falkner called, pushing his way through the crowd. 'Good day, Mistress Tinnys. You look charming as ever. A fine jewel you have there.'

'Indeed, Sir James, a gift from an admirer,' Rhose replied as she smiled up at Oliver.

'Can I borrow your admirer for a while? I want to show off my new stallion, Moscoe. He won the first race. You can place a wager on him. I have every confidence you would be in profit. Though Fletcher's Vulcan looks fit and came in second. Still two more races should see him off.'

'I thought to take my companion to see the runners. There's half an hour before the next heat.'

'No, Oliver, I shall be safer here. The horses unnerved me before. I think seeing them at a distance will suit me better.'

Rhose had no wish for Oliver to be present at her meeting with Sir Francis.

Chapter Twenty-three

Kersal Moor

Rhose strolled among the crowd intent on acquiring some refreshment.

'Well, you do look grand Rhose, how about a tipple of rum?'

'Nice to see you, Jenny. Did Alice procure a licence or are you avoiding the law?'

'Just trying to earn a bit on the side. Alice has us all out offering our services; you know what I mean. These three days should earn you a tidy profit. Not that I'm complaining. These strangers will be easy to fleece then they'll be off back to their wives, no questions asked.'

'You're a treasure, Jenny. You deserve better than Sugar Lane. No doubt you will be managing your own house soon. I'll sample your rum, though no doubt it's mine if everybody had their own.' Rhose laughed.

'Have you placed a bet? I'm favouring Sir James Falkner's, Moscoe, though I have a partiality to the grey, Sprightly, as well. And then there's Fletcher's Vulcan; it's hard to choose. Perhaps I'll stick to selling rum, I'm bound to make a profit there.'

The sound of a bell interrupted their conversation. The crowd rose as one and craned to see the race. From the hill Rhose watched as the horses chased round the course. Jenny's grey led

231

for a while but on the third lap it was overtaken by the horse called Moscoe. As they entered the final lap Moscoe was well ahead when from behind came the challenge.

'It's Sir Francis on Vulcan; he's the only owner riding. Look how the horse is straining every muscle to catch up.'

The crowd roared their favourite horse on. Rhose was deafened by cries of 'Moscoe, come on!' 'Vulcan, Vulcan, you can do it.' 'Yes, yes, he'll make it, Fletcher for Manchester!' With a final bell, the horses crossed the line. Vulcan had won by a nose. The crowd sighed, the lucky ones going off to collect their winnings. Jenny started to follow them.

'They'll have money to spend, and I've got things to sell. See you later, Rhose. Enjoy the final race. One each now, it will be a deadly contest. What a great start to the races – Lancashire against Cheshire.'

Frank, victory still pulsating through his veins, patted Vulcan's long soft nose as he handed him over for his rub down. He pressed a guinea into the stable lad's palm. 'Treat him with care. There's another heat to go so keep him calm. We'll take that as well I'll wager.'

'Aye, you may, but it's evens now.' Sir James Falkner's voice cut through the murmur of the crowd. He came forward with arms outstretched as ever and clapped Frank's back so soundly as to almost knock him over.

'Steady, Jamie,' he laughed as his knees buckled, 'I've not got my land legs yet.'

'Why my boy, you've just won me a hundred guineas! I always bet on the best of the opposition too. There's more to come if you ride like that again. Good luck to us both, I must see Moscoe is rubbed down now. We'll meet after the final race.'

Frank watched the broad back disappear then turned and hurriedly strode towards the hill. Mistress Tinnys had chosen the place of their assignation. He did not want to be late for the last ride. Instantly spotting her amongst the crowd, he could not help but acknowledge that she was a magnificent creature – a thoroughbred amongst women. She just needed to be broken in. As she saw him approach she moved to meet him and they strolled down the course in apparently friendly conversation. Racegoers congratulated Sir Francis as they passed.

'Mistress Tinnys, you have no hidden weapon today I trust.'

'We are both unarmed no doubt at such a gathering.'

'What would you have of me then?'

'A thousand pounds would suffice.'

'A steep price for a tavern keeper.'

'A small price for a young lady to be lost and my silence kept.'

By now they were approaching the starting bell and where an eager crowd were laying bets as they waited for the final race.

'Let us be brief, I have the ultimate heat to ride. I would have this nonsense out of the way. You ask too much!'

'Not nonsense! I hold your reputation in my hands.'

'Hussy! My reputation is above the scurrilous tittle-tattle of a highwayman's whore.'

'You go too far. The price has risen – fifteen hundred guineas and I would have it by the end of the week.'

'Damn you! Who'd believe the ranting of a bawdy drab?'

'Hold your tongue. I may decide no price is high enough: it would please me to see you scorned as you scorn me.'

'You slut!'

The nearby crowd turned to see where the raised voices were coming from. Francis was indifferent to their gaze.

'I have made my position clear. Fifteen hundred guineas at the Ring o' Bells before the week is out. I have no more to say.'

Francis seized her tightly by the shoulders, shaking her so hard that her head snapped back, his face thrust into hers.

'Keep quiet, you bitch or I'll have you silenced.' The mutterings in the crowd grew. With one last contemptuous glance Frank strode way.

Rhose did not know that Ned had been watching them attentively in the crowd. He could hardly contain himself as the exchange with Sir Francis grew violent. He guessed the cause of the argument and cursed the crush of the people around as he tried to push through. Soon the fop would be facing an opponent who could not be cowed with words. He watched with amusement as Rhose found Oliver and they joined the other watchers on the hill. The throng hurried to clear the track in anticipation of a thrilling finale. With the memory of their reunion fresh in his mind, Ned was prepared to bide his time. The bell sounded for the start of the last heat. Ned, ignoring the course, turned to follow Sir Francis but saw him enter the saddling enclosure. No matter, he thought, he would soon have his reckoning with that bully of women and girls.

Oliver leaned over to Rhose, glad to have her by his side again.

'Will you not agree to my proposal? If you come with me, away from this pestilential town, you would cease to be troubled.' Oliver took Rhose gently by the hand and raised it to his lips, ignoring the amused stares of the bystanders. Glancing over his shoulder, Rhose saw with a shock Susannah moving through the crowd below her, accompanied by the constables. The press was slowing their progress. They had not seen her yet and she could not let that happen. Rhose sighed, moving to place Oliver between herself and the searchers.

'Thank you, Oliver, perhaps you are right. It is time to leave Manchester. Forgive me! I am much distracted, so many things are pressing in on me. I have no more heart for the races. I would be alone to think.'

'I see this is not the time, or place, to expect an answer. Allow me at least to conduct you home.'

Rhose withdrew her hand from his and adjusted her shawl. 'I need to walk by myself awhile. You have given me much to consider.'

'As you will. I have a wager on this next race. I would see what profit my two hundred pounds brings.'

Angrily Oliver turned away. Rhose stepped from his side and vanished into the crowd. Oliver's annoyance was short lived. With a laugh to himself, he determined he would not let her go, but for now the race came first.

The atmosphere around the course became tense, voices hushed. The horses waited nervously for the off. The starting bell rang round the course. 'They're away.' Again Sprightly took the lead, the pack striving to take its place. Francis waited, he knew better than to let Vulcan fly too soon. The hoofs pounded the track, sandy clouds rising as the horses passed, obscuring the view. On they went, ears flattened, manes and tails streaming backwards as they raced past. A chestnut bay, Fair Forrester, took up the lead trailed by Vulcan and Moscoe, these three clear of the rest. Frank could hear the horses drawing breath as their nostrils flared wide, their jockeys urging them on to the last lap. Sweat glistened on the horses' flanks, flecks of foam flew from their lips. The roar of the crowd was tremendous but Frank failed to hear. His mind was on the finish; naught else mattered. Stride by stride he urged Vulcan past the bay. Where was Moscoe? As if to answer his question he was aware of his rival on the outside. Stride for stride the two horses rushed onward, their hearts pounding. Frank knew the bell must be near. Again, step-by-step, Moscoe drew closer. The bell clanged. The challenge was too late, Vulcan was the victor. The crowd roared at his success. 'Vulcan for ever!'

'Well done, well done!' George and John hurried over to help the exultant Frank dismount. 'We knew you'd win. You've made us all a tidy sum.'

'Congratulations! Your V – V – Vulcan hammered 'em.' Robert Johnson rushed over to join them.

'Well done, Francis,' Sir James called from Moscoe's side. 'What say we sink a noggin or two in celebration? The treat's all mine. You can join the ladies later.'

Frank was hoisted aloft on the shoulders of his friends. Sir James led them into the nearest booth already heaving with drinkers bent on toasting the victory. A few minutes later Frank reappeared; calling over his shoulder; 'Even a hero needs a piss.'

He hurried to an overgrown copse, unbuttoned his breeches and breathed a sigh of relief as the golden stream splashed into the bracken.

'Now, Fletcher, you and I need to talk.'

A voice spoke quietly behind him. He turned to see Ned leaning nonchalantly against a tree, hat down over his eyes, legs crossed, hands thrust into jacket pockets.

'Best put yourself away. You'd not want a scandal.'

As Frank hurried to button up, the highwayman stepped forward. His fist lashed out in a back-handed cuff that sent his opponent staggering. Frank steadied himself, wiping a smear of blood from his mouth.

'Had I my sword, I'd make short work of you.' He spat toward the other's face.

'Fah, you're all wind and piss. You're facing a man now, not a woman or a little lass.'

There was a moment's silence as they took the measure of each other. Ned, easy and assured, flung the hat from his head, took a step forward. Frank backed away, eyes flickering from side to side, arms forward ready for the assault. A voice rose from the hubbub of men emerging from the booth below.

'F-F-Frank, come on! Are you for the novice race? The grey's favourite to win.'

'Take care. You see I have friends within call. You dare do nothing in so public a place.'

'You think to frighten me? I too am not without friends.' Ned put two fingers to his lips and whistled. There was a rustling in the bushes as dishevelled figures appeared dimly amid the undergrowth. With dismay Frank heard the murmur of voices disappear toward the track.

'I'll see you on the gibbet and your whore in the stocks, God help me.' With this he plunged at the highwayman, catching him off balance. They fell into a patch of scrub oak. Frank on top, flailing with both fists then scrabbling to his feet. Ned, tangled in brambles, breath knocked from him, could do no more than curse as he watched his foe stumble off.

Soon Frank was mingling with the crush as it surged towards the track. The crowd eddied on to the course and broke into small, chattering animated groups. Frank searched in vain for familiar faces. Where were his friends, James, Oliver, John, damn them? Instead he only seemed to see the menacing shapes of Ned's tinker cronies shadowing him. He found his way barred by a field preacher extolling the virtues of a chaste Christian life. Stepping aside he felt a hand grip his sleeve. Instinctively he rounded on his pursuer, cuffing him round the head with an ill-timed blow. Ned's reply was a fierce grin and a hard right fist to the chest. Frank winded, staggered back as the left fist followed. He reeled against another body and rough hands pushed him forward.

A space had opened up around them. The fastidious were hurrying away but more were crowding in as 'A fight! A fight!' spread along the track. Gasping, Frank gathered his strength and hurled himself at his opponent. He smashed himself squarely into Ned's face. Bone cracked and blood poured from a broken nose. The crowd, turbulent before now, fell silent; expectant. A lone voice called for them to desist 'in the name of the Lord'. Ned wiped his face with a smear of his broad flat hand. Frank shook his head to clear it then launched an attack with a vicious round-arm punch. It did not land true. His exhaustion from the races was beginning to take its toll on him. Ned seized the arm with ease and Frank felt iron fingers clamp around his throat. Fingernails dug into the flesh. The breath squeezed out of him. A cry ran around, one voice above the rest: 'It's time yon bugger were taught a lesson.' Frank twisted and writhed to free his arm, ease the throbbing pain in his throat. He scrabbled his left hand through the sticky blood on Ned's face then jabbed his thumb hard into the eye.

The stranglehold was broken. Frank collapsed on to the turf smelling the crushed grass as he hawked and spluttered. Again he shook his head. There was ringing in his ears. His throat was on fire, his breath coming in agonizing gulps. He sensed rather than saw the crowd thinning out. Had rescuers arrived? He struggled to his knees and a boot cracked into his face. He fell forward on to the churned-up sod. He tasted the sickly sweet blood trickling into his mouth. He wanted to call out for help but

237

no sound came from his lacerated throat. Another kick rolled him on to his back. Frank raised his head. Through a haze of pain he saw Ned backing away. It was then he felt the tremor through the earth, heard the persistent drum of hoofs gathering momentum, saw the leading grey almost upon him. Saw the jockey pulling hard on the reins, trying to swerve. Banshee, he thought as he rolled away towards the crowd, raising one arm in protest as the hoofs came down.

Rhose hurried towards Manchester. The sand in her shoes made walking uncomfortable. As she began the long descent, she determined she must leave the town that spread out before her. Life was too precious to waste on an argument with Frank Fletcher. The constables, too, would be coming now Susannah had claimed for the reward for sure. Either Oliver or Laurence would take care of her, rich men both. Which should she choose – the kept mistress or the smuggler's paramour?

She glanced up to see a chaise resplendent in yellow and green waiting at the side of the road. The choice it seemed had been made for her. She stopped to catch her breath and heard hoofbeats behind her.

'Come, my pippin, you will not escape me so easily. 'Tis time we left this place.'

A strong arm whisked her off her feet and on to the horse. She laughed with true joy as she looked into the twinkling eyes under the familiar slouched hat. Oliver watched as the pair rode past oblivious of him. With a shrug of his shoulders and a wry smile, he turned the chaise away. Still he thought to himself, tomorrow was another day with all to play for.

Manchester Mercury November 10th 1760

PETER SMITH
of
SMITH'S COFFEE HOUSE, in Manchester,
in, the County of Lancaster

Peter Smith of Manchester begs leave to inform the Public, that he intends immediately on the removal of Mistress Rhose Tinnys, to begin Public Business at the Ring o' Bells Inn: All gentlemen, Travellers and others, who please to make use of the Ring o' Bells Inn, may depend of meeting Good Entertainment and Civil Usage

By their most obedient humble Servant
PETER SMITH

Sedan Chairs, Neat Post Chaises, able Horses and Careful Drivers upon the shortest Notice.

Afterword:
Manchester and the Jacobites

The Jacobites were supporters of the Stuart claim to the British throne after James II abdicated in 1688. They were mainly Roman Catholics and Scots opposed to the Protestant Hanoverian royal family, George I and George II.

Charles Edward Stuart, 'Bonnie Prince Charlie', led a Jacobite army from Scotland into England in 1745. Passing through Manchester he raised a volunteer body of troops, the Manchester Regiment. Beppy Byrom, a fervent Jacobite gave a vivid account of him in her diary: 'There is a local legend that Bonnie Prince Charlie had visited Manchester incognito in 1744 staying with the Mosley family.' His army turned back at Derby and retreated to Scotland. The Manchester Regiment was left, with others, to defend Carlisle, but the city was soon taken and the rebels captured by government forces. Many were executed but some, like Thomas Miller, were sent to serve in India.

The Scots were defeated at Culloden in 1746, and the Prince escaped to the continent, where he spent the rest of his life. It continued to be treason to support openly the Stuart cause, although sympathizers secretly drank to 'the King over the water'. Manchester newspapers continued to report violent clashes between Jacobites and Whigs (King George's supporters) throughout the 1750s and 1760s. England was again at war with France from 1756 to 1763. Jacobites were therefore suspected of being traitors as the French government had always supported the Stuart claim.